Stealing HOME

BECKY WALLACE

PAGE STREET
PUBLISHING CO.

PAGE STREET
PUBLISHING CO.

Distributed by Macmillan, sales in Canada by The Canadian Manda Group.

23   22   21   20   19   1   2   3   4   5

ISBN-13: 978-1-62414-764-7
ISBN-10: 1-62414-764-X

Library of Congress Control Number: 2019933675

Cover and book design by Rosie Stewart for Page Street Publishing Co.
Photograph of couple © Shutterstock / solominviktor
Author photo by Keira Sky Photography

Printed and bound in the United States

TO MOM, DAD, LIZ, JOEL, AND MEME,

For being the very best, overworked, underpaid, and sometimes unpaid minor league baseball staff. I couldn't have survived it without your help. Love you forever.

CHAPTER

MY RIGHT FOOT TAPS OUT AN IMPATIENT RHYTHM ON THE STICKY airport floor, my shoe suctioning to the tile in a *tap, slurp, tap, slurp, tap, slurp*. The businesswoman waiting beside me at baggage claim keeps glancing at my foot like she wants to grind it under the heel of her pointy-toed pumps. I don't blame her. But I can't make myself stop. The repetition makes me feel like I'm doing something instead of wasting time.

The woman shifts her fancy purse to her left arm and checks her phone. Mine starts buzzing in my back pocket, and I answer it, hoping for news. "Hey."

"What are you wearing?"

"Same thing I was wearing an hour ago. Why?" There's a long silence on our call. Can silence sound disappointed? If it can, my best friend, Mia, is sending me all sorts of disapproval without saying a word. I look down at my uniform—a team-branded polo shirt, khaki shorts, and worn but comfortable running shoes. I look *fine*. "It's not like I'm trying to impress anyone."

Mia makes a noise that falls somewhere between a gag and a growl. "Seriously, Ryan? Why not? He's hot and talented and rich. I'm not saying you have to have his babies, but a little flirting is perfectly harmless."

"It's not professional, Mi."

"Professional, smrofessional. He's a first-round draft pick. He's *gorgeous*."

I scan baggage claim for anyone matching Sawyer Campbell's description. Since I always get stuck with *personnel retrieval*—that's the official term for picking up freshly drafted baseball players from their flights—I check out their photos. Both the Photoshopped headshots the front office sends and the awful ones I dig up on their social media accounts. That way, I never worry about approaching the wrong guy.

At six-foot-three, two hundred and five pounds, and with a head full of tousled chestnut hair, Campbell should stand out in any crowd. Even without the hair. Some guys are tall, some guys are thick, but there's something about athletes that makes them hard to ignore. It's more than bulging biceps, vein-ridden forearms, and bubble butts. A real athlete—a professional athlete—moves in a different way than a normal person. Like they have an extra sense about the space their body occupies, which somehow translates to an above-average level of self-confidence.

No one in the airport moves with the sort of precision, aware-ness, or *ego* of a first-round draft pick. And Sawyer Campbell is the biggest deal my little hometown will ever see.

"If he thinks he's famous, then you know what he's going to be like."

Mia gags for real and says two words: "Hadley Pearson."

The mention of his name makes my face burn. No single player in the history of the Buckley Beavers has caused more contention on or off the field. Sure, he's a promising centerfielder with an impressive social media following. But last season he caused a fight in the dugout, posted a picture with a sponsor's daughter that was beyond scandalous, and almost got a DUI. All of that in the first four weeks of his professional career.

"Say a prayer to the gods of baseball that Campbell is nothing like Pearson," Mia continues, probably crossing herself like she does at mass.

"No one can possibly be that bad." I slide to the side so a guy in an army uniform can get past me with a huge camouflage duffel. Other people push through the crowd, snagging their bags, shuffling politely around each other with a sort of heat-racked exhaustion. But no one steps forward to grab the yard-long Easton bag gummed up with pine tar on the sides and handles. I don't have to look at the tag to know what it'll say: Sawyer Campbell.

"It looks like his luggage made it," I say as it chugs past me on the carousel. "Will you ask around and see if the head office called? Maybe he missed his flight."

Mia's filling in for me at the receptionist desk at the Buckley Beavers' ballpark office. She mumbles something that sounds like disgruntled assent, and then puts me on hold.

This wouldn't be the first time I haven't been notified of a last-minute change, but I check my phone anyway. After swiping four calendar reminders off my screen, I pull up the flight info for the thirty-fifth time. Flight 1474 arrived forty-two minutes ago.

The luggage carousel stops churning. The Easton bag, unquestionably full of bats and other equipment, comes to a halt a few yards ahead of me. The crowd of business folk, small families, and the soldier melt through the sliding doors and grow hazy with the heat rising from the cracked cement outside. I pace, tighten my ponytail, and pace again.

Still no Sawyer Campbell.

The awful on-hold music quits as Mia gets back on our call. "No one here knows anything."

We're understaffed and overworked. Calls get missed, sometimes. Emails get ignored. There aren't enough of us to address all the office-related tasks, especially on game days. "That's nothing new."

Mia laughs. "Even if he gets there right now, you're probably gonna be late for pregame. What do you need me to set up?"

A pit opens in my stomach as I try to name all the tasks I normally have to accomplish before the gates open in four hours. All of which are on hold because I'm standing in the airport. Waiting.

"Can you handle prepping the on-field promotions? And make sure the autograph table is set up on the concourse. The blue tablecloths are—"

"In the closet. I know, I know."

She *does* know. This season has been especially hectic, and so many things would have fallen through the cracks without her help. Two of our summer staffers quit last week when they realized that working at the stadium was less fun than they'd imagined. Until we find replacements, we have to pick up the slack.

"You're the best, Mia."

"I know that, too. People tell me all the time."

Then it's my turn to laugh, because it's both super arrogant and true. She really is amazing.

"Do you see him yet?" She's clicking around in the background, probably changing the screensaver on my computer. Again.

"You know how these guys are." I turn to face the elevators, hoping to see Campbell as soon as he exits. "They don't hurry unless they have to."

"Maybe someone recognized him from the cover of *Sports Illustrated*?"

"It's possible." I've picked up eight different guys in the year and a half since I've had my driver's license. And I know better than to be irritated that this Campbell kid is taking his sweet time getting down the terminal. Like so many players before him, he's probably basking in the high of his newfound—and likely short-lived—fame. Sad fact: Only sixty-six percent of top draft picks ever play in the Bigs.

Too many end up like my dad. Spend a season or two riding the bench for a major league team and a handful of years bouncing around the minors. Then—*bam!*—career over before they're thirty. They have to pick up the pieces—shattered dreams, broken bodies, destroyed relationships. Some go back to school. Some coach. A few do what my dad did: invest in a small-town minor league baseball team.

"Campbell's probably flirting with a flight attendant," Mia says.

"Ew. He's underage."

"Wouldn't stop me."

I roll my eyes even though she can't see me. Maybe she can hear *that* through the phone. "*You're* underage."

Another flood of people moves toward me, and I look for a salmon-colored polo. Or maybe lavender. Southern boys like Campbell have an odd addiction to pastel collared shirts. We haven't had a player from Georgia in a while. Maybe those boys like polo shirts in baby blue.

Or light green.

Not his shirt. His *face*. Campbell is staggering along the terminal wall like he's indulged in one too many tiny bottles of first-class vodka. Not that he's old enough to order it, but when the phrase *seventeen-year-old phenom* is attached to your name, a lot of rules get ignored. Like laws.

Any optimism that he's not like Hadley Pearson flickers and dies.

"He's coming."

"Is he pretty?" she squeals.

"He's drunk. Gotta go fix this before anyone else notices." I hang up before she can do anything but gasp. Pasting on a welcoming expression, I approach the man-child as he steadies himself on a concourse support beam. "Mr. Campbell?" Yep. Even though we're the same age, I stick to the formalities. "I'm Ryan Russell from the Buckley Beavers, and your ride to the stadium. If we could grab your bags and get going."

"Move."

His sharpness shocks me. "Excuse—"

I don't finish my question because his eyes widen like he's expecting a fastball to the face. Then Sawyer Campbell, the future star of the Texas Rangers, pukes all over me.

IF WE'RE BEING FAIR—AND I'M NOT FEELING ANY SORT OF FAIR— the barf splatters at my feet, but something warm oozes down my shin. My stomach clenches, my throat burns, my eyes water. My body wants to return the favor. Then my brain kicks in.

Directly behind me is an oversize stainless-steel garbage can. Likely where Campbell was headed before I stepped into the line of fire.

He claps his hands over his mouth, but it's too late for that. Much, much too late.

"I—" I stumble for words. I don't know what to say. I've been in awkward situations before. I've covered for players when they've said stupid things to reporters. I picked up our mascot when he got knocked down in the middle of the town Christmas parade. And last year, I caught Pearson in a compromising position with our *former* ticket office manager. Still can't bleach that image from my mind.

But I've got nothing for this.

"I…I'll be right back," I mumble.

The line for the women's bathroom stretches into the baggage area, but the ladies all slide aside when they see—or *smell*—me coming. I snag a handful of paper towels and pump them full of foaming soap, thinking to start on my leg. But when I look in the mirror, I realize with a breath-stealing sense of horror that there is a glob of something pinkish on my shirt.

"It's not that bad," I say aloud, and begin scrubbing at my chest.

"Oh, bless your heart," an elderly voice coos from behind me. "You get a touch airsick?"

"Something like that." The white becomes translucent because that's what happens when you get white T-shirts wet. And I can clearly see the lace at the top of my bra. And. And. And.

Stop. I take a deep breath. A bad idea considering the smell, but I still manage to pull myself together. Rinse hands. Tighten ponytail. Everything is going to be fine.

"Some of those kiosks sell shirts, you know." Every syllable out of the helpful geriatric's lips is slathered with Texas hospitality. Still doesn't change the fact that I have to walk out of the bathroom and face the guy who speckled me with his barf.

"Yes." I can't forget my own upbringing. "Thank you, ma'am."

I collect a few more towels and dash out of the bathroom, hoping to find my superstar still undiscovered. I don't know exactly how the newspapers or any other source would get footage of Campbell's *Exorcist* reenactment, but everyone in the world seems to be filming everything, every minute. Plenty of people watched him retch, but no one is standing close, holding out their phones.

Small miracles.

He's slumped onto one of those hard plastic chairs closest to the garbage can, handfuls of dark hair trapped between his fingers.

"Here." I offer up the paper towels.

"Thanks." He wipes off the toes of his Nikes and the tiny bit of puke that managed to splash on his jeans. "I can't believe..."

He lifts his head, and I take my first real look at Sawyer Campbell. Maybe it's the blush-stained cheeks and the way his hair stands up all over or that his eyes are so wide and blue and apologetic, but he doesn't look as perfectly airbrushed and muscle-bound and *manly* as the guy on the magazine covers. He looks young. Like a real, actual seventeen-year-old who barfed on a stranger in the airport.

My sympathy, however, is fleeting. Somehow, his fitted gray T-shirt—a V-neck instead of a polo—survived his puke-fit without a mark on it, and the smear on his distressed jeans will go unnoticed. Of course *he'd* go on some drinking binge and still be able to walk out of the airport without smelling vile. Life is just that fair.

"Can we get going?" I gesture to my soon-to-be-crunchy, barely-hiding-anything shirt.

His eyes drop to my chest, and color rushes up his face. Then *my* face heats to egg-frying temperature. I might as well have said, *Feel free to check out my boobs.*

"Oh. Yes." He swallows a couple of times before standing. Instantly, the color in his cheeks fades to a nasty shade of gray that blends nicely with the wall behind him.

I grit my teeth. "I'll get your stuff. Did you have anything besides your bat bag?"

"You don't have to. I'm going to be okay."

He doesn't look okay. He looks awful.

"Sit."

His face collapses into a frown, and he hunkers down in the chair.

"I'll bring the van around curbside." I point to the bench outside the sliding doors. "Do you think you can make it that far without passing out, or..."

"Yeah." He clears his throat like it's dry. "Probably."

Probably is going to have to be good enough.

I gather his bags—an enormous red duffel was the only other thing on the carousel besides his equipment bag—both labeled with his last name in permanent marker. With a grunt, I haul the monsters out to the van. The burning in my muscles ignites some inner reservoir of anger I've stored up against prima donna athletes and their ridiculous lifestyle choices.

Don't get me wrong: there are usually only a handful of jerks. The majority of the guys are hardworking, decent people. But we can't go an entire season without one highly talented, self-absorbed athlete who thinks he's untouchable. Like Sawyer Campbell.

My cell phone rings as I sling open the van's back door. I chuck Campbell's bags inside, hoping they're full of valuable electronics and Rolex watches, but they clunk like wood bats.

Too bad.

The words *Office of the General Manager* float across my screen, and a kitschy 1920s version of "Take Me Out to the Ballgame" fills the parking garage. I can't ignore the call no matter how much I want to.

"What's up, Dad?"

"Are you and Campbell on your way back?"

I wish. "Not quite yet." Do I out Campbell now? I bite my bottom lip as I consider it. I think about the way his eyes looked when he apologized, and I pity him a little. He is young and probably dumb. No one said you had to be smart to be a good athlete. This time I'll let it go with a warning. "We had a bit of a luggage issue."

"But you have his bags now? You'll be on your way soon?" My dad never sounds nervous, but there's a clear undercurrent of urgency in his tone. He manages the Buckley Beavers like it's a walk in the ballpark—that's a business joke.

Tonight is Thirsty Thursday, and the half-price beer promo fills the stands with loud drunks. A great promo for weekday revenue, but we're also hosting a huge party for the local Baptist ministry. Last time those groups mixed, somebody gave a sermon on the evils of overindulging in alcohol, and someone else got reminded to keep their judgments to themselves. To make sure everyone has a good time and wants to come back, we've got to make sure the groups stay seated on opposite sides of the ballpark. Add all of that to the pregame autograph signing, and a wasted athlete waiting curbside...

I wipe a trickle of sweat off my forehead. "We're loading up now."

"All right, Ry. Be safe."

I fire up the old Beavermobile and cruise back to the terminal at a careful five over.

Campbell has made it to the bench under the awning, legs spread wide like he owns the whole seat. If he ever becomes something big, you can bet your bluebonnets that someone will slap a placard on that bench. All because his butt touched it once.

Sports are sort of a huge deal in Texas.

He stands as I roll to a stop in front of him, seeming a little more stable on his feet. I don't give him credit for his power of observation, though. It's hard to ignore a full-size van with a giant beaver face painted on the hood.

"Nice ride," he says as he slides into the passenger seat and drops a backpack on the floor.

It doesn't matter if he means it like a joke or a passing remark, because the smirk on his face is so condescending.

"You know what, Campbell? This is *minor* league baseball. We don't have limo services to haul around drunk shortstops who probably won't live up to their hype." I shift the van into drive and stomp on the accelerator. His head snaps back with a satisfying *thunk*. "In the minors, everyone pulls their weight—the front office staff, the ground crew, and especially the players who want to stick around long enough to be promoted to Triple-A or above."

I open the console minifridge installed between the seats. Mascot costumes are wickedly hot, and we've lost a couple of Beaver-attired staffers to heat exhaustion. I toss a bottle of water at him, which he manages to catch before it rebounds off his chest.

"Drink that. Get yourself right." I shoot him my most venomous glare as I pull into traffic. "You've got hundreds of adoring kids who will be waiting at the park to meet a future all-star and not an alcoholic."

"I'm not drunk." His voice is low, his tone defensive.

"Whatever."

"I don't drink. I never have."

"That's what they all say."

Traffic—surprise, surprise—grinds to a halt. The eighty-minute car ride from Bush Intercontinental Airport to the field will surely stretch into a painful eternity. The silence drapes between us like a sign on the centerfield fence, weighted at the corners so it won't blow away easily.

"I think I have food poisoning," he says, after we've been parked for a good five minutes.

I focus on the bumper of the truck in front of us, trying to keep my eyes from straying anywhere near the passenger seat. "It's a good excuse. Make sure to use it if a reporter asks why you blew chunks all over the airport."

"Because everyone who throws up is drunk, right?" His voice has a dry ring of sarcasm to it.

I roll my eyes at him. "I'm sure you have a better explanation."

"I was starving when I woke up this morning and ate leftover chicken strips." He grimaces like he's remembering how they tasted on the return journey. "They'd been in the fridge for a few days."

For all I know Campbell is a good liar—he wouldn't have been the first guy to lie to me convincingly—but if he is telling the truth, I'll feel bad about it later. "Sorry for the accusation."

"I don't blame you." He gives a self-conscious half laugh. "I practically puked in your mouth."

I try not to think about how many times more horrible that would have been. "Ugh. Can we *please* not talk about this anymore?"

"Yes. Good plan." He drags a hand down his face like he's tired, but from the corner of my eye I see him gearing up again. Like he can't let it go. "I feel so bad. We really got off on the wrong foot."

"You puked on my right one. So..."

His face breaks into this cheek-dimpling smile, and something in the back of my neck relaxes. He's grateful that I'm teasing.

"Here." He opens his backpack and pulls out a package of Wint-O-Green mints and a tightly rolled navy bundle. "This'll probably be too big, but at least it won't…you know…stink."

He's offering me a lightweight T-shirt. Just looking at the clean material makes me itch to strip out of my nasty clothes.

"If you want to pull over and change, I won't look."

"That's comforting."

"I'll even cover my eyes."

There's a little smirk at the corner of his mouth, which doesn't make me feel any better. Still, I could climb over the seat and change in the back—that's what the space is intended for anyway. Usually it's used by our mascots. I take the material out of his hand. It's uber-soft, one of those shirts that's been washed a million and five times.

"Thanks," I mumble and pull off the road.

I'm not sure what my dad will say when I show up wearing a different shirt than I left in. But at least I'll be clean.

Well…cleaner.

Three

CAMPBELL'S SHIRT SMELLS LIKE HEAVEN AND FEELS LIKE BUTTER against my skin. I've had boyfriends, but I haven't had one long enough to acquire any of his clothes. And I'm not sure I'm the type of girl to wear a boy's clothes anyway.

But this T-shirt is perfect. Long enough to cover all but the hem of my shorts and comfy enough to forget I've got it on. Stealing it would be totally inappropriate, but maybe I could borrow it. For a long-ish time.

"Let's try this again," I say as I climb back into my seat. The neckline dips off my shoulder, and I tuck it under my seat belt to pin it in place. I offer him my hand to shake, all professional-like. "I'm Ryan Russell, assistant of game-day operations for the Buckley Beavers."

He takes it, and a grin spreads onto his face. "Sawyer Campbell. Nice to meet ya." His voice is like my favorite barbecue sauce, rich with southern flavor and as slow-moving as honey and molasses.

My job has put me in contact with some devastatingly good-looking men, but the better-looking they are, the worse they usually are to work with. I don't want to pre-judge Campbell based on his appearance, but experience is tough to ignore. Mentally, I put him on the line between the Okay Guy and Horrible Human categories. Only time will tell which heading he belongs under.

"Let me give you the official breakdown of how things work with the Buckley Beavers." I switch into tour guide mode, filling him in on housing assignments. "You can stay at the team's motel or wait for a member of the booster club to volunteer a guest room."

"Oh. I thought..." He finishes off his water bottle and crushes it into a tight wad. "Never mind."

A first-round draft pick will have plenty of folks offering up their extra rooms or garage apartments. I get the sense that he's a little bit uncomfortable with either choice, but if he's worried about accommodations, he's got enough money to rent an apartment or stay at a nicer hotel.

As we roll into Buckley's outskirts, I point out our few meager landmarks, the good restaurants, and the new outlet malls. There's one small movie theater with six screens that I never go to—the chairs are ancient. I'd need a can of Lysol just to sit down.

I don't tell him that part.

During home stretches, the players have a lot of free time on their hands and put to use what little entertainment Buckley has to offer. I'd rather have Campbell at the movies or mall than at one of our two bars. No players arrested this summer, thank you very much.

His phone chirps, and he groans at whatever the notification has delivered. He looks out the window and then grimaces. "What's a five-letter word that starts with Z?"

"What?"

"I'm playing a game with my brother." He looks at me like this should clearly mean something.

It doesn't. I don't have time for stupid games. I barely have time to return text messages. The upside of him being a Scrabble nerd is that he'll probably spend less time getting wasted. "Google it."

"That's cheating."

"And asking for help isn't?"

He tips his head in half agreement. "Zebra." He turns his phone to me, and from the corner of my eye I see confetti fire.

"Wow," I say without any enthusiasm. "You get a trophy for that?"

Campbell laughs like I'm funny and not offensive. "Sorry. You were telling me about Buckley."

"Right." I try to remember where I left off. "We also have a good library. The team does two story times there every month, one in English and one in Spanish."

"That's cool."

Most players have a stint in short-season Class A baseball—it's for the guys who were drafted in June after high school graduation or when their college seasons end—but the really promising athletes get to skip Class A all together, moving through the farm system to Class AA or Class AAA. They also don't get initiated into the fabulous world of sponsorships, promotions, and community relations programs.

I take a deep breath before launching into my memorized spiel. "I'm not sure what the contract details are between you and the Rangers, but most members of the Beavers are required to participate in sponsor-related activities, attend autograph signings and press junkets." I check to see if he's already glazed over but find him staring back at me with the oddest expression. "What?"

"How old are you?" He squints at me like I'm some sort of bug.

Ah. That question. "I'm seventeen, but the Beavers are a family business, so this is my fifth season working full-time for the team. I *am* qualified to do my job."

"Yeah. I can see that." He gives me a questioning eyebrow quirk. "You're sort of…intense."

Cannot count the number of times I've heard some variation of that. *Relax, Ry. Take a breath, Ry. You're no fun, Ry.* Whatever. I'm the master of getting stuff done. "You say that like it's a bad thing."

He holds up both hands defensively. "It's not," he corrects

quickly. "I'm intense. Intense is good. It's just that I don't know many girls who are intense about baseball."

"Baseball is my business." The words come out snippy and defensive. I don't mean them to, but the subject's a little sensitive.

"Do you like your job?"

"I can't imagine doing anything else." And I hope I never have to. After college—and during the summers—I intend to come back and keep working at the ballpark, eventually taking over for my dad. General manager by twenty-two? That's the plan. I'm going to be the youngest GM in the history of minor league baseball, and one of the few female GMs in the business.

"It's cool to meet someone who loves baseball like I do," Campbell says, his face lighting up like we've arrived on common ground. As we pull into the stadium parking lot, his face drops into a look of absolute awe, and I realize that maybe we have.

John M. Perry Park—Home of the Buckley Beavers—sits atop the city's highest hill like a crown on a monarch's head. It's built in an older style, with brick walls and exposed girders, like Wrigley Field in Chicago, but with only two decks and a grassy hill in the outfield instead of bleachers.

It's beautiful.

Larger-than-life banners of famous MLB players who've graced our field drape down the walls, and as I pull the van into a fenced-in side lot, a late-June breeze sends the images fluttering. A few cars speckle the enclosure, mostly food vendors and seasonal staffers. We're still an hour early for team arrival, but the field manager and other coaches always have a pregame meeting in the lower level conference room. I'll deliver Campbell to them and get back to work.

I jump out of the van and discreetly detach my shorts from the back of my sticky thighs. "Grab your stuff, and I'll introduce you to Mac, our clubbie, and—"

Campbell doesn't move. He stands outside the passenger door with his head tilted back to the pale blue sky. The goofiest grin I've ever seen stretches his face, like he's some little kid I've dropped off at Disney World. "This is..."

He turns his full-wattage smile on me. It's more potent than the self-conscious, the embarrassed, and the flirty smirks I've faced so far. My mouth wants to match his, to share some of the excitement he's clearly feeling. But I've got so many things to do.

"I'll play my first professional game at this stadium." He speaks with a sort of quiet reverence.

My foot lifts to start tapping, but his wonder...I can't ignore it, even though I want to. If today was my first day taking over the team, how would I feel?

Amazed. Grateful. Overwhelmed.

I swallow. "Do you want me to take your picture?"

"That would be great. My mom would love it. My family will—" He digs into his pocket and hands me an old iPhone with a cracked screen and then just stands there. In the parking lot.

Like this will be a picture worth sending home.

Boys are idiots.

"Come on. I have a better idea." I turn and stride off. I can give him three minutes. Three more minutes won't kill my schedule completely. "I'll take you to the main gates."

Apparently he's recovered from the barfing episode, because he springs forward like a puppy. If he had a tail, it would be wagging.

I take several pictures of him leaning against the gatepost, one with him draping his arm around the statue of Mr. Perry—the guy who donated most of the money to build the stadium—and one pointing to the posters on the walls.

Campbell is ridiculously photogenic. The dimples. The square jaw. The contrast of blue eyes against dark hair. I really want to hate him, but what kind of person can hate a puppy? Sure, they're sort of stupid and sometimes throw up on your feet, but the bounding happiness? The big puppy eyes? The wagging?

Sigh.

"We're going to be late."

I show him a secret passageway that snakes under the seats and connects to the left field ticket office. The door is heavy and a little corroded, so I give it a good shove. It pops open, and I trip over the body sprawled on the floor.

Four

"**M**IA!" I SHRIEK, HANGING ON TO THE DOOR HANDLE SO THAT I don't step on her head. "What are you doing?"

Mia has one thin arm thrown over her eyes and the other pillowing her head against the painted cement floor. Her long legs stretch out of her somehow-shorter-than-standard-issue khakis, feet bare.

The violations. I can't count them. I don't even try.

"It's so hot in here. No one turned on the air, and I was early, so—" Her eyes open a little, then widen when she sees I'm not alone. "So, so hot," she finishes in a half whisper.

Campbell brushes past me. "Did you pass out? Did you hit your head?" He offers her his hand to sit up, but she bounces to her feet. Her curly hair springs to life around her face.

"You're Sawyer Campbell." She takes his hand like she's going to shake it, but she doesn't let go. "You were phenomenal in the Junior College World Series. You batted twelve for fourteen. It was phenomenal."

"You already said that, Mi." I fold my arms at the tone of her voice. Let the idol worship begin.

"But you're all right?" Campbell asks with genuine concern. He looks to me to explain what's going on.

I point to the A/C vent Mia had prostrated herself under. "She's fine. She's always like this."

I know everything about the business of baseball. Mia knows everything about the sport of baseball—and every other sport. She'll probably be all-state in softball, basketball, and track our senior year, has the body of a professional beach volleyball player, and has already signed a full scholarship to play softball for the University of Texas. She also reads baseball scouting reports for fun and has her own personal subscriptions to *ESPN The Magazine*, *Sports Illustrated*, and *Baseball America*. She says it's to look at all the hot guys, but I know it's for the articles.

"I mean, you broke the record for home runs—"

"Mr. Campbell knows he's a big deal," I interrupt, and make a face at her from behind Campbell's broad shoulder. "He doesn't need you to remind him."

"Well, sometimes I do." He shrugs in a gee-whiz way that's so sweet it makes my teeth hurt. "It's nice to meet you, Mia."

And then Mia tucks a few stray curls behind her ear and shifts her weight from one foot to the other. She's smitten.

"He's got to check in with the trainers and coaches, and I've got things to do." I put both of my palms in the middle of Campbell's back and propel him toward the far end of the ticket booth, which opens onto the stadium's tunnels. "Tell Mr. Campbell goodbye, Mia."

"Goodbye, Campbell." She gives a dorky little wave I know she'll regret later. As I reach back to close the door, Mia whisper-yells, "Dibs!"

"Fraternization gets you fired!" I whisper-yell back, then turn face-first in to a solid wall of gray.

Campbell is standing so close it's impossible not to see how tall and muscled and gorgeous he is. For one brain-freezing moment, I see exactly what Mia is drooling over. In another couple of years, he could be the new face of Nike. He could be on billboards and commercials, and every girl in America would stop and watch Gatorade-colored sweat drip down his face.

So, so hot.

I stomp the brakes on that train of thought. No fraternization between staff and players. Ever. It's in the contract I sign every year. Sure, it's a super-patriarchal clause that screws over the woman in pretty much every situation, but workplace relationships are always messy.

Dad had to fire our ticket office manager last year for hooking up with Hadley Pearson in the ticket office and felt horrible about it. He wrote Pearson up and sent a memo to the head office, but even though Dad owns the team, he doesn't have any control over the players. Rumor was that Pearson had to pay some sort of fine and was benched for three games, but the punishment was pretty minor in comparison to what happened to the girl.

Obviously, since Pearson is still here and she's not.

It's not like I needed another reason to adhere to the fraternization policy, but since then I added it to my list of rules to help me earn my dad's job.

Rule #1: Never cringe at the worst tasks. Sweep the floors, pour the beer, and sometimes hide players' mistakes. Easy.

Rule #2: Know the business better than anyone else. If I know *everything,* no one will doubt me.

Rule #3: Never get involved with a player. No one in this male-dominated profession will take me seriously if they think I'm trying to sleep my way to the top.

"Sorry." I lower my hands from Campbell's chest. How long have they been on his chest? I clear my throat, and we shift apart. "Home team locker rooms are this way." I point out the elevator like I'm bringing a 747 in for landing. "After games, you'll take that up to the press box if you're needed for interviews or special events."

"Pretty similar process to what we did at State." He nods for me to keep walking.

I'd memorized Campbell's basic stats and faintly remember reading something about him being a sixteen-year-old college freshman, but I thought it was a typo.

"State?"

"I got my GED after my sophomore year of high school and went to the State College of Georgia last year."

I don't want to be impressed. A lot of guys are drafted right out of high school, but he couldn't have qualified for the draft till the year he turned eighteen. We've had a few players this young before, though most everyone on the team is in their early twenties. It's sort of admirable that he got a little college in before turning pro.

"Hmm." *Focus, Ryan. You don't care.* "Trainer first."

The tunnels narrow as we move under the grandstand. The training room and the small in-stadium gym are tucked under the home base seats. It's dark, with the only external windows looking into the dugout, but it was a clever way to use the space.

Heaving open the door to a room that even if the stadium burned to the ground would smell like sweat and athletic tape, I find our ancient trainer, Red, waiting for us.

He's staring over his bifocals, with his white eyebrows disappearing into his receding hairline. "Ryan Marie Russell, what in heaven's name are you wearing, girl?"

I ignore the question and the embarrassment that comes with it. "Red, this is Sawyer Campbell. He needs to be checked out before he can play."

"I know who he is. But if your mother sees you——"

"She won't." I cut Red off before he can dispense a grand-fatherly warning like he does Advil and ice packs. I straighten the collar of my borrowed shirt, sending the V-neck plunging between my boobs. Not an improvement. "Will you please take care of Mr. Campbell for me?"

"Of course I will." He gives the man-child a cursory glance. "You best get topside."

"Yes, sir." I turn for the door before this can get any worse. "See you for the anthem."

A hand brushes my arm, gentle, not obtrusive. "I'm really sorry about——" Campbell waves to my borrowed shirt with his free hand. "I'll make it up to you."

I offer him my biggest, fakest smile. "No worries. At least nothing worse can happen to me today."

MIA HAS MOVED FROM THE FLOOR TO THE CHAIR AT THE TICKET window, and her mass of curls is twisted up and held in place with a ballpoint pen. It's left a series of blue ink marks above the neckline of her T-shirt.

"You've got stripes." I smear them a little.

She cringes at my touch. "Please tell me you did not lick your finger."

"Ew. Germs. No."

"Speaking of germs and spit, Sawyer Campbell." She nods like that sentence is supposed to make sense. I know exactly where she's going with this, but I simply shake my head. "If he wanted to share spit with me or—"

"I can probably get him to puke on you, and trust me when I say that's an unpleasant experience."

Mia has an almost cartoonishly pretty face—giant eyes, full lips, defined cheekbones—and her face moves like a cartoon too. Her eyes grow so wide that her eyelashes smash against her eyebrows. "There's a story here. Please tell me that it's better than I'm imagining."

I open the narrow cabinet against the room's rear wall, searching for the box of leftover shirts for the Beaver Buddies—the official apparel of the junior fan club—stored somewhere among unprinted ticket stock and programs. "Are you imagining Sawyer Campbell throwing up on me at the airport?" I shake out a child's medium, the largest in the box. "'Cause that's exactly what happened."

"Shut. Your. Mouth." She bursts into the sort of hysterical, snorting laughter that's impossible not to join.

I retell the story as I shove the box back into the closet. "I tried to clean up in the airport bathroom, but my shirt was unsaveable. So, he lent me this." I straighten the sleeve of Campbell's shirt once more.

"Wow." She folds her arms over her chest and leans back

as far as the chair will let her. Her animated face has turned to scheming villain. "You're wearing Sawyer Campbell's shirt. That's *intimate*. For you."

"I wear your clothes." Sometimes. I'm five-foot-six. She's six feet even. Her shorts look like capris on me. I peek out the ticket office window, making sure no one can see in, and shuck Campbell's tee. "Nothing intimate about that."

"Maybe this is the beginning of something?"

"I don't have relationships with baseball players."

"You don't have *relationships* with anyone."

She can't see my irritated expression because the fan club T-shirt is too small—no surprise there. I manage to get my head through the hole and one arm lodged in a sleeve when the outer door of the ticket office flies open. I peek over my shoulder with an awkward twist of my neck and find, to both my relief and my horror, my mother standing in the open doorway.

"Ryan, pull your shirt down!" She sweeps into the office, her perfectly styled hair blowing forward as the door slams. The overpowering smell of her gardenia perfume saturates the space instantly.

"Don't you think I'm trying?"

She gives the shirt a vicious yank, nearly ripping off my earlobe in the process. "Standing here in your bra for the whole world to see? Surely your father has taught you better."

Since the divorce, any behavior she deems even slightly

inappropriate is my *father's* fault. "It was an emergency." I snake my other arm through the sleeve and catch my reflection in the window. The shirt is snug over my boobs, but it's long enough to cover the waistband of my shorts. "My other shirt got ruined."

"Doesn't your father keep a few extras around? When I worked here . . ."

Please, not now. If I have to listen to another lecture about how much better the team was when she worked on the staff, then I'm going to have to ask one of the pitchers to bean me in the head. Repeatedly.

"He might, Mom, but I didn't want to bother him. He's probably wrapping up his sponsorship meeting right now."

"We've talked about this before. You're the general manager's daughter. You don't have to dress like seasonal staff." She offers a simpering smirk over my shoulder. "No offense, Mia."

"None taken, Mrs. R." Mia's words are a little muffled because she's holding Campbell's shirt to her face.

I rip it out of her hands, but my dirty look makes her smile wider.

Mom is sorting through the shirts I put back, organizing them with her typical speed. Some habits are harder to quit than others. "We bought all those nice skirts and blouses. You can still be cool and look a little more professional."

"I can't squat in the dirt with the Beaver Buddies in a skirt, Mom."

She waves at her fifties-era halter dress. "Honey, when you own the team, you don't have to *squat in the dirt.*"

Mom received a fifty percent ownership of the Beavers as part of the divorce. She quit working in the front office, traded in her khakis for vintage dresses, and became a not-so-silent partner. Some weeks, she'll appear out of the blue to "check on things at the park" and flirt with the high rollers in the suites. She says it's good for our sponsors to be able to meet with a representative from the team and air their grievances or express their delight.

She isn't wrong, but having her around makes every staff member twitch with nerves. Including Dad.

Mom grabs the end of my long ponytail and twists it into a bun on top of my head before letting it fall loose again. "Just think about it. You don't want to be a field rat your entire life."

I bite my tongue to hold back commentary about her entire married life being spent as a field rat. She used to squat in the dirt and run promos and sweat in the miserable Texas heat with the rest of us. But Mom has bigger plans for everything now—including me—and none of them involve baseball. I roll up Campbell's shirt and hope she doesn't see my white-knuckled grip on the material.

"Speaking of your father, I've got a few things I need to discuss with him."

"He's probably headed to the press box, Mom. Where he's always at before a game starts."

She swipes a quick kiss across my cheek, surely leaving a red lipstick smear, and sweeps out of the office like she owns the place.

And I guess, technically, she does.

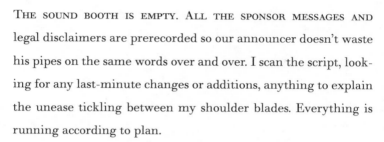

THE SOUND BOOTH IS EMPTY. ALL THE SPONSOR MESSAGES AND legal disclaimers are prerecorded so our announcer doesn't waste his pipes on the same words over and over. I scan the script, looking for any last-minute changes or additions, anything to explain the unease tickling between my shoulder blades. Everything is running according to plan.

Except for the shouting coming through the door that connects to the owner's booth.

The polite thing to do would be to turn away, like some kids do when their parents fight. I never had delusions of marital bliss between my parents, so I set down the script and ease closer. My parents' relationship had been rocky for years before they finally decided to split. The yelling doesn't bother me anymore. I don't really remember a time when they talked to each other at anything less than full volume.

"You can't do this, Marie! It's not fair to us. It's not fair to this organization," Dad says as I swing open the door. He towers over her petite five-foot-five frame. Not that she's ever been intimidated by him.

She's got her Ice Witch voice on, sounding detached and composed. "Let's talk a little less about *fair* and a little more about *logic*. The Rangers can withdraw their contract. You'll lose the team, Matthew. You'll lose ev-ery-thing."

"I've got it under control——"

"Selling half the team gets us *both* what we want."

"Selling half the team?" I ask, letting them know I'm standing behind them. "Mom, what are you talking about?"

Dad looks up, surprised. His cheeks are flushed, and the vein at his temple pulses. Mom steps back and waves for my dad to answer the question.

"It's nothing, honey." His hands drop from his hips. "Your mom has some ideas about investors, and we're just working through them."

Typical Dad. Trying to protect his baby girl from the big, bad world. I turn to Mom for a straight answer.

She actually manages to look guilty for a moment, but squares up her shoulders and plows forward: "I wanted to take you to dinner and tell you. But...I'm seriously considering selling my portion of the team."

I hear the foul-ball warning announcement—a shattering of fake glass to remind patrons to pay attention to the game. I only have two minutes to get down to the field. But Ice Witch has frozen me to the suite's industrial carpeting. "Why?"

"The Rangers require our facilities to meet certain standards, but the upgrades are expensive, and I honestly don't want the hassle of finding that kind of money." Mom smiles, and it's as fake as her new boobs. "Selling my portion will bring on investors with the kind of capital to make improvements. And it means I'm out of this business. Finally."

She throws a dark look at Dad that he doesn't acknowledge.

"It would mean a lot of other changes," he says, mouth flat, way too serious for a game day. "To the way we manage everything here."

"What kind of changes?" I ask, but I have a sick feeling I already know. Promotion overhauls. New sponsors. Staffing adjustments.

Mom curls her arm around my shoulders. "The investors will be here in ten days to check out the stadium. I promise that you and I will discuss all of this before I make any final decisions." She nods to the big picture windows that showcase the field below. "Right now, you've got to get those Little Leaguers on the field."

I'm shivering despite the heat. "But—"

"Go, Ryan," she says, pushing me toward the door.

Convenient for her that I have to "squat in the dirt" or those kids would never get on the field. "Fine." A part of me wants to stay and fight for an explanation, but my sense of duty wins out.

I understand the implications. If she sells her shares to one of those big-time conglomerates that own a ton of profit-churning teams, they could force Dad out of his position as general manager. It would be the end of our traditions, our long-running promotions, and our family business.

And if someone else is in charge, there's no guarantee they'll ever let a girl like me—or any girl—run the team on her own.

CHAPTER

Five

I T'S MIDNIGHT WHEN I GET HOME. AND NO MATTER HOW LATE I pull in, Dad's always an hour behind me. He'll pick up burgers and fries from our favorite all-night drive-thru, and we'll hash out the game and promos over grease and ketchup. Then he'll fall asleep on the couch to the sound of ESPN's top ten plays.

But as I step under the scalding water of my shower, I gear up for a discussion. I'm going to tell him that we have to fight Mom on this, that this time he can't sign the papers and walk away. This is more than dissolving our family. Selling her portion of the team could destroy my future.

As I turn off the water, I hear the deep rumble of voices. At first I think Mom's come home to stage her coup, but she hasn't been through the door in at least four months. And as I wrap a towel around my head, I realize the voices are too low in volume and pitch to be my parents.

Who did my dad bring home?

I didn't grab a bra, just my cami and pajama shorts. I open the bathroom door and hear Dad laughing, another deep voice continuing a story.

"Dad?" I call. "Who's here?"

He doesn't answer, still laughing.

Our house is a rambler, with all four bedrooms like spokes around a big kitchen and living room. I peek around the corner and see none other than Sawyer Campbell sitting at our kitchen bar, an enormous burger in his hands and both elbows on the counter. Dad's next to him, same position, completely at ease with this boy he barely knows. I can't get to my room without dashing past the archway that opens onto the kitchen, and I don't really want Campbell to see me in my pajamas.

"Ry?" Dad yells now that he's done laughing. "Come say hi to Sawyer. He's staying with us for the night."

We've put up players before, but not since Mom left. I got the sense it would be inappropriate without another woman in the house. So what makes Campbell so special?

I stick my head further around the corner, trying to keep my body hidden in the shadows of the hallway. "Hey." I hope that my monotone carries my lack of enthusiasm.

Dad is beaming, and he's got barbecue sauce at the corner of his mouth. "Come eat. I know you're starving."

I am, and my traitor stomach rumbles at the sight of a double bacon cheeseburger and a huge carton of fries, but I don't want to do dinner without my bra. It's not like I'm super busty, but still.

"Did Sawyer tell you his dad and I played together in college?"

Either Dad is ignoring the way I'm keeping my distance, or he doesn't care. Sawyer's got his focus on his fries and a container of ketchup.

"No." *Please, Dad, read my body language this one time.* "He didn't mention it." Or that he was staying with us.

"His parents are the best people. I worked on their family's watermelon farm for three summers. Did your dad sell out or are y'all still running it?"

"Still running it." Campbell nods without looking up from his food. "Some years are tougher than others."

"Some things never change." Dad takes a swig of his beer and looks up at me. "Your food's getting cold. Eat."

It's a command, and like the obedient kid I've always been, I stomp into the kitchen and snatch my burger, despite the zit glaring on my chin. I stay standing, keeping the length of the island between me and Campbell.

"I haven't seen your parents in ages." Dad points at Sawyer with a fry. "They coming out to watch you play?"

"Mom's coming later in the season, and she's excited to see you and your family."

"Your dad going to make it?"

Sawyer shakes his head. "He can't leave the farm. You know how it is." There's something unhappy in the line of his jaw. Guiltily, I find myself hoping Wonderboy has some family issues, and then immediately hate myself for wishing my problems on someone else. Then I soothe my self-loathing with another fry. It's a healthy way to deal with my emotions, I know.

Dad pushes a couple packets of mustard toward me, knowing I'll want them for my burger. "Did you know that Sawyer is from Cordele, Georgia, watermelon capital of the world?"

I try to channel one of Mom's Ice Witch glares to tell Dad he's being super weird, but must miss the mark. Or he ignores it. What exactly is he doing? Dad doesn't introduce me to guys. And he doesn't bring random people home and feed them fast food late at night. Why does this feel like...I don't know...some sort of blind date? "Watermelons, huh? That's interesting." Poor Campbell blushes, and I feel like an actual witch. I eat another fry, clear my throat, and make an effort. "Is this your first time away from home?"

"I lived in the dorms last year, but that was only twenty minutes from my parents' house." He nods, wipes his fingers on his napkin, then nods again. "But, yeah, this is the farthest I've ever been from my family for more than a couple of days at a time."

"Did Sawyer tell you he was homeschooled up until his first year of high school, but by then he was so far ahead of his classmates he graduated early?" Dad slaps Sawyer across the back like he's so *darn* proud of this kid he just met.

"Nope." I drench my fry in ketchup so I don't have to see the way Campbell's cheeks darken to a lovely shade of vermillion.

"Well, I promised your folks we'd take good care of you. If you need rides anywhere, to church or the park or whatnot, I'll make sure Ryan can get you where you need to be."

Oh, fun. So on top of my regular assignments and trying to figure out how to save the team, now I'm Campbell's personal chauffeur.

"That's really not necessary, sir." Campbell shoots a look at me, but his eyes dart away fast. "I can take a Lyft or walk——"

"Of course not! Your family took care of me, and now it's my chance to return the favor." Dad looks up and, maybe for the first time in the entire conversation, he really sees me. His forehead creases when he notices my wet hair and pajamas. This time he reads my angry eyes and responds with a shoulder shrug that tells me I'm overreacting. "Tomorrow, we'll get Sawyer all set up at the team motel and we'll go from there."

We finish eating while Dad continues telling us stories about Campbell's family and the summers he worked on the watermelon farm. I don't really understand the ins and outs of melon harvest, but it sounds miserable. Then Dad says something that has Sawyer laughing so hard he has to cover his mouth with his fist.

Despite myself, I find myself smiling at the image of a much younger version of my dad blowing up overripe melons with fireworks. Or lining them up along the Campbells' fence for target practice.

As I roll the orange-and-white-striped wrapper of my burger into a tight ball, I catch Sawyer watching me. He doesn't look away like he's embarrassed that he's been caught. Instead he gives me an apologetic smile. I'm not sure if he's sorry for looking at me or for my dad's long-windedness or for this whole situation, but it zings straight into my gut like I misjudged a line drive.

Dad's silent, and his eyes weigh the tension between Campbell and me. "It's getting late." He finishes off his Bud Light. "Lots to do tomorrow. Ryan, why don't you show Sawyer to the guest room? Then we can all get some sleep."

The guest room. The room next to mine. Across from the bathroom we'll share. I try to fight the nervous chill creeping down my back, but it's a losing battle. *It's for one night. No one will ever know he's been here.*

"Sure."

Campbell clears his mess, then picks up his duffel and follows me down the hall. Can he see the hairs on the back of my thighs? Do I care? Why do I care?

"Let me grab you a clean towel." My voice sounds soft in the darkened hallway.

"I'm sorry to put you out." He runs his free hand through his hair, making it stand up.

I give him a half smile that I hope doesn't look too much like a wince. "It's not a problem."

When I swing open the bedroom door, I'm grateful that the cleaning ladies come every week. The room smells like fresh linens, and it looks homey, if a little shabby. Mom loves that beat-up white furniture look. The queen-size bed is covered with a handmade wedding ring quilt that had been a gift when my parents got married. There's a low dresser and a matching armoire but not much floor space. Campbell's arm brushes my shoulder when he enters. I don't want to notice the way he smells, all pine tar and sunflower seeds, but I can't help it.

He's hot. So what? Lots of guys are hot. My fingernails cut little crescents into my palms. "If you need anything else, let me know."

He drops the duffel on the foot of the bed, then moves it to the floor like he's afraid it might dirty up the quilt. "Thanks. I promise I'll be out of your hair tomorrow."

The awkwardness buzzes between us like a swarm of summer mosquitos. We're both shifting nervously, like we want to swat it away, but neither of us makes the first move. Whatever easiness we found in the Beavermobile and as I took pictures of him at the field is long gone.

"Sleep well." A smirk tweaks at the corner of my mouth, and this time it feels closer to real. He does seem more Okay Guy than Horrible Human. And our families are—or once were—

close. I'll think of him like a hot cousin. That way I can accept that he's good-looking but feel icky when I think about it.

I keep repeating the phrase *hot cousin* over and over in my head as I brush my teeth and settle into my own bed.

Then I remember that my mom wants to sell my team, and every thought of Sawyer Campbell poofs out of my mind.

I HIDE OUT IN MY ROOM THE NEXT MORNING UNTIL I HEAR DAD and Campbell leave to pick up breakfast and then head to the field. Some days I beat Dad to the office, some days he beats me. There aren't set hours since a lot of our work isn't done at a desk, but everyone's expected to check in by ten.

Being a chicken means that I have to dig through the cupboards for food—we don't eat at home regularly during the season—and come up with a crumpled protein bar and some instant coffee. On top of the burger last night and the run I skipped this morning, my body hates me. I'll work all of it off running up and down the stairs at the stadium between promotions, but it's not the same as eating well and getting five or more miles in. I make a promise to myself to do better tomorrow.

Friday nights usually have huge attendance numbers. There's not much else to do in Buckley. Tonight, we've got three corporate dinners and a postgame concert with a popular Christian rock band. The ticket presales are over eight thousand, and we have a good chance of selling out. The weather's great, not miserably humid for a Texas June.

Dark thoughts from my too-short conversation with my mom linger in my head, but when game time arrives, everything goes smoothly. The nine-year-old national anthem singer remembers all the words. The promos get on and off the field without holding up the game. Bucky the Beaver delivers flowers to a lady in the wheelchair row, and she tears up.

Her gratitude twists something in my chest. *This.* This is why I have to run this team. I don't want some outsiders to come and change the simple things that work so well, to take away our traditions and replace them with outrageous gags meant to reel in news coverage and sponsorship dollars. I *will* fight my mom over this.

I pull out my phone—I stopped texting her months ago, but this feels like the right time to break the ban and tell her exactly what I think.

You can't sell the team. It will kill Dad. It will destroy my hopes of ever running the Beavers. DON'T DO THIS.

No response.

As I jog back to the field to get the Race Around the Bases

promo in place, I can't shake the feeling that storms are on the horizon. Sky's clear. A perfect night for baseball.

This season our mascot is played by Mason Wheeler, a sophomore drama kid from my school, who absolutely loves his job. I should laugh when the little kid who races Mason/Bucky trips over second, stumbles into the beaver, and sends our mascot rolling into the outfield. The crowd's eating up Mason/Bucky's antics. Even Mia, who always leaves the ticket booth after the third inning to help me with the between-inning entertainment, almost pees her pants laughing. I know from a miserable personal experience how hard it is to stand up in that Beaver suit. Campbell is the closest player, and he hams it up, getting the mascot back onto his giant webbed feet. Bucky holds his back like he's injured; Campbell dusts dirt off the beaver's enormous rump before sending the mascot toward the dugout with a friendly pat.

Instead of joining the crowd in their adoration, I swallow hard and wipe my sweaty palms on my khaki shorts.

If Mom sold her interest, all of this would change. All of it.

MIA AND I ROLL THE PROMOTION GEAR INTO THE STADIUM DURING the ninth inning, planning to reorganize everything so tomorrow's props are easier to reach.

"So." She only starts sentences like that when she knows I'm not going to like what follows. "Whatcha doing tonight?"

"You mean after the concert, stadium cleanup, and counting the till?"

She huffs and jiggles the lock on the closet because it won't unlatch. "Yes. After all that. What are you doing?"

"By then it will be after midnight and I'll stink like ballpark and hot dogs and—"

"Come swimming tonight," she interrupts, as the closet bursts open and props tumble out. "People are coming over and we're going to play night games and swim. You won't need to shower before, because the chlorine will wash away your stench."

I know exactly what kind of *people* Mia is talking about—people of the male variety, namely athletic guys from school. They flock to Mia because she has the amazing capacity to be both a tomboy and a cool girl, and to date all of them without making any of them hate her.

"It'll be replacing one stench with another." This is where *I* excel. Saying no without actually saying the word. "How about I call you when I'm done here?"

She pulls a pencil out of her hair—no marks on her neck today—and it falls down her back like a waterfall. "I know you don't *want* to come, but that doesn't mean you shouldn't come."

Just like I know her "So" sentences, she hears my *no* even though I really don't want to disappoint her. "I do want to come—"

"Except that you don't." She sighs and shakes her head, disappointed despite my efforts. "You've become this little ball of stress and anxiety and schedules. I think you need to be seventeen for a little while."

You know how a dog's fur bristles when it feels threatened? The hair on the back of my neck stands up, and just like that I'm irrationally angry at my best friend. Mia's words sound too much like something Mom said at dinner last week.

I don't want you to have regrets.

You need to get away from this town and see what else is out there.

You won't be a kid forever. You need to enjoy it.

Mia offers me a sad smile and bumps my shoulder with hers. "The invitation is open even if you always ignore it."

Guilt pinches. I suck as a friend from March to September. Mia knows it and still hasn't abandoned me. "What if I come for an hour? Once I make sure that Campbell's housing is arranged, I can probably ditch—"

"Wait. WAIT." She holds up both hands, as if she's stopping a freight train. "Where is Sawyer Campbell staying?"

I can see where this conversation is headed. "No, Mia."

"But with my brother gone, we have an extra room. Or Campbell could stay in the pool house. Either way, I could build up a totally platonic..." She trails off, her eyes all dreamy. "I'm lying. I will quit this job right now if it means I get to hook up with Sawyer Campbell."

And she would, too. Mia works for the team because it's the

only time we get to spend together in the summer. It's not like she needs the money. Her parents own the largest air-conditioning company in Texas. If there's one business that will never fail, it's the one that makes Texas habitable.

"Traitor," I say, faking a punch at her face.

"Why am I—"

My radio clips off her words. Meredith, our public relations director, is calling me with the list of players the media wants to interview. Mia turns back to the jalapeño sausage costume and straightens its sombrero and skinny mustache. The guy who'd worn it for the race got tripped by the Italian sausage, and they steamrolled each other to reach the finish line.

"Who do you need, Mer? Over."

"Just Campbell," her voice crackles through.

"That's it? Williams pitched six good innings. Over."

"Yep. Just Campbell."

I roll my eyes. This is another problem with having big names in a small town. The guys who work their butts off every day are overlooked for the guys with bigger signing bonuses. Not that Campbell didn't play well—he hit a homer in the third and doubled in his second at bat—but Williams struck out eight straight and only gave up one run. He should have gotten his moment in the spotlight.

"Ew," Mia says as she hangs the lederhosen-wearing sausage back on its hook.

"I'll get the sanitizing spray."

"Not that." Though she wipes her hands on her shorts. "You're making that face."

"Which face?"

"The face my abuela makes when a dog poops on her lawn."

I laugh. Abuela Rodrigues has two main expressions: exuberantly overjoyed and thoroughly disgusted. For some reason, Abuela long ago decided she liked me even though I only understand every fifth word of her rapid-fire Spanish. Every time Mia and I drop by, she tries to stuff me full of homemade alfajores cookies—not complaining—and glares at her granddaughter. As if Mia has failed to feed me properly.

Wrinkling my nose up, I sniff like Abuela Rodrigues does. "I thought this was her smell-a-fart face."

"It's very similar to the dog-poop face. And you make it every time you hear Sawyer Campbell's name."

"Every time you say Sawyer Campbell—and you *always* use both of his names, by the way—it triggers my gag reflex. I think I have PTSD from almost tasting his barf."

She tilts her head to the side, her dark eyes full of mischief. "You want him."

"I do not." *Hot cousin. Hot cousin.*

"You. Want. Sawyer. Campbell."

Her voice is so loud, and the tunnels echo so much. If I wasn't channeling Abuela before, I am now.

"I can't blame you." Mia takes the can of sanitizer out of my hand. "He's glorious."

"You're ridiculous." I turn my head out of the direction of the spray. "I'm going to go escort him upstairs."

Mia laughs. It's a vicious, evil laugh that makes me blush and want to punch her for real. "Have fun in the elevator."

Small space. Campbell close. Why did she put that in my head? "You're awful."

"Glor-i-ous!"

Seven

UNLIKE WITH MAJOR LEAGUE BASEBALL TEAMS, OUR POSTGAME press conferences don't take place in the locker room. Parts of the stadium have been refurbished in the ten years that Dad has owned the team, but the locker room is almost as gross as my high school's and smells only marginally better. That might be why the Rangers want it upgraded.

There's no cell reception under the stadium, and while our clubhouse manager carries a radio, he never answers it. Dad elected me to ferry the players from the locker room to the press box a few years ago, and the routine stuck.

I pound on the heavy steel door before cracking it open a bit, instantly suffocated by the combination of sweat and body spray. "I need Campbell!"

"I bet you do!" One of the guys—probably Pearson—responds from inside.

Sigh. Minor league baseball is its own ridiculous fraternity, and most of the guys don't outgrow their stupid jokes in the year or two they play at Perry Park. "Send him out. Please."

There's a crack of a towel and some laughter. I let the door drift shut without any guarantee Campbell will get the message.

But he comes out a few minutes later, hat in his hand, hair a mess.

My hands in his hair. His arms tight around me as I press him against the elevator's glass wall. Anyone outside could see us, rising above the stadium, but—

Mia! She's fired as my best friend. I gulp away any thoughts of kissing Campbell and push the elevator button a half a dozen times. The engine is one of the other things that hasn't been updated.

"Did Meredith give you talking points?" I ask him without making eye contact. *Push the button. Don't look at Campbell.* "Keep your language clean. Spread your compliments around. Stay positive."

"Does pushing the button over and over make it move faster?" His eyebrows are up, mouth quirked.

"Maybe." I hold the lighted button down, hearing the elevator creak closer. *Not that I want to get into this tight space with you any sooner. Yes, I do. No, I don't.* "It always looks better when you talk more about your team than yourself."

"I have done this before." He sounds a little...put out, maybe?

"Great." I give him a closed-lip smirk that doesn't come anywhere near sweet. "But it never hurts to be reminded."

"Right." He nods as the doors slide open, so I can enter first. "Thanks."

"Of course. It's my job." My job. *Which does not involve imagining your hair in my hands—what is wrong with me?*

If my team-approved polo showed any more of my skin, Campbell would be able to see that my chest is as red as it was the time I went to the Schlitterbahn water park and only put on sunblock once.

The doors creep closed, and I push myself against the wall, as far from Campbell as possible. He keeps sneaking looks at me as we rise, leaning back against the handrail, hands spread wide. "Did I do something wrong?" he asks.

"What?" The word pops out of my mouth with a little emphasis on the *t*.

"I mean besides throwing up on you. Like, did I break some rule I don't know about? Did I say something that offended you?"

"No." But even to my ears it's sharp. I *sound* offended.

He shifts off the handrail. "Don't take this wrong, but I get along with almost everybody." His big shoulders curl forward, a little self-conscious and kind of adorable. "If I said or did something wrong, you'd tell me. Right?"

Campbell says it like we're friends. Like we know each other.

I try to take the fact that I've worn his clothes and he's seen me in my pajamas out of the equation. *Focus on the professional.* "If you screwed up, I'd let you know."

A little laugh pops out of his mouth. "I believe that."

"Then why'd you ask?"

"Because you act like I did something to you *personally.*"

I swallow hard, hoping the heat in my chest hasn't crept all the way to my cheeks. "Of course not. Sorry. Sometimes I get wrapped up in work."

He nods, chin pushed out. "Sure." He's mulling this over, but I can see he doesn't really believe it. "I get it."

"It's just..." I hesitate, trying to figure out the right way to phrase what I'm thinking. "When I'm too friendly with the players, it looks bad."

"Like with Ollie?"

"Like Ollie the catcher, Ollie?"

Whatever I'm doing with my face—all scrunched and a little horrified—makes Campbell laugh. "Yes, Ollie the catcher. Before warm-ups, I heard you guys making plans for Saturday."

I wipe the air in front of me, like it's something I'm trying to clean. Ollie is, to use my mother's word, *darling*. He has one of those really circular faces that will never look grown-up, and dimples so deep you could lose a finger in them. He's not bad-looking. He's just...stocky. Solid. Ollie. "I take him to the library to read to the kids because he's fluent in both Spanish and

English. He's actually really funny and the kids love him."

"But you don't?"

"No! We're *friends*."

Campbell raises his eyebrows at my response, waiting for me to explain further.

How long is this elevator going to take? Doors. Open. Now. "Ollie is my coworker. Our relationship will always be platonic."

"And ours won't be?" There's a laugh in Campbell's words.

That's when the doors choose to pop open, revealing all the reporters waiting in the foyer beyond. "I—"

He steps out of the elevator, but the look he sends me over his shoulder turns my insides to lava. "See you later, Ryan."

And before I can say anything else, the elevator doors slide closed.

I DIVE INTO MIA'S POOL, STAYING UNDER UNTIL MY LUNGS BURN. Oxygen deprivation doesn't make my worries about the stadium disappear. I surface to a pulsing merengue beat. Mia's parents don't care how loud we play our music in the Grotto—that's what Mia and I nicknamed her pool because it has stone privacy walls and a faux waterfall slide—as long as half of the songs are in Spanish.

"Hey!"

Swiping a strand of hair out of my eyes, I turn toward the voice.

"You okay?" Lucas Chestnut treads water beside me, real

concern pulling between his eyebrows. "I thought maybe you hit your head or something."

Only the tops of his shoulders clear the water. Broad, muscular, typical high school athlete shoulders. "I'm fine. Just seeing how long I could hold my breath."

Water droplets have collected in Lucas's eyelashes, making them look ridiculously long around his dark brown eyes. He's cute. That's why I let Mia convince me to date him for a few months last fall, hoping he'd grow a personality. He didn't.

"I thought I might have to rescue you." He sweeps an arm around my waist and tows me close. My bare belly is pressed against his side, and our legs tangle under the water. "I wouldn't mind resuscitating you."

For one heartbeat, I'm tempted. He's a nice-enough guy, a good student, a great kisser. But I know resuming things with Lucas would be a mistake. For both of us. "I'm good. Thanks for the offer." I shove against him, but he doesn't budge.

He grins, like this is all part of the game. "Offer stands even if you are breathing."

"Not interested."

"Come on, Ry—" His words cut off when a Nerf football blasts into the side of his head. He spins, looking for his assailant, and lets me go.

Mia's standing on the side of the pool, hands on her bikini-clad hips, feet spread wide like she's a statue of some Greek goddess. "Game's starting." She motions for him to get the ball. "You're on my team."

He snags the football and swims away without a backwards glance, and I remember *exactly* why we broke up. His phone, his friends, whatever sounded fun at the moment was more interesting than me. We couldn't have a conversation without him checking his Snapchat or texts every few seconds. He documented everything we did together: our food, our shoes—one time he even tried to take a selfie while he was kissing me good night. It was like he cared more about what other people thought about our relationship than what I thought.

"You playing?" Mia yells, still looking all avenging goddess, and I know she started this game of two-hand touch to save me from Lucas. Or my own stupidity.

I did not want to come tonight. She would have forgiven me if I stayed home and pored over every sports business journal I could scrounge up, but I owe it to her to be a better friend. For this rescue and so many others. "Sure."

The teams are pretty even. Mia and I are the only girls who play. The other softball players either keep to the waterslide or hang out in the pool house where the A/C is blasting and there are plenty of drinks to go around. Even though I don't play team sports anymore, I inherited enough of my dad's athleticism to stay competitive, catching passes that earn some cheers and juking out of reach.

The night has turned steamy, but my muscles feel looser than they have in months. Even better than after one of my too-few training runs.

Lucas lines up across from me, shirt still off. He *does* look good, and he knows it. "Are you running cross-country again in the fall?" he asks.

"Yeah." I'm not in shape to win races, but my participation is important for college applications, though I'm only going to apply to A&M. It's the only school close enough that I can come home for April and September games. "I haven't been running with the team."

"If you want someone to train with..." He leaves the offer hanging.

"You can't keep up with me." And when Mia hikes the ball, I prove it.

Mia's team destroys mine, but we're laughing and breathless as the game wraps up. I've missed this. I've missed being with her, eating her mom's chivito sandwiches, and singing off-key to the songs on her playlist.

"Thanks for making me come." I slide into the water, and though it isn't that cool, it still feels better than the humidity. "It was fun."

Mia drops onto the side, waving to the last of the partygoers as they leave. She kicks water at me. "That's because I know how to have a good time."

"Speaking of that, what time is it?"

She leans back, stretching for my bag and pulling out my phone. The light makes a blue rectangle on her face, and I watch her eyes widen in shock. "You've got eleven missed calls in the last five minutes, and three text messages. All from your dad."

"What?" I splash out of the water. "He knows where I am."

Dad's not a worrier so...

"Need you at the stadium, ASAP," I read the message aloud. "Call me. It's an emergency."

CHAPTER

T HE STADIUM LIGHTS ARE OFF, BUT THE SPOTLIGHTS FROM THE
Christian concert throw bright beams over the walls. Music
pours into the parking lot, where I leave the Beavermobile. The
bass thumps in time with my heart as I break into a jog. Dad's
last message said he'd be in the training room, but he hasn't
answered my calls. The lack of cell service under the stadium
has always been a pain, but this is the first time it's given me a
reason to panic.

Dad's standing inside the glass door, arms folded across his
chest, and I take a relieved breath. I didn't know what to expect,
but my mind conjured up a dozen scenarios. Most of them stupid. Dad wouldn't have been texting and calling me if he'd had
a heart attack or broken his neck falling down the stadium stairs,

but those were my first thoughts.

When I step inside, I don't notice the training room's ever-present stink. Directly across from the door, Campbell is sprawled on his stomach on one of the pleather-covered training tables. Blood drips off his leg in a steady stream and plinks on the cement.

Our field manager, Duke Kartchner, stands to one side of the table, talking to someone on the ancient landline. The curly phone cord is pulled taut, stretching from Red's office between the training area and the gym. Duke is sort of a slow-moving man—round belly and a lip full of tobacco—and in the five years he's been assigned to the Beavers, I've never heard him speak with such concern.

Ollie's leaning against one of the other tables, hat backwards, arms folded, frowning while a glove-wearing, scissor-wielding Red snips off Campbell's sock.

"It's not that bad," Campbell says, voice muted as he speaks into his folded arms.

I don't know him that well, but the lie is clear. The muscles in his back stand out through the material of his thin workout shirt, and his hands are clenched into fists.

Whatever happened to his ankle, it hurts.

"Dad?"

He slides to the side, then drapes an arm over my shoulders and kisses the top of my head brusquely. "Thanks for coming so fast."

"Sure." I look between Dad and Campbell. "Why do you need me?"

"It's just a cut." Campbell lifts his head, and his face is pale. "I only came in here for a Band-Aid. Can't you slap some tape on it?"

"Quiet." Red peels back the sock's two halves. "Be still."

"Oh, no," Duke says, more to himself than to the person on the phone. "It looks like raw hamburger."

Ollie makes a face like a cockroach crawled across his dinner and turns away, but Dad steps forward, absorbed in the gory sight. "The EMTs are still here for the concert. Do we need the ambulance?"

"You're making a big deal out of nothing. I don't need an ambulance." Campbell's laugh is forced. "Come on, Mr. Russell. You know we get worse injuries on the farm."

"EMTs can't do anything for this, and he's not going to bleed to death." Red looks up and catches my eyes over his bifocals. "Go wash your hands and help me, Ry."

Everyone turns to look, and I wish that I would have taken off my swimsuit instead of throwing my shirt and shorts over the top. My butt is wet, and I'm sure there are boob circles from the padding in my bikini top.

"I—"

"Don't dither," Red snaps. "You took sports medicine. I helped you with your homework. We're making a compress. You're going to glove up and apply pressure. Not difficult."

I snap into action because that's what I do best, and find myself wearing latex gloves and looking *into* Sawyer Campbell's body. A gash a half-inch wide and two inches long cuts clean across his Achilles tendon.

"What happened?" I ask as I accept a roll of gauze from Red. He puts a pad across the gaping hole.

"It was an accident," Campbell answers around gritted teeth.

"He convinced me to stay late and hit a couple buckets of balls," Ollie says, facing me now that Campbell's wound is covered. "You know how the doors to the batting cages automatically lock when they swing shut? My arms were full, so Campbell stuck out his foot to stop the door and..."

Ollie finishes the sentence with a shrug. I can see for myself what happened. The doors to the batting cages, like the rest of the doors in the stadium, are made of heavy-gauge steel. They're supposed to be break-in resistant, fireproof, tornado-proof, and apparently foot-proof.

"The edges of those doors are sharp." Red signals for me to slide my fingers out of the way so he can tape down the gauze. "At least it's a clean cut. Nothing a dozen stitches won't take care of."

Duke turns the mouthpiece of the phone upward. "We have to take him to the ER. The team orthopedic will have to look at it."

"A surgeon?" Campbell's voice squeaks a little.

"For caution's sake, son." Red strips off his gloves. "The

organization has to look after its investment."

Any color left in Campbell's face drains away. It's a shade I recognize, and I look for the closest trash can.

"Now, don't you worry." The old man's tone is gentler than I'm used to hearing. "I'll grab you some crutches. Ollie, you and Ryan get him loaded into the van."

"I'll drive." Dad mimes for me to hand over the keys. "We can call your mom and let her know what's going on."

Campbell doesn't really need any help getting into the Beavermobile. He seems a little pissed off as he hefts himself over the bumper and onto the bench seat. Ollie hands up the crutches and shuts the door.

I pull an ugly face at Ollie. "This should be fun."

He gives a tired-sounding laugh. "Keep me posted?"

"If you want."

"I do." He takes off his hat, smooths back his dark hair, and puts it back on his head. "I feel a little responsible for the kid."

"First of all, he's not a kid. He's the same age I am. And second, no one thinks you're responsible for *anything*."

"Nope." He gives me a gentle push toward the passenger-side door. "Everyone expects you to be the responsible one."

THE HOSPITAL'S WAITING ROOM IS QUIETER THAN I EXPECTED. Besides one older couple, some fake potted plants, and a *Wheel*

of Fortune rerun on mute, I've got the place to myself.

"He's asking for you."

I jump, realizing the voice is directed at me, and look up from my phone and into a nurse's wide grin. I guess those funky hospital shoes make her extra stealthy, because she didn't make any noise until she was right in front of me. "Excuse me?" I ask, blinking my gritty eyes.

"That sweet boy, Sawyer, says he'd like you to come back and sit with him for a few minutes." She winks at me. "I know you're not family, but I'll overlook it tonight, seeing as you brought him in and he's got no one else."

My dad helped get Campbell all arranged and has been outside ever since. I can see him pacing in front of the building. He's been on his phone the whole time. With Campbell's mom, Brenda, and then the head office, and the surgeon's office.

I tighten my still-wet ponytail and follow the nurse toward the giant ER doors. They glide open, bringing with them the hospital smell—chicken soup and disinfectant. She leads me to a room with a curtain door, but before she can fling it aside, I grab her wrist.

"He's still dressed, right?" Visions of Campbell in an open-backed gown flash across my mind. It's not quite as pleasant as you'd imagine.

The nurse gives a belly laugh that Campbell is certain to hear through the partition. "Honey, his injury is on his ankle. We didn't strip him down for that."

She nods for me to enter, and I push beyond the curtain. Campbell's lying on his stomach, big body filling the entire bed, feet dangling off the edge, and shoulders wedged between the roll-off bars. They haven't touched Red's compression wrap, but his other sock is missing. He's tucked a pillow under his chest to prop himself up, and his head is turned so the phone is balancing on his face.

"Hi," I whisper, and make some sort of circular motion with my hand.

"It's my mom," he mouths, then rolls his eyes. "Do not fly out here. It's too expensive and it'll make Dad mad."

His signing bonus had to be several million dollars. How much could one ticket set him back? There's a chair close to the bed, but I don't feel comfortable walking in and sitting down. "I'll go."

"Please don't."

I'm not sure if he's talking to me or his mom, so I hover against the wall.

"Ryan's here. You'll listen to her." He holds the phone out toward me. "Tell her I'm okay."

I back away from his phone like it's venomous. "I don't know that you're okay, and I'm not lying to your mom."

He covers the phone with his hand. "Just tell her the team will take care of me."

"No." My eyes narrow. "Is that why you called me back here?"

"Please, Ryan. It's the middle of the watermelon harvest, my dad needs my mom's help, and I'm not there this year to do my share of the work." He's pleading, eyes wide and bright. "Please."

I hesitate before taking the phone. It's warm from his touch, and a streak of dirt smears the heavy case. "Hello, Mrs. Campbell!" My voice is too loud in the small space, and I clear my throat nervously.

"This must be Ryan! You sweet girl. I'm sorry my son has got you out so late. I'm sure you'd rather be sleeping. I'm so, so grateful he's got such good folks to help him out."

I don't know Brenda Campbell. Maybe she's an awesome actress or she's polite on the surface. But her voice is like a hug, wrapping around you and welcoming you into her family. "I'm happy to help, ma'am."

"My son, bless his heart, is trying to convince me that he's going to be fine. But I'm his mother. I *know* him." Her tone is full of worry, and the last word quivers a little. "He tends to ignore injuries because he and his dad think there is some silly sort of honor in never admitting they're in pain. It's simple bullheadedness, if you ask me."

"Tell her I'm fine." Campbell pulls a teeth-gritting face he must think will coerce me. Ha.

"Well, Mrs. Campbell, I'll be honest with you..."

"Please don't," he mumbles into the pillow.

"His ankle looks like it's been through a shredder."

"Gah," Campbell groans, and drops his fist onto the mattress hard enough that it makes the bed shake.

"But our trainer is an old family friend. I've known him since I was a little girl, and Red promised that if Campbell was careful and stayed off it for a week or so, he'd be fine."

Mrs. Campbell sighs into the phone. "That's what Sawyer said. But he's not good at staying down. It will take a lot of babysitting to make him stay on crutches."

"I can think of a few million reasons he'll stay on those crutches, ma'am."

She laughs at my boldness, and I continue. "I haven't known Camp—er, Sawyer—for very long, but I don't think he's stupid." I give him my dirtiest look, which only seems to amuse him. "He's going to want to get back to the field as soon as possible, but he knows and Red knows and the head office knows that he'll need time to fully recover before he tries to walk on that foot."

She sighs. "Forgive me, Ryan, but he's my baby. Big as he is, he'll always be my baby and I can't help but worry. He pushes himself so hard. Being injured gnaws at him."

I can only walk three steps before I have to turn and start back in the opposite direction. Campbell's eyes follow me as I pace. Ignoring him doesn't work, and there's something about knowing he's watching me that makes goosebumps rise along my arms.

"I totally understand, ma'am, and I promise if something

happens—" The phone beeps in my ear, and I check the screen. Someone named *Jay Street* is calling. Well, Jay Street will have to wait until I'm done making promises to Campbell's mom. "If there *is* something worth worrying about, I'll call you. Personally."

I could be brokering a sponsorship package for all the assurances I'm offering. And a southern accent I don't actually have keeps slipping out of my mouth. Apparently, people are more likely to buy lies and fence signage if you've got a drawl.

"Oh, Ryan, thank you. It does my heart good to know that you and your daddy will be watching out for him."

"Sure thing, Mrs. Campbell."

The phone beeps again. This Jay person is persistent. Campbell holds out his hand for the phone, a smarmy grin on his face.

"Someone named Jay Street keeps trying to call," I say, and Campbell's expression collapses.

He takes the phone out of my hand. "Mom, I've got to go. Jay is on the other line. I'll call you back." He switches to the other call as she's still saying goodbye. "Jay, yeah—"

Campbell's words are immediately cut off by a very loud male voice. I try not to listen, but it's hard *not* to hear.

"I was going to call you—"

This person isn't great at waiting for people to finish a sentence, simply overriding everything Campbell tries to say.

"I know," Campbell manages to break in. "I know it's bad."

I thought I'd seen every shade of Campbell's paleness; I was wrong. His face goes as white as the pillowcase, and he tries to sit up, bumping into the bars, face flinching. I step closer to the bed, wanting to help in some way, but he stops moving. Except for the fist holding the edge of the pillow tucked under his chest. His grip tightens and tightens, wrinkling the material and smashing the fluff inside.

His eyes pinch shut like he's in pain, but I don't think it's from his ankle. I'm pretty sure whatever Jay said is tearing Campbell up on the inside. I've only known this kid for a day, but it still hurts to watch his reaction.

"I swear I'll stay on top of it. This won't slow me down at all," he promises. "I'll be back in a week and——" He listens for a minute more, then says, "Okay."

The call must end, because Campbell lets the phone drop onto the mattress, then his head follows. He mumbles a string of obscenities into the sheet.

Do I sneak away? Pretend I didn't witness some sort of epic meltdown?

Instead, I aim for funny. "Jay Street sounds like a *real* nice guy."

It must have hit the mark at least partway. Campbell gives a snort–laugh before lifting his head. "He's my agent."

"Oh." *Oh.* I know agents are supposed to work on their clients' behalf, but sometimes they work *over* their clients. Arranging sponsorship deals. Building their images. Dropping them off at rehab.

"But you're not wrong about him." Campbell looks at me over

his shoulder, maybe a little less pale. "He called to remind me of my injury clause."

Sometimes teams give a list of activities players are not allowed to do because it could cause an injury. Like skiing and riding motorcycles and other potentially dangerous stuff. "But you were taking batting practice."

"It wasn't team sanctioned."

"It wasn't?" I can't imagine any coach forbidding his players to practice. Campbell isn't the first guy to stay after the game and hit some balls, but maybe because he's a first-rounder he's not supposed to?

"And Jay is pretty sure that the Rangers won't hold it against me, but..."

"But they might?" I finish for him.

He nods.

"They couldn't cancel your contract, could they?"

"Probably not cancel it completely, but if this messes up the way I play—" He cuts off with a frustrated head shake. He doesn't have to say anything else.

"You're going to be fine. In a couple weeks, you're going to be back, knocking the ball out of the park, turning double plays." I swallow, trying to muster my reassurances, but I must have used them all up with his mom. My voice comes out soft. "It's just a bump in the road."

"I can't afford any bumps in the road." His hand is gripping the corner of the pillow again. "My family *literally* can't afford it."

I raise my eyebrows, but he's not looking at me, and he doesn't need the cue to continue.

"Remember how your dad and I talked about my family's watermelon farm last night? And your dad asked if we'd sold out?" Pink spots burn bright on his cheeks. He's focused on the mattress, speaking to it instead of me.

"Yeah. You said some years are tougher than others." Which is true for both farms and farm teams, apparently.

"Well..." He glances at me then turns back to the bed. "I didn't want to say anything to your dad, but my signing bonus is the only thing that's keeping the farm afloat."

"Oh." My heart clenches like his fist is wrapped around it instead of the pillow.

"I don't want anyone to know. My dad would be embarrassed."

"I won't say anything. I swear."

He turns to look at me and holds my gaze, eyes intense. "This injury. It could ruin so much more than my baseball career. You know?"

My dad relies on me for a lot, but I can't imagine being responsible for my family's livelihood. From our conversation last night, I know their family has run the farm for generations. They live in a little old house right on the edge of a watermelon field. Would they lose all of that if Campbell couldn't keep playing? A little panic wells in my chest just thinking about it. How much worse must he be feeling?

"Look," I say, leaning forward so our faces are level. "I've seen guys come back from so much worse than this. I'll be here to help you, and so will my dad. You have nothing to worry about."

Behind me, the whisk of the curtain stops whatever Campbell's about to say.

"Doctor's coming in." The nurse smiles at me sweetly. "Which means that you've got to go."

I stop long enough to squeeze Campbell's forearm before I leave the room. "I'll be here when you need me."

CHAPTER

Nine

T HE MOTION LIGHT POPS ON WHEN I PULL INTO THE DRIVEWAY OF
my one-story house. Its big wraparound porch and two rocking chairs look inviting, and the lights in the entryway shine
brightly through the window above the door.

Campbell hasn't moved since we left the hospital. His arm
is over his eyes, knees cocked all funny to fit his bandaged foot
and crutches, hair standing straight up. There was no question of
taking him to the motel after this. Dad had promised everyone—
Brenda, the Rangers, and, at some point, the agent—that we'd
take care of Campbell.

"We're home." I touch his shoulder gently when he doesn't stir.

He rubs his eyes with one fist like a sleepy toddler and levers
himself upright. "Your dad make it back?"

"His car's in the garage. I'm guessing he's probably dozed off on the couch, waiting for us." I jog around to Campbell's side of the van and hand him his crutches. "Let me get your stuff out of the back."

"Please don't." He shifts all his weight to one crutch and balances precariously on his good foot. "If you hand the bags to me, I can take them in."

"Don't be ridiculous." I laugh a little as I struggle to get them both onto my shoulders.

Campbell crutches ahead of me and pushes the door open, frowning. "It's just...this is the second time in two days that you've carried my bags." He shakes his head and gives a brittle-sounding laugh. "I'm not used to having other people do stuff for me."

"Don't let it threaten your masculinity. I promise I'll find something heavy for you to move when your ankle is better."

He grunts like I'd punched him in the gut. "That's not what I meant—"

"I know. I'm teasing."

Dad must have been waiting for us because the inner door swings open. He sweeps the bags off my shoulders and carries them both—in one hand, of course—to the room Sawyer occupied the night before. The bed is neatly made. Dad would never have thought to fold down the quilt and tuck the sheet over the top, so I know Campbell must have done it.

"Go get Sawyer some extra pillows so we can elevate that foot," Dad says, and I scurry off to get everything set up.

I return with a good stack in time to hear Dad say, "Tomorrow the head office is sending a surgeon to check out your ankle and make sure everything is closing properly." Dad slides aside so I can arrange the pillows on the bed. "Ryan will make sure you're comfortable and get you to the park or wherever you need to be."

Oh, will I? I give my dad a look that says as much, which he either ignores or misses completely.

"In a few days, when you're feeling better and are off the narcotics, we can move you to the motel."

"Sounds good, Mr. Russell." Campbell leans his crutches against the wall and lowers himself slowly to the foot of the bed.

"I'll grab you a couple bottles of water."

Dad disappears down the hallway, while I stand awkwardly in the narrow space between the bed and the closet. "Do you need anything else?" I don't really want to paw through his bag for a toothbrush or clean underwear, but I have been *commanded* by my father to help Campbell.

"Will you throw my bag on the bed for me? I think that will be easier."

I heft it up beside him. "Yell if you need anything." I knock on the wall that divides our rooms. "I'm three feet away."

It brings a smile out of him. "Thanks for everything. I'm probably going to be indebted to you for the rest of my life."

I swallow, my throat strangely dry. Where's Dad with those bottles of water? "I'm sure I can find *some* way for you to work off your debt."

"I bet you will." He reaches out and takes my hand and gives it a thank-you squeeze before letting it drop.

As I walk the short distance to my own bedroom, my stupid heart gives a little flutter.

EVEN THOUGH I'M TOTALLY AND COMPLETELY EXHAUSTED, I CAN'T sleep. I toss. I turn. I flip my pillow over to the cool side. I speed up the fan. All in an effort to avoid thinking about the boy two sheets of drywall away.

It's not just that he's attractive—that's undeniable—but I can't help thinking that our situations are sort of similar. And for as much as I worry about losing the stadium and the team, it sounds like he has a lot to lose too.

Once I start thinking about my mom selling her half of the Beavers, my brain won't let it go. I get out of bed and turn on my laptop, starting a Word document of everything I know, what I've learned from the trade magazines, and the research I've done so far.

Community Bonds: Get the city to raise taxes to help pay for stadium renovations. Take months/years to get the city to back anything to raise that kind of money. Lose partial/full control of facilities.

That option is out. We're up for contract renewal with the Rangers next year, and renovations for the stadium have to be underway. Plus, I've only got nine days—or eight, now?—to figure out how to find the money so my mom won't sell the team.

Which leaves us with two options: private donors or big-name sponsors. I make a list of every person and company in Buckley that might put up that sort of cash.

It's a very short list.

Besides the Perry family, who paid for the original stadium, I don't think there's anyone in our town rich enough to throw around that kind of money. The biggest companies in Buckley are the hospital; Advanced Machining, a manufacturer that makes metal products for big building projects; and Mia's dad's business, Rodrigues Heating and Air.

I've got to be missing something. Or someone. I pull up a satellite map of Buckley, hoping I'll be reminded of a business I've forgotten. But there's nothing besides neighborhoods, grocery stores, and some farms on the outskirts of town.

I can sort of see what Mom means about the hassle of trying to find the money. But if she sells the team to some conglomerate, what exactly is going to happen to the Beavers? There isn't much on the Internet about how those groups work or what they do to the teams they purchase, but one article snags my attention. It's eight years old and about some tiny team I've never heard of, but it confirms all my worst fears.

The team was sold to an ownership group based back East, and every member of the staff was laid off. The next year, the team was relocated and the stadium left empty.

The article includes two pictures: the first is of the stadium when it was still in use. The building was old, but it had character and charm. Neatly trimmed hedges and cypress trees shaded its baselines. Its grandstands were simple but functional. It looked like a place that families in South Carolina had visited for cheap entertainment for generations.

The next picture is taken from the same angle, but instead of cheerful signage on the walls and a parking lot full of cars, the stadium is growing some sort of weeping mold. Weeds spring from the cracked sidewalk, graffiti tags the gates, and the hedge is growing out of control.

It looks lifeless. Like something the swamp is trying to reclaim.

If it's up to my mom, will Perry Park look like this in a few years? Has she thought about what selling her interest would do to the rest of us? Of the lives she'd ruin if all our employees are put out of work? Including mine?

I lie back in my bed, balancing my laptop across my stomach, and close my eyes against the screen's glare.

Does Mom hate Dad so much?

I slam the screen shut, but my brain won't click off as easily. An anxious sort of energy has me kicking off the covers and getting out of bed. It's almost six o'clock, and the sky outside my window is starting to brighten. I might as well go for a run.

Mom and I have exactly two things in common: we look scarily similar—small boned, sharp featured—and we both can run. She and Dad were college athletes. She raced cross-country and long-distance events, and he was a pitcher. They met during her freshman year when he was a junior, and they had me the next winter. From that point on, they were inseparable.

Right up to the point when they couldn't stand each other anymore.

Mom and I have never liked the same books or movies or clothes. We don't talk about boys or even sports. But we trained together. Even that first year, after she moved out of the house, she'd pick me up to go run the local trails every weekend.

I stopped inviting her along last fall. Not only did I need to push myself harder than she wanted to go, but she also kept trying to talk to me about what happened between her and Dad. I didn't want to hear her opinions about him, the team, and how no one finds true love at eighteen. It started to feel like she only ran with me so she could use the time to *market* herself like some political candidate—make promises she didn't intend to keep and sling mud at her opponent.

Dad never said a bad word about Mom. He never had to explain himself. He wasn't the one who left.

I carry my shoes through the house and sit in the rocking

chair outside to put them on. Dad doesn't love me running alone when it's not quite light out, but I send him a text letting him know my plan. I'll deal with the fallout when I get back.

Without any particular destination in mind, I start running. I let my body pick a familiar route and lose myself in the stretch and pull of muscles, the rush of my breath, the color of the sky as it lightens from purple to pink and then pale yellow.

Six miles later, the stadium walls loom above me. The sun casts the front of the building in shadow. The windows to the front office are dark. No one will be there for at least a few hours.

I stop on a grass-lined parking lot divider and *look*. No mold. No graffiti. It's as beautiful as it was when I showed Campbell around two days ago.

And it's going to stay that way.

It will.

My legs feel shaky as I turn away from the building, and I check my watch. If I started it at the right time, my run wasn't as slow as it could have been, considering my lack of sleep. I try convincing myself that the run is what's making me feel like I'm about to puke and not anything else. I sit down on the curb, knowing I can't make it home like this. I could probably walk it, but that would take forever. So I pull out my phone and call the one person I know will rescue me no matter what time it is.

Mia's black Volvo rolls into the parking lot ten minutes later. She looks almost as bad as I feel. Her curly hair is twisted into a wild knot on top of her head, and she's wearing her glasses. The super-thick lenses make her already-huge eyes look owlish.

She's got horrible eyesight—as in, legally blind without correction. Her parents didn't find out until she was in kindergarten and she'd started falling behind in her schoolwork. Her teachers never guessed that she couldn't see, because her personality was so big that they figured she was goofing off in class.

Her mom, Ms. Vivi, still tears up when she tells the story of the day Mia got her first pair of glasses and looked around the doctor's office, amazement on her face. "Mom, the world is so *big*. And your teeth are enormous!"

Kids used to make fun of Mia's glasses. Not that she let their taunts get to her, but I know she hates them. I also know that she loves me enough to let me see her with them on.

"You better have a good story for me," she says as I climb into the passenger seat. "You left my house with no explanation, and I pick you up from the stadium, a hundred hours later, looking like you've been hit by a car." She pauses and really looks at me. Her nose wrinkles. "Did you get hit by a car?"

"No, I—" And then I burst into tears.

This is one of the things I love about Mia. She listens. She doesn't analyze what I'm saying or offer solutions until I've told her about my mom's plans to sell the team, the conglomerate, and stadium graveyard. By that time, we're sitting in my driveway with breakfast burritos from her favorite taco truck. She believes greasy food works as well as ice cream for emotional eating. She's not wrong.

"So," she says around a bite of queso-slathered hash browns. "What are you going to do about it?"

"What *can* I do? It's not like I'm involved in these decisions."

"Well, why aren't you?"

"Because..."

"Look, what I know about the actual business of baseball is not very much." She folds the bottom of her tortilla so scrambled eggs don't land in her lap. "But I know a little about family businesses. Marc and I will inherit my dad's company if anything happens to him. It's in the will. You're almost eighteen. Your parents have probably worked something like that out."

"I'm not killing my parents, Mi."

She bursts into hysterical laughter, and I join her. It feels so good to laugh that tears prick my eyes.

"Okay. So," Mia says once we calm down. "What does your dad say about all of this?"

I drag my hand down my face, feeling the grit of salt and sweat slide with it. "You know my dad. He doesn't want to change anything."

Before Mom left to become a personal trainer, she convinced him to use the stadium for a couple of little things during the off-season, like a baseball camp for members of the Beaver Buddies and hosting the community fun run. But Dad hates the extra stuff.

He never wanted to own an events facility—just a baseball team.

In his mind, the Beavers should be the only entertainment Buckley needs.

"Have you talked to your mom about it?"

"I sent her a text."

"That's not the same." Mia shakes her head like she's disappointed in me. "You stopped *talking* to her sometime last year."

Right after Mom insisted that I apply for schools far from Buckley or she wouldn't help pay for tuition.

Mia hands me a hash brown. "You need to look at your mom and tell her you don't want her to sell the Beavers."

"She knows."

"You *think* she knows, but you haven't really explained why."

"I shouldn't have to." I dressed up as my dad for career day every year. Every "When I Grow Up" essay said the same thing: *I want to be the general manager of the Buckley Beavers.* My mom *knows.*

"Remind her." Mia shoves another piece of bacon in her mouth. Girl can eat. "But don't complain. Go to her like...those people on *Shark Tank.*"

Mia's totally obsessed with that show. She secretly wants to start her own fancy pillow-making business—she calls them "designer textiles"—but thinks it would be a total flop. When every new season of *Shark Tank* starts, Mia convinces her mom to make a whole bunch of delicious desserts to eat while they watch. I've stayed a couple of times for Ms. Vivi's treats.

"Don't be one of those people who gets annihilated," Mia continues. "Prove you've done your research."

"Like this article I found about a conglomerate shutting a local stadium down?" The sad image of the moldy grandstand sends my stomach spinning. I toss the remainder of my burrito back in the greasy paper sack and try not to think of our park in such a state.

"Yeah, and anything else you can find that will support your side of the argument."

It's a good idea. A really, really good idea. "I've got lists of potential sponsors. What if *I* find the money to cover the renovations?"

"Then she'll have no reason to sell," Mia says, but then she grimaces. "How long do you have?"

"Eight days."

She bites her lip, considering. "That's tight, but not totally impossible. I'll talk to my dad and see if he has any ideas."

Then I see the time on the dashboard: 7:15.

"Holy crap. I've been gone forever." I pop open the door. "I forgot about Campbell." He's probably going to wake up soon and need help. Would he ask for it if he did?

Mia grins, and there's mischief on her face. "Sure you did."

I pull a face at her then hop out of her car. "Thanks for breakfast!"

"Details!" Mia shouts after me. "I expect every *intimate* detail!"

I ignore her as I jog up the steps but pause when I catch my reflection in our front door's glass. Some girls look cute when they work out. They sweat a little. Their cheeks get pink. Their clothes cling in all the right places. I am not one of those girls. Sweat pours off my head like a downspout in a Texas rainstorm and drenches my tomato-red face before gathering in the pit between my boobs. And my tears have left my face puffy and blotchy.

The instant I step into the house, the A/C glues my already-short running shorts to my clammy thighs and sends goosebumps dancing up my arms and other places. Why do I not own any padded sports bras?

And there's Campbell, standing at the far end of the kitchen island.

"Hey," I say, crossing my arms. 'Cause that doesn't draw more attention to the problem area. "I thought you'd sleep awhile longer."

He shifts on his crutches, clearly uncomfortable, and I wonder if the awkwardness is *between* us, or if I'm causing it. "Are you..." He pauses and looks at my face one more time. "Okay?"

My breath catches in the back of my throat. "What?" It's not a question as much as it is an embarrassed reaction.

"I mean..." He leans one of his crutches against the counter so he can run his fingers through his hair. It's standing up worse than usual, and he's wearing ratty basketball shorts and a 5K T-shirt with a watermelon on the front. "Did you fall?"

"No." I cough into my elbow. If I don't, I will either die from embarrassment or from asphyxiating on my own spit. It's a toss-up at this point.

"Did something happen?" His forehead bunches with worry. "Is it a guy?"

"What? No." I reach for the cupboard next to the fridge and consider grabbing the oven mitt hanging on the magnet to wipe down my face. "Can I get you breakfast? Coffee or something?"

Of course, there's next to nothing to eat. Our selection of breakfast cereal is ridiculously low. There's maybe one handful of Cinnamon Toasties, and they're a little squishy. I'll offer them to Campbell if it will make him stop asking questions.

"I know what crying looks like." He says this like it's supposed to make sense in the context of the conversation we're *not* having. "If anyone hurt you, I'll trip them with my crutches. We could make it look like an accident."

His words are so earnest—there's really no other way to describe his tone—that I stop my faux perusal of the cabinet and look at him. Besides the smirk that's failing to mask his concern, Campbell looks like crap. Maybe worse than me, and that's saying something. Dark circles. Red-rimmed eyes. The whole sleepless, mussed thing.

"Are *you* okay?" I ask.

"I'm fine. You know, besides this." He tips his head to the side, motioning toward the bandage on his leg. The blood has soaked through the gauze covering the stitches, and the arch of his foot is purple.

"Oh my gosh. Sit down." I motion toward the bar stool. "Does it hurt?"

"Not too bad." But he cringes as he lowers himself onto the seat.

"Is that why you woke up? Need pain meds?"

"My brother called." He pulls his phone out of his pocket and sets it on the counter. "We're always up early."

"Is everything all right? At home, I mean?"

Maybe I shouldn't have brought it up, because his face flashes pink. "Good enough, considering."

I don't say anything else, instead opening the fridge even though I know there's nothing edible in it. An ancient coffee creamer, mustard, and something that sort of resembles a grape-fruit. I don't know why I expected there to be anything. There wasn't yesterday when I looked, and we don't have a magic gro-cery fairy. At least not anymore. I don't remember when Mom stopped dropping off bags of my favorite snacks and fruit.

"So," he prompts, breaking the silence. "Are you going to tell me who made you cry?"

"Are you going to let it go if I don't?" I pull open the freezer's drawer, so I don't have to look at him. There's a sleeve of ice-encrusted waffles that I might eat with enough Nutella spread on them, but I wouldn't force them on anyone else.

"I don't know. Maybe." He's tapping his crutch against the counter softly. The metal makes a *tink, tink, tink* that I swear is hammering at my ability to keep my worries locked inside. "I mean," he says, followed by *tink, tink, tink*. "You heard all my darkest secrets last night."

"Your darkest secret is that your family's watermelon farm is struggling?"

His smile is fleeting, there and then gone, like the lights at the stadium that pop on brilliant and blinding for a second before dimming. "Probably."

"Is this one of those 'you showed me yours, so I show you mine' things?"

The grin is back and doesn't disappear. "Your words, not mine."

Ugh. He's cute. I want to not like him, but instead I think I like him a little more. And maybe if I say all of this stuff about the stadium out loud my brain will be able to wrap around the details.

"Okay." I start a little hesitantly, trying to summarize, leaving out all the messy bits. "My mom is thinking about selling her portion of the team, but if she does, then my dad could lose controlling interest. The stadium needs renovations, and if we don't come up with the money for them, the Rangers could pull their contract. If that happens, then we'll potentially lose both the team *and* the stadium." It comes out in a breathless rush, but I manage it without the tears I shed in Mia's car.

"That's a huge deal for you." He doesn't say it like a question. He doesn't try to escape from this super personal thing I've dropped at his feet.

"Yes." I put a little laugh into my voice, hoping it disguises any other emotion trying to leak through. "Managing this organization is the one thing I've always wanted to do."

He nods, waiting for me to continue. And even though I barely know him, I keep talking, pouring out the information about the conglomerate and the stadium cemetery. He's a good listener, nodding along, but not in a glazed way. I think he's actually hearing me.

"I've seen one of those before," he says. "In a book somewhere."

"Sad, right?" I swallow hard, embarrassed that I've said anything at all, but also weirdly relieved that I've been able to talk about losing the team more clinically, like a professional would. "Mia thinks I should lay out all the negatives and data for my mom when she's back in town, and that should convince her not to sell."

"Do you think that'll work? Will she listen?"

I want to say yes, but the truth is, I don't know. She certainly didn't give Dad's pleas to stay a second thought. I give Campbell a shrug. "I'd have to do something brilliant. Like get someone to sponsor the whole renovation—or at least show my mom that there's potential to make that happen—but my dad hates the idea of changing *anything*. So, whatever I did, I'd have to…" I lower my voice and look toward the master bedroom. I know Dad rarely wakes up before nine, but today would be the day when he surprises me. "To do it all without my dad finding out."

Campbell grimaces, but the crutch-tapping stops. "Let me help you," he says at a near whisper.

"Why would you want to?" I move a little closer, the bag of waffles puddling between us on the counter.

"Because I'm good at this stuff. I used to go out with my college's sports marketing staff all the time to meet sponsors and advertisers. They love meeting players, having lunch, getting their pictures taken."

He's not wrong. We schedule a special batting practice for our sponsors to meet players every season. They love standing out in the field next to a player, chatting about nothing. And Campbell's a first-round draft pick. That's gotta be worth something to people.

"It's not like I have anything else to do for the next two weeks."

It might keep Campbell from wallowing in his own self-pity, and since I've already been assigned to chauffeur him to doctor's appointments I'll have a reasonable excuse to take him places and disappear from the office.

Maybe I'm taking too long to decide, because Campbell leans a little closer. Keeping his voice soft, he says, "You help me get back on the field as fast as possible, and I'll help you do whatever it takes to save your stadium."

Our gazes tangle and hold for an instant too long. We stand in the kitchen, separated by only a few feet and a melting bag of waffles, but I feel a tug. A connection.

"Morning, y'all," Dad says as he stomps into the room, totally oblivious to this *thing* that's formed between Campbell and me.

I shake off the moment, because that's all it was. A moment of stupidity. I won't let it become anything else. I won't entertain the what-ifs. Campbell plays for the team, and I'm still a member of the staff. It's against every rule, both the Beavers' and my own.

"I was going to feed Campbell a waffle, but that might give him food poisoning. Again."

Dad takes the bag off the counter. Printed on the bottom in blue ink is an expiration date. "They wouldn't have tasted much better...seventeen months ago." He tosses the whole sleeve into the garbage. "I don't know why your mother ever bought those. None of us would eat them anyway. We should have kept the box. That might have had more nutritional value."

Campbell laughs, but the joke falls flat to my ears.

"I'll run and grab breakfast burritos from Rudy's," I offer, even though I don't have room for a second breakfast. "Bacon or sausage?"

Dad votes sausage, but Campbell asks for bacon.

That blip of connection tries to re-form, but I remind myself that I'm going to *work* with this boy. I can't have a crush on him. Even if he has excellent taste in breakfast meat.

Ten

After breakfast and showers, I drive Campbell to the stadium to meet with the doctor the Rangers are sending, and then I head up to the front office. Our actual work space is the very last part of the stadium my dad will update. The carpet is a lush emerald green that shows every crumb and paper scrap—we got it at a huge discount from one of our sponsors, for obvious reasons. The off-white walls have more scrapes and holes and associated stories than I care to think about. But the doorways are tall, almost grand, and surrounded by beautifully carved moldings. A row of narrow windows gives a partial view of the stadium's green grass, and the slim ones above the office doors have flower patterns cut into the glass. My mom used to say, "She's an old lady with beautiful bones."

It's true. Our office space has something special and old-timey about it.

My favorite part is the receptionist desk where I sit. It's the first thing you see when you enter from the front door, like something you might find in an old bank or fancy library. The entire thing is carved wood, at least four feet tall and twice that long. I have to pump my chair all the way to its highest setting to reach the scarred work surface. Mom told me the desk and the matching table in the conference room were part of the original building and they're probably worth a fortune. I believe it, but I hope that Dad will figure out a way to keep them when we update the offices.

Or whoever owns the team.

I push that thought aside. I've got a dozen windows open on my desktop, most with searches like "largest employer in Buckley" and "Texas hill country's richest residents." Even though I'm dying to set up some lunch meetings with potential sponsors, I've got my everyday tasks to attend to first. Print ads need to be approved before our hospital visit—I do it, because Dad can't spot grammatical errors—then I have to send all the action shots and player info sheets to our graphic designer for baseball cards. Last year, Meredith tried to handle it, but she confused two of our pitchers. In her defense, both guys were blond, the same height and weight, and used black mitts. Unfortunately, one was a right-handed pitcher and the other was left-handed. No one noticed until the baseball cards went to print, and it cost a fortune to reprint the corrections, and was a huge pain to shove them in the little plastic packages. Mia helped me with the stuffing, but I still had paper cuts on every finger.

Mom never made mistakes like that, and I've picked up her knack for noticing little details—like which hand guys use to throw the ball. Dad and Meredith turned the project over to me this year.

The phone has rung a few times, and I've directed a handful of ticket buyers to our sales team, but it's probably going to be a slow night. It's hard to fill the stands, even when we have good promotions or giveaways. Lots of empty seats means low concession sales, which equates to little revenue. It's the worst sort of chain reaction.

I shift my focus to the player profiles when I hear a too-familiar noise: crutches on the cement walkway that connects the stadium to our office.

For one moment, I consider diving under my desk. I don't know why.

Liar. You totally know why.

The more I've thought about having Campbell help me—be around me—the more I worry that people will assume there's something going on *between* us. If our relationship doesn't seem professional, people might treat me more like a groupie than a member of the staff.

In some ways, my mom had to deal with this too. Even though she worked every bit as hard as my dad, she was still "the general manager's wife" way more often than she was Marie Russell, vice president of the Buckley Beavers.

With all that in mind, I have a hard time digging up an expression that doesn't let my worries leak through. "How'd the appointment go?"

His forehead furrows. "Didn't anyone tell you?"

"No. What?" I'm cut off by the ringing of my desk phone. I hold up a finger. "Hello, Buckley Beavers. How may I direct your call?"

"Hey, Ry." It's my dad calling from the training room. I can tell by the way his voice echoes. He'd met with a sponsor this morning and must've gone right into the stadium afterward instead of stopping in the office first. "I need you to take Sawyer to Arlington. I know it's a long drive, but I've already arranged for one of my friends from the head office to take you on a tour of their stadium, so you can see how things are done at the big-league level."

"Wait...what?"

"The ortho is afraid that the wound and resulting scar tissue might affect Sawyer's Achilles and doesn't want to sign off on treatment until the Rangers' staff doctor can approve it. And his agent wants a second opinion."

"But I have to leave for the children's hospital in thirty

minutes and I was hoping to get at least part of the baseball card info imported."

"Mer will go to the hospital instead. How long will the import take?"

"Like five more hours. Minimum."

He blows out a long breath. I imagine he's standing with his feet spread apart, one hand on his hip, debating. "When is it due back?"

"Tuesday. And with an away game tomorrow, I'd hoped to get caught up on some other things." *Or start some other things.*

"I hate to ask you to go, but I've got no one else on the car insurance who can leave now."

Now it's my turn to sigh. "What about Steve?" He's our laziest sales guy—who also happens to have an MBA in sports administration—and I know he's on the insurance.

"He's got a lunch meeting with the new packaging plant."

Well, good job, Steve.

"Meredith's handling pregame press, and there's no way she'd make it back before the gates open."

"Who's setting up the promotions?"

"Mia can handle it."

She can. I know it. But I hate that it makes me feel like I'm the only person on the entire staff who can be replaced so easily. "I'll call her before I leave and give her the game updates." I sound pouty to my own ears, and I force it down, remembering

Rule #1: Do the crummy jobs. "When do I need to leave?"

"Right now."

I click my mouse a little more vehemently than necessary, closing all my windows and the baseball card file. The little Save box pops up, which is good since I forgot to name it.

"Fuel up the Beavermobile. I'll text you the address."

"Fine." My computer is taking its sweet time saving. The little circle is spinning and spinning. I look up and realize that Campbell is still there, frowning at me.

"This is screwing up your plans, isn't it?" He sounds legitimately apologetic. Some guys would've huffed over not being my first priority.

"It's fine. I'll finish this all later. No big deal."

When a file error pops up, it becomes a much bigger deal. I shake my mouse, even though I know that's not going to do anything. "Nononono. Don't do this," I whisper to my computer.

"What's wrong?" Campbell rests his weight on his forearms, leaning over the top of the desk to see my screen.

"This computer is old and sometimes it doesn't like to save." Especially when I'm impatient with it. Stupid, vindictive computer.

Campbell comes around the side of the desk and puts one hand on the back of my chair, hovering over my head to get a better look at the circle that won't stop spinning. From this angle I can see the underside of his jaw, a thin white scar that traces the bottom of his chin, and the dark stubble he didn't bother to shave. His face is quietly intense, as he clicks three keys with his left hand.

"Let me get out of your way." I stand up, shoulder dragging against his side. He doesn't seem to notice the contact the same way I do, eyes still narrowed at the screen as he drops into my chair.

Two years ago, we had a pitcher who graduated from Harvard with a degree in something like rocket science. On the days he didn't pitch, he entertained himself in the bullpen by working on two calculus problems at the same time. So I know that some of the players are incredibly intelligent, some are talented musicians and artists, but sometimes it still catches me off-guard when they have skills and interests far outside of baseball. Especially the ones as gifted as Campbell.

Or maybe that has more to do with me and the way I focus on baseball.

My computer screen flashes blue, rows of white text scrolling upward. I bite back a groan, but Campbell's fingers slash across the keyboard, typing in something that looks a lot like code.

"What are you doing? Is it all gone?"

"Hold on." Campbell clicks something and my file reopens. He shoots me a look that's full of self-satisfaction. "I was able to bring back everything but the last ten minutes or so."

"Thank you." I cover my heart like some old lady. "You saved me hours of work."

He shakes off my gratitude. "Considering I'm about to cost you twice that much time, it's really not that helpful."

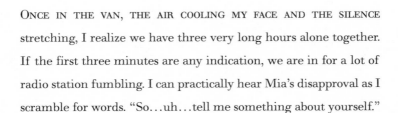

ONCE IN THE VAN, THE AIR COOLING MY FACE AND THE SILENCE stretching, I realize we have three very long hours alone together. If the first three minutes are any indication, we are in for a lot of radio station fumbling. I can practically hear Mia's disapproval as I scramble for words. "So...uh...tell me something about yourself."

"Like what?"

I sneak a glance and catch him looking at me. He turns away immediately, like he's a little embarrassed to have gotten caught.

"Tell me about your family."

"I've got a twin brother and two younger sisters."

"You have a twin?" My voice goes up an octave. "Identical?"

"Not exactly."

"There's fraternal and identical. Surely you know that."

"Yeah, but he has cerebral palsy. So even though we are technically identical, most people don't see it." He's looking out the passenger window, but I have a feeling he's not really seeing Mumford, Texas, whiz by.

"Oh." How do I respond to that? Is "I'm sorry" the wrong thing to say?

"He's one of the smartest, funniest people I've ever met." Campbell pulls out his phone and scans through his pictures until he finds the right one. "He's the one who taught me how to recover your computer file, by the way."

"Tell him thank you." I shouldn't look down at the picture while I'm driving, but I've got the cruise control set, and there's no one on the road. The picture is of Campbell and his brother in a car. Campbell isn't looking at the camera but making a sideways peace sign, and his brother is giving this crooked grin. They do look a *lot* alike, but his brother's face is thinner, cheekbones more pronounced.

"That's the night I got drafted. We drove around our tiny town yelling out the car windows." Campbell's eyes focus on the picture, and I can see him reliving the moment in his memory. His expression is soft, wistful. "Sterling was as excited as I was. Maybe more."

"His name is Sterling?"

"Yeah." He takes his phone back, swiping to the next picture.

"Sawyer and Sterling," I say, trying to keep the conversation going. "That's super—"

"Cheesy?" he asks, raising one eyebrow in my direction.

"I was going to say 'cute,' but feel free to speak for me." I sound more annoyed than I really am. "Plus, I think it's a rule that twin names should match in some way."

"Like Phil and Bill? Those are my uncles' names."

"Shut up! You have twin uncles?"

"No." He's laughing, and it's such a nice laugh that I want to hear it again.

"Well, there are twins that go to my high school. Krystal and Shanda Leer."

"You're lying. Krystal Shanda Leer?"

"I'm not."

We spend the next chunk of time coming up with the worst possible names for twins. Easton and Weston. Misty and Stormy. Adan and Dana. He Googles to find some more and then starts laughing so hard that he's not making any noise.

"What?" I slap his arm lightly.

"I can't. It's so bad." He covers his mouth with his fist, laughing into it. "Jenna and Talia."

My forehead wrinkles. "I don't get it."

"Say it fast."

"Jenna Talia." And then like two little kids, we're giggling about body parts.

When we stop laughing, he just sort of looks at me. "My mom wanted to make sure I thanked you and your dad for everything you guys have done so far." He moves his arm to the console so it's right next to mine. "It made her feel so much better to know that people were watching out for me when she couldn't be here."

We're not touching, not really, but there's this electric field between us like two magnets being drawn toward each other. My pinkie finger twitches, brushing against his skin and then falling back to its position.

What am I doing?

There should be no finger-touching, no electricity. I drop my hand into my lap.

"Okay," I start, and then stop. How do you go about telling someone that nothing is ever going to happen between you without sounding completely self-absorbed? I run the scenario through in my head a dozen different ways, but they all end badly.

Clearing my throat, I start again. "I'm happy to help you, and I'm so glad you're going to help me reach out to sponsors." It is so hot in the van. Is the A/C even working? I'm sweating. Why am I sweating? "I've got a couple of ideas for good leads, and I know they're all going to be thrilled to meet you. But..."

"But?" He shifts his crutches and our elbows bump.

Elbows. It's an *elbow*, Ryan. Still, I tuck my arm tight to my body to avoid any further bumpage. "But I'm a little bit worried that people might see us together and think that we're, like, *together*." I literally could not sound stupider, so I plow on ahead. If I'm going to word-vomit all over myself, I might as well do it right. "And having you talk to sponsors as, like, my boyfriend is way less impressive than having you talk to them as Sawyer Campbell, first-round draft pick. So we need to be super clear with everyone..." *Especially yourself, Ryan.* "That this is a business relationship only."

He seems to consider my words for a second, mouth partway open. "Yeah," he says, finally, head nodding slowly. "I agree."

"Oh. Good." That was not nearly as painful as I'd imagined,

and yet I can't ignore the little blip of disappointment. I didn't want him to disagree. That would be ridiculous.

I am ridiculous.

"Actually, I'm really glad you said something." He shifts his crutches again. "I know we're going to be spending a lot of time together and I didn't want you to get the wrong idea."

Now I've totally got the wrong idea.

"I need to be completely committed to getting healthy as fast as possible. Eating good food. Getting plenty of sleep. Getting in workouts wherever I can."

From my peripheral vision, I can feel his eyes on me.

"Everything has to be all baseball, all the time. No distractions."

Distractions like a girl. I know what he's saying even though he doesn't say those exact words. "Of course."

"Cool."

Except that nothing about this is cool. I've turned the A/C all the way up and can still feel the prickles of sweat on my neck, and he's shifting around in his seat like it's full of ants.

It was necessary to make the rules clear, but I wish I could have done it without making things weird between us.

BASEBALL HAS ALWAYS BEEN PART OF MY LIFE, AND YET I'VE never been to an MLB game. It sounds pitiful, but our minor league season always overlaps with the major league one. And on the rare family trips we've taken, hitting up ballparks in the off-season never seemed like a real break from work.

I'm not prepared for the way the stadium appears off the expressway, this mammoth redbrick building with glorious white stone archways and glistening windows. It steals my breath like a punch to the throat.

Campbell must see the awe on my face as we turn into the parking area. "Have you never been here before?"

"Never to any major league ballpark."

"It's a game day. Wanna stay and watch? I bet I can get tickets for free."

I'm tempted—by so much more than staying for my first MLB game—but I know better. "I guess we'll see how long your appointment takes."

"You know they're building a new stadium, right?" He turns and points south. "This one will only be open for a few more years. You should enjoy it before they tear it down."

His words are said with such good intention—*Have fun. Enjoy this.*—but they drive a spike right through my heart. "If they tear down a building this beautiful, what will people with more money and big ideas do to Perry Park?"

Campbell's happiness fades. "We'll find a way to convince your mom. Maybe the answers you need are here?"

He says "we" like he's really invested in this, and I'm grateful enough that I squeeze his hand, just once, before I climb out of the van.

EVERYTHING IN THE FRONT OFFICE IS SLEEK AND STREAMLINED. Polished wood dominates the design, but the carpet, couches, paintings, and other decorations carry the team's colors and logos. The receptionist desk is as tall as mine, and two professionally dressed women wearing headsets sit behind it. They alternate between directing calls and greeting guests. And they do it with amazing efficiency, switching between Spanish and English like they've been programmed to do so.

"Hi. Ryan Russell to see—"

"We've been expecting you." The receptionist flashes beautiful white teeth behind perfectly red lips. I suddenly feel shabby in my khaki shorts, team-branded polo shirt, and high ponytail. "If you and Mr. Campbell will take a seat." She points to the leather couches behind us.

Campbell has barely set his crutches down when a woman in a charcoal pencil skirt, black scoop-neck blouse, and four-inch-tall stilettos comes clicking down the hall. Her dark brown hair is parted down the middle and tied at the base of her neck in a super-sleek ponytail. She stops in front of us, exuding confidence like expensive perfume, and I realize she's only a couple of years older than I am.

"Welcome to Ranger Stadium! I'm Amerie Pierce, and I'll be showing y'all around today." She picks up Sawyer's crutches and offers them to him like he's helpless. "Let's get you up to the training area, Mr. Campbell, and then I can show Ms. Russell around the ballpark."

She launches into what must be a memorized script as she guides us toward the elevator, describing important elements of the architecture and the memorabilia that hangs along the walls. She has a special key that gets her to floors restricted from fan entry, and the elevator zooms to an upper level.

"Do you need any further assistance, Mr. Campbell?" she says as the doors spring open to a world-class gym and training area. A couple of guys are working out, but I don't want to gawk at the incredible facility or the players. More than likely, some of them came through Buckley at one point.

"I'm good." Campbell seems a little overwhelmed by the poshness of the training room or the ballpark or the thought of meeting his future teammates, but adds a hasty "thank you."

I almost follow Campbell out of the elevator, but realize Amerie hasn't moved. "Text me when you're done and we'll figure out where to meet."

He gives me that small, nervous smile that makes him look seventeen. "Will do."

"Good luck." I'm tempted to hug him, but I settle for the little wave that always makes me feel incredibly stupid.

The elevator doors close as Campbell crutches across the room, and once it drops a few feet Amerie turns to me, eyes wide. "Wow. He's...wow."

The crack in her professional façade throws me a little, and I give a half laugh.

She leans against the elevator rail and rocks back on her heels like it isn't a gravity-defying feat. "You are crushing on him so hard."

"What? No." I shake my head and make an X with my hands. "I'm not. I've only known him for like two days and—"

"It's okay. It happens, and I don't blame you even though he's off-limits." She drops back onto the part of her shoes that are intended to be walked on. "Does he have a girlfriend?"

"I don't think so." Because I'm pretty sure he would have mentioned that during our painful "business partnership" conversation.

"It's always best to assume guys like him are with someone. He's probably left some gorgeous girl back in Mississippi, or wherever, but hasn't talked about her," she says with a pinch of bitterness, and I can't help but wonder if she's speaking from personal experience. "It'll give you another reason to keep your distance."

I don't need the reminder, but once she's put the idea of Campbell having a girlfriend into my head, it sticks like brisket between my back teeth: small, irritating, and something I can't quite ignore.

When we exit the elevator, she's back to being super professional, returning to her perfect posture and scripted tour. Maybe everything that's said in the elevator *stays* in the elevator or something.

The stadium is nothing short of amazing. The suites are a million times nicer than ours, with real leather chairs and huge flat-screen TVs. Some even have their own bars. I expected everything to be glamorous and over-the-top, and I'm not wrong. But it gives me such a sick feeling that I can barely enjoy all the behind-the-scenes things Amerie is showing me.

"So what do you do for the Beavers?" she asks politely as we walk down a long hallway behind the bullpen.

"Officially, game day operations."

Her nose squishes up. "You mean you work for your dad?" She shrugs like she recognizes the way she said it might be offensive but doesn't actually care. "I'm only an intern."

"Really?" She seems too polished to be a temporary employee.

"Yep. So we've basically got the same job."

I almost counter but then I realize that she's not wrong. I get stuck with all the jobs no one else wants to do. I work more hours for less pay. And sometimes my job includes driving injured players to faraway stadiums on a game day.

I'm a glorified, permanent intern.

Every year in the spring, Dad always makes a big deal about inviting sponsors to take batting practice on the field. He pitches and the staff, players, and I shag balls. There are hot dogs and beer and cotton candy, and it's an amazing time. Three or four years ago, one of our construction partners was out in left field with me, catching the balls that flew that way. He's a huge dude—big enough to make Campbell look small—and we went after the same ball. I don't know if he thought I wouldn't get to it or if he couldn't see me, but he ran over me. Knocked the wind right out of me and left me gasping for air on the warning track. I shook it off like it was nothing and hurried to the dugout, claiming I needed a drink. Really, I needed a place to cry alone.

Realizing that I don't matter any more than an intern leaves me feeling like I've been laid out by that three-hundred-pound construction foreman all over again. I shake it off, finding a smile for Amerie, but maybe later I'll find someplace private to cry.

MY PHONE BUZZES WHEN WE LEAVE THE BULLPEN—APPARENTLY THE Rangers don't have any problems with reception in their stadium—and it's Campbell. He's finished and wants to join us on the tour.

"Why don't you tell him we're done and to meet us back at the front office?" Amerie suggests.

I feel like I've seen all there is to see anyway, and we circle back through the building. Campbell is leaning on his crutches in front of this big architectural drawing of the new park.

"Ry, check this out." He touches the glass, pointing out the plans for a glassed-in building that's separate from the stadium. "The new ballpark is going to have an events center."

Amerie jumps in, suddenly interested in telling us everything about it. "We're adding an entire events staff—caterers, florists, decorators. It will be used for everything from business conferences to weddings." She pauses and touches the glass-covered picture with her finger. "They're still looking for a naming-rights sponsor for the additional buildings."

"They can do that?" I ask, surprised.

"Sure. It's not officially part of the ballpark. Some teams even have different names for their playing fields. Something like John Smith Events Center at Globe Life Park."

"You're getting money from selling the same space twice?" Campbell asks, forehead creased.

Amerie puts her fingers on his forearm. "No, it's all contracted very carefully, so the sponsorship packages don't overlap. Plus, the naming rights cover the cost of running the building until it turns a profit as an events center."

Ideas are bouncing around in my head. New things I've never considered and seriously doubt my parents have. Not only could something like this make our park even more appealing, but it would be amazing for the community. More jobs. More opportunities to partner with local businesses.

No reason to sell to a conglomerate.

I'm ready to go, itching to do some research. "Thanks for the tour, Amerie. It was nice to meet you."

"You too!"

We're almost to the doors when she calls Campbell back.

"In case you're ever in Arlington and find that you need anything—tickets, recommendations for dinner—*anything*." She offers him a business card, then pulls her long ponytail over her shoulder, smoothing its already shiny length. "My cell number is on the back."

I start walking before I can see what happens next. Because it doesn't matter to me.

Not at all.

CHAPTER

Twelve

THE VAN'S ALMOST COMPLETELY COOL BY THE TIME CAMPBELL makes his way out. He drops a slightly crumpled business card into the cupholder between us. Amerie drew a little heart next to her phone number, and I'm tempted to throw it out the car window.

Good Texans don't litter. Plus, it doesn't matter who Campbell does or does not call. If he wants to hang out with a gorgeous girl who happens to work for the head office, I'm not going to say anything. It's not my business.

I'm not going to turn *her* in for fraternization.

"What were you thinking when she showed you the new park?" Campbell's voice is a bit too enthusiastic, like he's trying to cover for spending so much time flirting with Amerie. "You looked like..."

My phone is taking forever to come up with the fastest route options to get home, and I want to avoid as much traffic as possible. I look up from the screen to find Campbell making the stupidest, happiest expression.

"I did not look like *that*." I try not to smile, but seriously, his face.

"Like a kid on Christmas?" He puts his hands on his cheeks, elated shock between them. "And yes. You did." Then he shifts his crutches into the gap next to his seat. "If the solutions to my problems dropped into my lap, I'd probably look like that too."

Two things hit me all at once: First, Campbell is a better person than I am. Like, a genuinely good human being who puts everyone else's worries before his own. And second, I didn't even ask how his appointment went. Which provides more evidence of me being awful. "You didn't tell me. What did the doctor say?"

The sun is starting its descent, glaring across the cars in the parking lot and firing up the sky behind his head. He's silhouetted against the window, but it doesn't disguise the tension in his shoulders or the frustrated set of his chin. "Six more days on crutches, plus three more of 'carefully monitored movement' before I can get back to the field."

Ten days is an eternity for a freshly drafted player. It's ten days of bingeing Netflix and eating crap and upper-body workouts for those who are still willing to try. I've seen it before. They get left behind when the team travels—no point in paying for them to go—and they get all greasy and grouchy and spend too much time hanging out with Red in the training room.

"Well, that sucks. I'm sorry."

He shrugs like it doesn't matter that much, but he doesn't smile it off or change the subject right away, letting the silence in the van linger a little too long. Not playing eats at him. Campbell's good at pretending he's okay, shaking away dark thoughts and muscling up some optimism. But I understand exactly how he feels, because thinking about losing the team torments me in the same awful way.

Maybe he needs a distraction? Maybe we both do.

Not that kind, brain. Seriously.

"Are you hungry?" I show him the map on my phone. It's smattered with traffic slowdowns and at least two car accidents. It will take us an extra forty minutes to get back to Buckley if we leave now. "Or do you want to stay here and watch the game tonight?" I'm hesitant to ask because I don't know if it will make him feel better or worse, but at least I can give him the choice.

The corner of Campbell's mouth ticks up a little, and he reaches into his pocket. "What do you think took me so long?"

I don't answer *that* question.

He offers me two tickets on row one. It doesn't matter where they are in the park—they're amazing seats. "We don't have to stay, if you've got stuff to do."

I've always got stuff to do, but we're not going to get home at any reasonable hour anyway. What's one more late night in an endless string of late nights? And more than that, I'd really like to watch this game. With him. Even if I probably shouldn't.

"If this is going to be my first MLB game, I might as well have a great view."

"LET'S GET SOME FOOD BEFORE WE GO DOWN TO OUR SEATS," Campbell says as we move along the mezzanine to the third base side. The crowd is thin so early before the game. Only the real die-hards and the kids who are hoping to catch some batting practice balls move past us.

"Fine, but I'm buying." I speed-walk to get in front of him.

"No, you're not." He crutches faster, and somehow getting to the concession stand line becomes a race. I could beat him if I run, but that doesn't seem fair, so I'm walking as fast as my legs can move. He's figured out how to use his crutches like gorilla arms, propelling forward in huge swings.

"Campbell!" I say with an exasperated sigh. "Is this a competition?"

He laughs but doesn't look back, beating me to the counter by a few steps. Leaning his crutches against the stainless-steel edge, he balances on one foot and digs out his wallet.

"You got the tickets." I try to edge in front of him, but he doesn't budge.

"I didn't have to pay for them."

"Still."

Then he waves two food vouchers at me. "And I don't have to pay for food either."

I fake-punch him in the left shoulder. "Why didn't you say something?"

"Because I wanted to beat you. And even on crutches, I am the *champion*." He gives a little chest thump, and I give him a look that tells him he's ridiculous.

"Now," he says, checking out the food offerings. "What do you want?"

"I want a rematch and a footlong. But not in that order."

We both end up getting hot dogs—well, he orders three—and blue Powerade. But I'm stuck carrying all that crap as he maneuvers down the stairs toward our seats. As it turns out, our seats are right on the third base line, close enough to the field that if I dangled over the rail, I could snatch a handful of red dirt.

We end up talking about stadium signage and LED advertising, and all my baseball-business nerd hangs out. He's unsurprisingly awesome about it—listening and asking questions like he actually cares—and even starts taking pictures of the field so I have reminders of which companies the Beavers could hit up for sponsorship packages.

"I went on a recruiting trip to the University of Texas a few years ago. They have an events center a lot like the one the Rangers are planning. They were hosting some sort of seminar there."

I put the information in my phone and start a search.

"You could host camps."

"We already do spring and fall sports camps." I'm listening, but only halfway. My brain is absorbing so many ways to generate funds for a smaller version of the Rangers' building that I can't give him my full attention.

"I was thinking more of special needs sports camps." He's thumbing through his phone, looking for a picture. He turns it my way, and I look up from my screen, realizing I've pulled a total Lucas Chestnut, more focused on my phone than on Campbell.

In the picture, Campbell is standing next to a dark brown horse, wearing dirty jeans and a sweat-stained baseball hat. He's beaming—like, smiling so wide his face might break—and his hand is on the back of a little boy who is sitting in some sort of specialized saddle. The child is looking down at Campbell with hero worship on his face. The cuteness makes my heart clench and stay that way.

"Every fall, my brother and I volunteer for an equestrian therapy group. It gives kids with disabilities a chance to try something they normally couldn't. And I always thought that if I make it big—" He gives a self-deprecating laugh. "Which is still debatable—that I'd like to give kids with special needs a chance to really play baseball."

Up until this moment, I've imagined kissing Sawyer Campbell for all the wrong—*but really enjoyable*—reasons. But right now,

I want to throw my arms around him and hold on. I swallow down that feeling and look away, afraid he might see it on my face. "That's a really cool idea."

He bumps my arm off the armrest that divides our chairs—to make sure he has my attention or to be irritating, I'm not sure which. "Would that be something the Beavers could do? Something you could talk to your dad about?"

It might be exactly the sort of thing to break Dad's no-extra-events policy. "Yeah. I think I could."

AFTER BATTING PRACTICE ENDS—IN WHICH I CAUGHT A FOUL BALL and Campbell cheered my form—an usher comes down to check our tickets. I get that he's doing his job, but he doesn't crack a smile until he gets a good look at Campbell. Then the poor usher is so overwhelmed and embarrassed that he makes a big deal and asks Campbell for a picture.

From that point on, I become Photo Girl. Taking pictures of Campbell with any Rangers fan (or staffer) who realizes who he is. Little kids from a few rows behind us bring Campbell a hat and ball to sign. The lady to our left has me take at least ten pictures, until she's happy with the way she looks so she can post it on her social media accounts. People sneak toward us until the third inning, when the usher becomes more of a bouncer and turns them away. It's a fire hazard to have them in the aisle, after all.

Campbell was gracious and humble and truly engaged the entire time, but I can see that the crowd has worn him out a little bit. It sort of amazes me that someone who is so clearly talented can also be a little shy.

"Do you have to deal with this a lot?" I ask as I hand him back his phone. He wanted some pictures to post for his friends and family back at home. His accounts are private. I checked before I picked him up at the airport.

"Sometimes." He takes the baseball I caught out of the cupholder and bounces it off his elbow, then catches it before it falls too far. "Spring training was hard. There were people who tried to convince me to invest in their companies or ask me for money for something. Or..."

I take the ball out of his hand. "Or what?"

"It's just...sometimes it's hard to know what to believe. I wasn't really sure if the people I met there wanted to get to know *me* or the Rangers' first-round draft pick. You know?"

"Yeah."

"The fans are great for the most part. But I'm never sure what to say to them."

"You did fine." I don't give him talking points or suggestions— Agent Jay will probably do that, and I like that Campbell's not overly practiced. It made him seem real. *Attainable.* Which is something I shouldn't be thinking about at all.

To distract myself from Campbell's shoulder against mine,

or anything else Campbell-related, I start making a list on my phone of all the promotions we've seen so far. He leans closer and helps me fill in the blanks. Then the crowd around us starts cheering, and I realize I'm at a baseball game but I'm not even watching.

Looking up for the replay, I expect to see a home run or at least a double, but instead my face and Campbell's fill the jumbo screen. Around our image little hearts pulse and the words KISS CAM flash like a strobe light.

"Oh, crap," Campbell says, and then laughs, covering his eyes.

I don't know what to do. The crowd around us is chanting. "Do it! Do it! Do it!" The camera won't pan off of us until we do *something.* That's how this promotion works. I turn to Campbell, mouth open, head shaking, and the words *We can't* form on my lips.

But before I say anything, he leans in and kisses me, hard and fast. It's on the corner of my mouth, more cheek than lips, but the crowd cheers anyway—probably at my stunned expression— and the camera moves on to a new couple.

"Sorry," he says, but nothing about the way he's smiling is an apology. "Seemed like the best way to solve the problem."

"Right." I sink lower into my chair and stop myself from wishing it could have been more.

CHAPTER

Thirteen

EVEN AT SEVEN A.M, IT'S HOT. LIKE, SO HOT I CAN ACTUALLY SEE heat rising from the asphalt as I hit the hill behind my house for the seventh time. I'm running fast, even though I'm exhausted. We left before the game ended but still didn't get home from Arlington until after midnight. Instead of going to bed I logged all the information Campbell and I learned into an Excel file, and then looked for ways to make the Rangers' sponsorship ideas work in Buckley. I stayed awake half the night analyzing everything we could do and the other half making lists of all the ways I could fail. What if I can't convince any sponsors they want to back an events center at the ballpark? What if I manage to convince sponsors, but then my dad hates all of my ideas? What if my mom ignores all of my work and sells the team anyway?

Is there a competition for overthinking? Because I'm the champion.

The lack of sleep is really starting to take a toll though. I jog up the hill once more and head back to the house, coming home a half an hour earlier than usual. The house is so silent I can hear the cicadas buzzing in the trees outside. Dad's still in bed. Campbell must be too.

My tank top is soaked with sweat. I use the hem, where there's still a dry spot, to mop off my face, then drop it directly in the washer. I walk through the house like this all the time, but maybe I shouldn't with Campbell staying here. My bikini's smaller than what I'm wearing now, but I still feel like I have to sneak to my room. I ditch my shoes and socks in the kitchen and pad barefoot across the tile.

Still no noise.

As I turn in to my hallway, the bathroom door flies open, and out comes Campbell on one crutch.

I gasp and my hand flies to my chest. And then my brain registers what he's wearing. Or not. Since he's only got a white bathroom towel tied low around his hips.

Oh. My.

He's frozen. I'm frozen. We're standing in a dark hallway, half-dressed. *Less* than half. Staring at each other.

He takes in my sports bra, my shorts, and he swallows. The knob of his throat bobs as he *looks,* mouth open a little bit. And

I see something in his expression I didn't expect: want. Hunger.

Problem: I feel exactly the same way. My heart is galloping under my hand, racing toward options that I shouldn't even consider.

We start speaking at the same time: "I didn't think you'd be back so soon."

"I thought you were still asleep."

His eyes jump to the picture on the wall, but then drift back to me, falling down my body once more. "I'm sorry." He blushes. "I should have taken my clothes."

I'm still so hot from my run that he probably can't tell that I'm flushed all the way to my hairline. "I'll just..." I point to my door behind him.

The hallway has never felt smaller, especially when we slide past each other to get to our respective rooms. He smells amazing—clean, piney. Like freshly cut wood and soap. His hair is even darker when it's wet, making his eyes look bluer. Water droplets cling to his shoulders, to his chest. One falls on my arm as he turns to pass me, and every muscle in my body clenches.

His door closes first, but mine follows a split second later. I lean against it, letting it support me as I puddle to the floor.

This is what "weak in the knees" means. I'm breathless, light-headed.

Very little of that has do with running hills.

Because I'm a chicken, I hide in my room, forcing myself to

open my research and trying not to relive that moment in the hallway. But my brain won't let it go, filling in the blanks of what might have happened had I stepped closer to him instead of away. If I'd brushed the water droplets from his shoulder. If his hands had found my waist. If my mouth had skimmed his.

No, brain! No.

All my mind power has to be devoted to the Beavers. I've got sponsors to find and a ballpark to save. Maybe it's time I have a conversation with myself about the danger of distractions.

Distractions named Campbell.

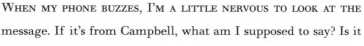

WHEN MY PHONE BUZZES, I'M A LITTLE NERVOUS TO LOOK AT THE message. If it's from Campbell, what am I supposed to say? Is it better to pretend nothing happened?

Luckily, the message is from Mia. She's giving me the details of Sunday dinner. I eat with her family almost every week. I'm not really sure how it happened. There was no official invitation extended, no time set. She always texts me at some point on Sunday afternoon—unless we have a day game or a double-header—and tells me what her mom is making. Or, in today's case, what her dad is grilling.

Dad's got brisket on, she sends a little after ten.

And because I can't help myself, I respond with *Campbell looks great naked.*

My phone rings immediately.

"How do you know that?" she shrieks before I even say hello.

"Shhh!" I hiss back, walking to my bedroom door and peeking out into the hallway. His door is shut, but I don't know if that means he's in the living room with my dad or a few feet away. "He's gonna hear you."

"Is he there? In your room?" Her voice is a little rough, like she's been sleeping. More than likely, Ms. Vivi dragged her out of bed to go to early mass, and Mia went back to bed as soon as she got home. "If you're joking, I swear——"

"I'm not joking," I say, stepping into my closet and shutting the door. Ridiculous? Yep. "I got home from my run right as he was coming out of the bathroom in a towel."

"And?" she prompts.

"And nothing. That's it." The silence stretches for so long that I wonder if the call dropped. "Mia?"

"You are the *worst*. Here I was hoping that for once in your life you'd broken your stupid rules. But you were leading me on."

I frown. "What's wrong with my rules?"

"Everything. Nothing. They're just restrictive."

"I have them for reasons."

"I know. But when God hands you the perfect boy, you're supposed to say thank you and forget the rules. *All* of them."

If she's bringing up God, then she's definitely been to church today. "For some reason I think God would disagree with you."

Mia gives a fake cry that morphs into a laugh midway through. "Probably so."

"Campbell and I have worked out an agreement—"

"Of course you have."

She can't see my eyeroll, but she knows me well enough to know I did it. I tell her everything that's happened in the last twenty-four hours, minus the awful "no distractions" conversation with Campbell, because there's really only so much humiliation I can handle. "I emailed Advanced Machining and was able to swing a lunch meeting on Tuesday. I'm taking Campbell with me." I kick the high heels I wore to prom into the far corner, so I have a place to sit. "The marketing director sounded excited in his email."

"Hmpf." Mia sounds less than enthused. "What's Campbell doing for dinner today?" When I hesitate, she says, "You are bringing Campbell." It's a command, not a request.

"Why?" I tip my head against the wall and run my fingers through my sweat-soaked hair. "So you can stare at him the whole time?"

"Of course. Why else would I invite him? It's not like my family is nice or anything."

"Never."

She laughs. "Dad says to be here by one. He thinks the new smoker will have the meat done by then."

It takes a minute to get brave enough to text Campbell, but I figure that's safer than knocking on the door to his room. Even if it is in my house. He might be on the phone with his family. He might be sleeping. He might not be dressed.

He responds right away. *Are you sure you want me to come?*

Thought you might want to get out of here, I say. And then: *Also there will be brisket.*

When do we leave?

The Rodrigueses always invite Dad to dinner too, but he's only come a couple of times in the last year. I know Sundays are a big catch-up day for him—being the general manager means overseeing every aspect of the Beavers except coaching the players— and since Mom left he's handled it all on his own. But maybe brisket will tempt him to leave work behind for a little while.

I exit my closet and tiptoe past Campbell's bedroom door, but he doesn't burst out in a towel again. Then I mentally punch myself for being a little disappointed.

Our home office has French doors, and I can see Dad through the glass. He's got a fat stack of folders on his left, his laptop squared in front of him, and a beer on his right. Dad refuses to get bifocals—he says those are for old people—and is squinting at something on the screen.

I tap on the glass before I swing open the door. "I'm going to go to Mia's for an early dinner. You coming today?"

He looks up like he's surprised to see me. "Not today. Gotta clean up the books."

"Don't we have an accountant for that?"

Actually, I know we do. His name is Bill Miller, and he's got the freakiest memory of anyone I've ever met. He handles our payroll and billing and can remember pretty much every number he's ever seen. I bet he'd make an awesome calculus tutor.

"Bill could do this, but he's expensive." Dad takes a swig of his beer and sets it back down. "Your mom wanted some financial updates, and I figured I could run them for her and refresh my memory while I was at it."

My skin prickles like I've opened up the stadium's deep freezer. "Why does Mom need 'financial updates'?"

Dad doesn't answer me right away, measuring his words like he always does when he's going to say something he thinks I won't like. Which only makes me worry more. "She's serious about selling the team, Ry. She needs the financials for that investment group."

"And you're *helping* her?"

He rubs the bridge of his nose and gives a tired sigh. "I don't exactly have a choice. As part owner, she can request a full workup of sales, assets, you name it, at any time. I don't want to help her, and I don't want her to sell the team, but it's less messy to give her the information she wants than for her to send her lawyers after the numbers."

"Why is she like this?" I step all the way into the office and shut the glass doors behind me. Not that they do much to dampen the sound. My parents used to fight in here all the time.

"Working for the team was..." He pauses, and I can see

him taking the edge off whatever he'd planned to say. Despite not being married to Mom anymore, Dad is so careful about everything he says about her. I used to think it was because he harbored a hope that she'd come back, but sometime last year I realized it's more about the kind of person Dad is. "Owning the Beavers was never your mom's dream. It was mine. Baseball was always what I wanted. It took me a long time to realize that despite all the work she put in to keeping the team running, it didn't make her happy."

"It doesn't mean she has to ruin it for the rest of us."

Dad shakes his head slowly, but I'm not sure what that means. Maybe he doesn't have anything else to add.

"I guess you won't make it to the Rodrigueses' for brisket? Even for a few minutes?" I reach for the door handle, knowing the answer before he says it.

"Not today. But there are doughnuts in the kitchen." He gives me a sad half grin, seeing the disappointment I'm not doing a good enough job hiding. "Tell them all hello and that I'll try to make it next week."

"Sure, Dad." I know that when Dad says he'll "try" that he'll make a good effort. But he also didn't promise, because he's afraid he'll break it.

I guess an effort will have to be good enough. It's certainly more than Mom does.

CHAPTER

I PUT ON AN EXTRA COAT OF MASCARA BUT STOP MYSELF BEFORE I blow-dry my hair. I don't need to impress Campbell, and I shouldn't want to. I also shouldn't want to eat bacon every day, but that doesn't stop me from salivating every time I smell it.

My hands freeze in the middle of twisting my elastic around my ponytail. Did I mentally reduce Campbell to the level of bacon? Ew. He's so much more than breakfast meat. He's more than an amazing-looking guy. He's sweet and smart and a little bit shy.

Listing his qualities isn't helping either. I need to get out of my head and out of this house. When I open up the bathroom door, I can hear the *SportsCenter* jingle playing from the TV in the living room. There's a greasy box on the counter from my favorite doughnut shop, but I don't see Dad anywhere.

Campbell, however, is standing on his good foot, with his other foot propped up on one of the barstools. A gauze patch, some pre-wrap, and some athletic tape are spread on the counter.

I watch as he peels back the old bandage, body twisted awkwardly so that he can see what he's doing. He's got his tongue pinched between his teeth in concentration, and I can't decide if this is the cutest or stupidest thing I've ever seen anyone do.

"What exactly are you hoping to accomplish here?" I ask, voice light, trying not to say anything that will remind him of that moment in the hallway.

"Change my bandage."

"You couldn't wait to ask for help?"

"You were taking forever in the bathroom, and——" He tries to reposition his injured foot but bumps the tape, and it rolls all the way across the room. Campbell sighs, defeated. "What I meant to say was, 'Will you please help me?'"

"Good recovery." I walk into the living room and pull out the ottoman. "Sit. Dangle your foot off the edge."

He does as I ask, stretching his leg out toward me, and we tuck some pillows under his knee. Kneeling next to the ottoman, I check the bottom of his foot. It's even more purple today than it was yesterday, which is to be expected but is still ugly. His stitches are as beautiful as anyone's could be in the situation, but the wound is draining and totally disgusting.

"Sorry it's gross," he says, reading my stink-face.

"Sorry it happened."

"Sorry you have to take care of it."

Then I look up at him and smile. "It's part of our deal." I try to be as gentle as possible as I tape down the gauze patch, but I worry that every movement hurts.

"Speaking of the deal," he says and then lowers his voice, looking toward the office. Then he mouths, *Can your dad hear us?*

"Why?"

He leans over, grabs the remote, and turns the volume up a few clicks. "Come here."

Now I'm worried. Little worms of anxiety are squiggling around in my stomach, but I sit on the seat cushion next to him, one leg tucked under my butt.

"I had an idea this morning." The way he's talking makes me lean closer so I can hear every word. "Remember how I told you about the charity that Sterling and I work for? I think it's totally possible to launch something like that at your park. I did some research this morning and…" He pauses to pull out his phone and show me what's on the screen. There's a little boy in a wheelchair wearing a baseball helmet lined up next to a batting tee. "Teams all over the country use their facilities in the off-season to help kids with disabilities participate in sports. What if you gave one a home? How could your dad disagree with something that helps kids in need?"

My head is a little buzzy, like I haven't had enough to eat, but I know it's more than that. There's something here. I can feel it. "Sometimes people don't see the marketing potential in working with the Beavers. But maybe they'd be more willing to sponsor something that *affects* people in their town and their customers?"

"Exactly. I know I'm not a big enough deal to draw a huge following, but I've got some contacts and—" Campbell stops, meeting my eyes, and the excitement in his fades. "Do you think this is a stupid idea?"

"No," I rush to whisper back. There's something about a whisper that makes a regular conversation far more intense and personal. Maybe it's the proximity. Maybe it's the way you're watching the other person's mouth so you're positive you capture every word. "This is wonderful. Exactly what I was hoping for."

"Oh. Good, then."

"It's just…are you really sure you want to do this? This project will take a long time." *Longer than a week. Longer than a season. It's a commitment.*

"Of course. This is something I've always wanted to do. Give back to the community." He sets his phone down between us, wrist resting against the hand that I'm using to hold myself up. "And if this is something you really want to do, I think Buckley is the perfect place to do it."

I tell my dad that we're leaving early to go to Mia's, but really we climb in the van and drive to the grocery store. In the parking lot, Campbell makes a couple of calls to the organization he worked with back in Georgia. It's not surprising that no one answers since it's Sunday, but Campbell leaves voice mails.

While he's on the phone, I send emails to the five different organizations that all specialize in recreational therapy, asking for more information.

"I guess we wait until tomorrow and hope someone answers?" he asks as he fiddles with the van's door handle.

A hopeful bubble fills my chest, making me feel buoyant. "Yep, but first ice cream."

Even though Ms. Vivi never lets me bring anything to Sunday dinners, I always try to find something I can offer as a thank-you. Campbell and I pull into Mia's driveway with two sweaty containers of Blue Bell Ice Cream. It was on sale and they had Dutch Chocolate (Mia's favorite) and Strawberry & Homemade Vanilla. Campbell doesn't "mind" chocolate. Whatever that means. I'm not picky. I'll eat both.

I let myself in through the side door and find Ms. Vivi sautéing something that smells so good my stomach does a happy dance. She greets me with a hug and two kisses, one on each cheek, and gives Campbell the same welcome. If he had any hesitation about coming with me, it's melted away by her kindness.

She fusses over him, volunteering ice packs and Tylenol and cold beverages. When he turns down all her offers and she refuses our attempts to help, we're shooed out of the kitchen.

"Everyone is watching the game in the movie room," she says, turning back to her frying pan. "Go. Relax."

The Rodrigueses' house is gorgeous. They have a formal living room on the main floor and a game room with an attached movie theater on the upper floor. Two rows of reclining leather couches are positioned on risers in front of a wall-width screen. Ms. Vivi painted the room dark gray and hung framed black-and-white posters from classic movies down both walls. A real popcorn machine sits in one corner. This is another reason I don't go to the movie theater in town: Mia's house is so much better.

Actually, a lot of things are better at Mia's. Even before my mom left, I felt a little jealous of what the Rodrigueses have. Not the house—the traditions. They have parties scheduled with their extended family at specific times throughout the year. They have food they make for certain occasions and games they always play.

We see my dad's parents once or twice a year. They live in Alabama, where my dad is originally from, near his younger brother's family. My uncle has three kids, all younger than me, who Nana and Papa take care of several days per week. My mom and Nana never got along. I know it was Nana's fault—she accused my mom of getting pregnant with me on purpose to "steal Matthew's money"—but she apologized years ago. Still, there are things that can never be taken back.

Our rare trips to Tuscaloosa were always stilted and uncomfortable. Mom spent her time out shopping with my aunt or reuniting with college friends so she and Nana wouldn't occupy the same space for too many hours per day. They did a good job of acting cordial in front of everyone, but it's not the same as being smothered by Abuela Rodrigues's hugs and invited to work with Mia's mom and aunts in the kitchen—laughing, dancing, gossiping.

I know things will change when Mia goes off to UT and I go to A&M, and I'm a little sad when I think about it. I'll miss my best friend and her family more than I've ever missed my own.

Mia is curled up in the back row of recliners with a fleece blanket tucked to her chin. Her dad is asleep on his stomach across the front row, snoring slightly, completely oblivious to the frigid temperatures in the room.

"Hey, guys!" She flings open her arms to hug me, and I realize she's wearing a tie-dyed T-shirt from a fifth-grade stint at vacation Bible school and shorts that used to be sweats. She didn't dress up for guests or for the hot guy who was coming to her house for dinner, and I love her for it.

I plop down next to her, and Campbell takes the seat on the far side of me, immediately fidgeting with the buttons on the chair.

"How was the game last night?" Mia shares the edge of the blanket with me. "Don't you love the stadium? Did you have the loaded baked potato? It's my favorite."

I let Campbell answer, since Mia's already heard my version. He doesn't mention the crowd of people who hounded him for autographs, or Amerie, or the Kiss Cam. But he does bring up everything we learned about the new stadium.

Mia pokes me in the leg from underneath the blanket, as if Campbell has said something substantial. I'm not exactly sure how to decipher the leg poke, but I'm sure I'll hear about it later.

"Can you get me tickets?" a drowsy voice from the first row asks. It doesn't belong to Mr. Rodrigues.

"Marco Polo?" I stand up and peer over the recliner's back.

Mia's older brother smirks up at me, one eye squinted against the screen's glare. "What's up, Nolan Ryan?"

"No one told me you were going to be——" I don't finish my sentence because he reaches over the couch, locks his arm around my neck, and scrubs his fist against my head.

I screech–laugh, trying to get my fingers into the curve of his elbow. When I can't break his hold, I settle for pinching him hard on the underside of his arm until he yelps and lets go.

This is a typical Marc welcome and has been since we were on the track team together. He decided that if he had to see me at school, practice, *and* at home, he was going to treat me exactly like he treated Mia.

Which explains why her hair is a little more voluminous than usual.

"'Sup," Marc says, raising his chin at Campbell. They exchange names and fist bumps.

"How come you're home from school?" I yank out my elastic and put my hair back into some version of a ponytail.

"I'm not taking any classes during summer semester."

Mia kicks the back of Marc's seat. "And because he missed us."

Marc responds to that with a noncommittal grunt.

"Are you that mean to your sisters?" I ask Campbell while push-ing against the reclined couch-back with my feet. When it snaps perfectly vertical, Marc mumbles something like "Knock it off."

Campbell takes my ponytail and swings it so that it whacks me across the face. "All the time."

DINNER IS AMAZING. THE RODRIGUES FAMILY MAKES CAMPBELL feel like we've all been friends for centuries instead of five min-utes. Ms. Vivi serves the ice cream and then kicks us out of the main house so she can clean up without interruption. We take our bowls to the pool house and hang out there.

A couch and a love seat form an L around a Ping-Pong table and are a barrier in front of the mini-kitchen. A soccer game is on the flat-screen mounted to the wall, but none of us is interested in either team, so Mia and Marc start a Ping-Pong tournament. Their matches are always intense, full of cheering, taunts, threats, and the occasional victory dance.

Campbell and I sit on opposite ends of the couch, watching Mia perform some sort of celebratory shimmy after beating her brother in the first set. We're all laughing, and for a little while I'm able to distance myself from my worries of Mom selling the team.

"Check this out," Campbell says, tilting his phone toward me.

I have to slide down the couch to see what's on the screen. Our shoulders are touching, but I convince myself this is friendly. Not a big deal.

"What am I looking at?" I lean in a little closer, squinting at the blurry image. There's a weird glare at the bottom of the picture, like it's a picture of a picture.

And I realize that's exactly what it is. Two babies—one chubby, with a ton of hair, and the other completely bald—lay side by side on a frog-patterned blanket. The fat baby is giving a big droolly smile at the camera.

"That's me," he says, pointing to the big baby. "And that's you."

In the picture, I'm turned toward him, staring like he's the most interesting thing I've ever seen. Things haven't changed that much.

My parents don't have a ton of pictures of me before they got good cell phones with half-decent cameras, so it's weird to see myself so small. But the thing that snags my attention and holds on is the woman sitting on the ground in the background.

"Holy crap." I take the phone out of his hand. "That's my mom."

She's super thin—much skinnier than I am—and so young. I knew she was technically a teen mom, but this is the first time I've seen her as a teen *and* as my mom. She's not the focus of the picture; her face is turned partway from the camera, and her hair hangs long and silky, almost to her waist. She's laughing.

Mom quit school when she had me. Gave up her cross-country scholarship. Moved from town to town while Dad bounced around in the minors. I know it wasn't easy. She never finished her education, too busy moving us from city to city, and had very few friends until we moved to Buckley. Then working for the team sort of took over her life.

"When was this taken?" I ask, trying to remember a time when my mom ever looked so...*cute*.

Campbell takes the phone from me and texts his mom. "During your dad's last semester at Alabama. You and your mom came to visit."

"Huh." I don't know what else to say.

He bumps me with his shoulder. "Mom says we were always meant to be friends."

Mia gives a snort-laugh, and I realize she's been listening to everything we've said, but it costs her the game. Marc beats her with a wickedly angled shot.

"I play the winner," Campbell yells.

"Dude. You can barely move." Marc spins his paddle in tight circles before serving the ball to Mia. "Plus, you couldn't beat me with two good legs."

Campbell swallows down the taunt, but I can see by the way he holds his shoulders that it didn't go down easily. "You want to test that theory?"

Marc coughs, then slams the ball with a little more force than necessary. "Bring it."

Campbell stands without his crutches and limps, heel off the floor, toward the table. I draw a breath between my teeth and look at Mia for a suggestion. She shrugs at me and falls, sweaty-faced, into the spot Campbell relinquished.

"Do you think this is a good idea?" I toe one of Campbell's crutches toward him.

He ignores it but smiles at me like he's a knight headed into a tourney. "I think this is a great idea."

I'm not sure what he thinks he's fighting for. Is honor still a thing?

"Boys are stupid," Mia says loudly. But she mumbles under her breath, too soft for them to hear: "Not exactly Hadley Pearson, huh?"

"Nope."

"Are you rethinking your rules yet?"

"Never."

She knows I'm lying, and she laughs so hard that the boys look over to see what's so funny. Campbell eyes me like he's missed something, and that expression is enough to send heat flashing all over my body. And I realize Mia's not the only person I'm lying to.

CHAPTER

Fifteen

MY BRAIN HATES ME. IT TAKES FOREVER TO FALL ASLEEP, AND I don't stay there long. At three a.m., three full hours before I'd planned to go on my run, I wake up with something plaguing my thoughts: Lucas Chestnut.

Not for any of the reasons most girls wake up thinking about boys in the middle of the night. Lucas's dad owns Chestnut Oil Products, one of the largest manufacturing companies in all of Buckley. They make parts for pipelines or maintenance or something oil related, and apparently it's lucrative, because their house is even nicer than Mia's. Their shop is situated outside of town, so it didn't come up on my initial search.

One weekend Lucas and I had plans to go paintballing, but he canceled at the last minute to go golfing with his dad. His dad sponsors a team every year to raise money for an autism research group. I didn't mind that Lucas went. Sometimes stuff comes up, especially stuff related to your family business. Plus, I didn't need a date to shoot people with an air-powered rifle.

All those thoughts—minus the paintballing—combine with Campbell's suggestion to host special needs camps at Perry Park. If Mr. Chestnut was willing to shell out money for a golf team, would he be interested in sponsoring a facility that could help similar groups? Turning the ballpark into a year-round events center would mean upgrading the rest of the stadium, including the locker and training rooms. It would knock out all the Rangers' requirements *and* increase revenue in the off-season.

Really, it's a matter of pitching the idea in a way that helps Mr. Chestnut see how partnering with Perry Park could help his business and community.

I flop back on my pillow, trying to estimate how much work I'll have to do in less than a week. And that's *if* I can arrange a meeting with Mr. Chestnut.

Is it even possible?

Dad always says if it's not worth working for, it's not worth doing. And this would be worth it.

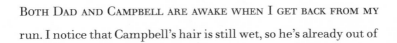

BOTH DAD AND CAMPBELL ARE AWAKE WHEN I GET BACK FROM MY run. I notice that Campbell's hair is still wet, so he's already out of the shower—thank goodness—and Dad is working at the kitchen counter. ESPN is blaring in the background, but Campbell pops to his feet as soon as I step into the living room.

"Hey, guys." I toe off my shoes, hoping I'm not releasing foot stench into the air. "You're both up early."

Dad grunts and pats the stack of papers next to him. "I've gotta get this all sent off to your mom before I head to the office. You wanna pick up breakfast?"

"Sure. Rudy's?"

"That's fine." He checks over his shoulder to where Sawyer is lingering by the couch. "What can we get you?"

"Is it okay if I come with?" Campbell asks, crutching toward the door, totally ready to go.

I freeze, wishing I could covertly sniff my armpit. "Sure."

Campbell tilts his head, communicating *something* with his eyes. I don't think he just wants to eat his burrito while it's hot.

"Let me grab my keys."

As soon as the door to the van shuts, Campbell is talking. "Susan—the director of the recreational therapy group in Georgia—already replied to my email." His enthusiasm pours out. Campbell usually talks slowly, all southern drawl, but he can't seem to get the words out fast enough. "She's going to call me in an hour and give me all the information we need to get a program started here in Buckley."

It takes all of my self-control not to dive across the console and wrap him in the biggest hug ever. Instead I steal Mia's victory dance and hold my hand up for a high five. Safest way to celebrate for sure. As we drive, I tell him all about my middle-of-the-night epiphany concerning Mr. Chestnut and Chestnut Oil Products. He agrees that it's a perfect fit. This is the first step. Now we have something concrete to lure in sponsors.

Rudy's is one of the more famous Texas BBQs. They serve your meat on sheets of brown butcher paper and give you a half loaf of bread to go with your brisket or ribs. The restaurant's interior—livestock water barrels filled with ice and bottled drinks, wood picnic tables, and garage doors instead of walls—gives it a roadside-dive sort of appeal. But they serve the best breakfast burritos, maybe even better than what Ms. Vivi can cook up, and that's saying something.

The burritos are in a warming bin to one side of the checkout counter, and once they're gone, they're gone. Luckily, we've arrived early enough to get a good selection, and I carry them to the cashier while Campbell crutches a step behind me.

I'm bouncing with energy from our conversation, actually outpacing him as I deliver our foil-wrapped breakfast burritos to the counter.

"Wait, Ryan," he calls. "Let me pay for breakfast. You and your dad have done so much for me."

I wave him off, credit card already out, but he reaches around me and snatches it out of my hand. He's close, chest against my shoulder, and I can smell whatever it is that makes the T-shirt I still haven't returned so delicious.

"Please." He offers my card back and pulls out some cash. "It's the least I can do——"

"I bet it is," says a voice behind us.

My stomach plunges to my feet as I look over Campbell's shoulder. Hadley Pearson is grinning like that awful cat in the *Alice in Wonderland* movie. I know what he thinks is going on. With me pressed right up against Campbell, my body language isn't exactly providing contrary evidence.

"What's up, Pearson?" I say as I move a little farther down the counter and away from Campbell, which probably looks worse. "Aren't you out of bed a little early?"

Pearson is one of those guys who's talented—gifted with speed and good instincts for where the ball is going to fly—but he doesn't work hard to get better. He's not like Ollie and Campbell, who play a whole game and then stay late for practice. Pearson is content to coast.

I dislike him too much to care what he thinks of me. I've spent my entire life around young athletes with underdeveloped frontal lobes—I learned that fact in my sports medicine class and it explained so much. I open my mouth to spit some sassy comment in his direction, but I see Ollie standing a few steps behind him. And the expression on his face looks like he swigged curdled milk. He shakes it off quickly.

"Less than a week?" Pearson says, focused only on Campbell. "That's impressive."

He offers Campbell knuckles, but Campbell ignores them and accepts his change from the cashier—a girl I recognize from the grade below mine. And *she's* smiling like she's caught in the middle of one of those telenovelas that Mia's abuela loves so much.

"It's not like that." Campbell faces Pearson, and the manly guy from the cover of the *Sports Illustrated* is back. Even on crutches, he's kind of intimidating. "She's been driving me to my appointments."

"And then stayed close to take care of you." Pearson's mouth drops into a poisonous smirk as he scans my skimpy running clothes and Campbell's wet hair. I'm tempted to punch out his perfectly straight teeth. "Ryan's known for being good at her job."

"Knock it off." Ollie bumps Pearson's shoulder as he moves toward the burritos. He doesn't even look in my direction.

This. This is exactly what I've been worried about. The insinuation. The suggestion. The rumors are as bad as if Campbell and I *had* done something.

I don't even stop by the condiment bar to pick up Rudy's famous pico. Instead, I grab my bag and rush back to the van— away from all of them.

Except…does that make me look guilty?

A few moments later, the restaurant doors fly open, and Campbell crutches across the parking lot toward the Beavermobile.

Looks like the pissing match with Pearson is over.

He stuffs his crutches inside the van. "Are those two always like that?" He reaches for the bag on the console and sorts through it until he finds his bacon, egg, and potato burritos.

"Pearson is." I usually don't let his crap get to me, but I've got a sharp spot in my throat, like I've swallowed a tortilla chip without chewing.

"And what about Ollie?"

I gulp hard, hoping the feeling will leave. "No. He's one of the good ones."

Campbell's looking at me over his burrito. I can feel his eyes on me. "Are you sure he's not...or *were* you ever——"

"I already told you nothing has ever or will ever happen between me and anyone who plays for the Beavers."

He's silent, but I can see him searching for words.

"What?" I snap, and he still doesn't say anything. "Now you see exactly why I was so worried. Your teammates are the biggest gossips I know. What do you think they're going to say? How many people do you think are going to hear about this?" I wave my hand toward the bag. Even though I'm not really hungry, food might be exactly the right thing to soothe this weird pain burning in my chest.

"They're leaving on a four-game road trip," he says, tossing me a bacon burrito. "They'll forget about it before they get back."

Since Campbell doesn't make eye contact as he says it, I'm pretty sure he's not telling the whole truth.

CHAPTER

Sixteen

Advanced Machining has a complex of aluminum buildings hidden behind a brick and stone office front. I've been here twice before with my dad, to drop off-season ticket packages. He doesn't usually deliver them personally, but Advanced Machining is one of the biggest employers in our town. It drives him nuts that he's never been able to sell them on sponsoring a giveaway or having an outfield sign. Sure, people in our town aren't exactly Advanced Machining's target market, but most companies are looking for ways to build "community partnerships." The last time I was here, Dad pitched a whole bunch of ideas, but according to their CEO, "Baseball isn't the right fit."

Maybe tying their business to a stadium renovation will be. Could they see value in providing the ceiling beams that support the new events center's roof? Or having an entire wing designed to showcase their craftsmanship?

I've pushed yesterday's incident with Ollie and Pearson to the back of my mind. Okay, fine. Not quite to the back. Every now and then Ollie's face peeks into my brain's peripheral vision, and I'll rehash the whole thing for a minute before I can shift focus.

I've got to get my game face on. Campbell and I spent most of Monday afternoon preparing a really informal one-page proposal of what we're hoping to accomplish with an addition to the facility. No numbers. Very few specifics.

Dad calls meetings like this "fishing expeditions." You throw out all sorts of bait and see what it'll take to make a potential sponsor bite. If I can get verbal interest, a promise for a second meeting, I can take that back to my mom. And eventually my dad.

When we pull into the parking lot, Campbell gives me an encouraging grin. "They're not going to say no."

"Of course not," I say, trying to ignore my shivery nervousness. I let him lead the way into the building, while I handle the boxes of bagels, cream cheese, and sandwiches. The marketing director, Jim Stein, didn't have time to meet me for an outside lunch, so I brought food to him.

Bonus points, please.

The receptionist shows us to the conference room where Jim will meet us. Everything in the building has a cabin-y feel, but the conference room takes the decor to a whole different level. It has dark exposed beams, a stone fireplace that has definitely never been used, and a table that looks like it was made out of an enormous tree trunk. I can even see the tree rings under the high-gloss shine. I set down the boxes, and Campbell sits in one of the leather armchairs on the table's right side.

Jim comes in a minute later. He's probably in his early fifties, with steel-gray hair and a gut that suggests he really enjoys Thirsty Thursdays at the ballpark. His eyes immediately fall on Campbell, who jumps back to his feet.

"In all the years I've been meeting with the Buckley Beavers and watching y'all's games, I haven't had a chance to meet a first-rounder." He shakes hands with Campbell. "You're the real deal, huh?"

Campbell gives a nervous-sounding laugh. "I hope so, sir."

"Sorry to hear you're hurt. But stitches heal up nicely." Jim spares a glance for me. "Nice to see you again, Ryan. Your dad coming along?" He looks around the room like he expects Dad to appear out of nowhere.

"No, sir," I say, turning the bagel box toward him. "Just me today. I wanted to talk to you about—"

"Let's eat first, sweetheart." He drops into the chair at the head of the table. "Business is always better on a full stomach."

Sweetheart. I'm sure he didn't mean anything by it. It's a Texas thing. *Sweetheart. Honey. Love.* I've been called those names a thousand times, but today it stings like a fire ant bite. Not painful, but irritating.

"Of course." I open the box and pass him the sandwich that he requested. "I brought plenty of other bagels for the rest of your staff."

"That's nice," he says, taking a bite. "Tell me, Sawyer—it is Sawyer, isn't it?—you're only seventeen?"

"Yes, sir. I'll be eighteen in December." Campbell picks a red onion off his sandwich and sets it on the box lid. "Actually, Ryan has some ideas—"

"And Ryan roped you into this meeting with that pretty smile of hers?" Jim winks at me like it's a joke, but it feels so patronizing. Two fire ant bites.

Campbell looks at me like he's not quite sure how to respond to that. "Um. Ryan has a nice smile, but no. Why don't I let her—"

"After I finish my sandwich, son. You kids are always in such a hurry." He shakes his head and then takes another bite. "You played in the Junior College World Series?"

The rest of the lunch goes pretty much according to this script: Jim talks to Campbell, recognizing that I'm in the room only when Campbell says my name, then Jim winks again and turns the conversation back to Campbell.

And I swear he's taking his sweet time eating to piss me off. Ten full minutes after I finished my sandwich, Jim balls up his bag of kettle chips and shoots it toward the garbage can in the corner. It falls short. He clicks his tongue in disappointment but leaves it where it fell.

"All right." He sucks a tooth, likely trying to get that wad of lettuce out. "Give me your spiel."

"No spiel, Jim." I'm done with calling him "sir" for the day. I push the proposal sheet in his direction. I used chunks of text straight from the information Campbell's friend emailed, so it has a more finished feel than if I'd whipped it together yesterday. "Campbell is from Georgia, and while he lived there he volunteered at a camp for children with special needs."

Jim's finger ticks against Campbell's picture at the top of the page. "That's nice. What does that have to do with me and Advanced Machining?" His eyes are focused on Campbell, waiting for his answer, but Sawyer turns to me to answer the question.

"To host camps similar to this one, we need to expand and renovate Perry Park. It would make sense to use a company in our own town to supply the girders and framework for that events center." I lay out all the information I have, and Campbell volunteers a story about some of the kids he's helped and how that's only one way the events center could be used in the off-season.

At the end, Jim kicks back in his chair, hands folded across his belly, and weighs us with his eyes. "Well, I have to say I'm surprised. This isn't at all what I was expecting."

I clear away the sandpaper lining my throat. "Do you think

this is the type of project that Advance Machining could get behind?"

He purses his lips and nods slowly. "It might be."

I keep my squeal of elation trapped inside. "I'd love to schedule another meeting with you and everyone on your team."

"Sounds good." He pulls his phone out of his front pocket and scrolls through his calendar. "I'm out of town for the next two weeks. The following week is bad, but how about a month from today?"

It's not ideal, but it's something. "That sounds good."

"Bring your daddy with you next time."

I freeze. Hopefully I can get Dad on board before then. And maybe he won't kill me for visiting one of his personal contacts without him. "Sure thing. I'll put it on his schedule."

Jim didn't give us a couple million dollars on the spot, but he didn't shut us down either.

Even though my hands are empty now, Campbell holds the door open for me as we leave—because manners are his thing—and I grin as I pass him. He's frowning.

"What's with the face?" I ask once we're out to the parking lot.

"I don't like that guy. He acted like you weren't even in the room."

"Usually I come with my dad on sales calls and that's pretty much how everyone treats me." I click the lock and stow the crutches for Campbell, trying to revel in the possibility of something good coming out of this instead of being super annoyed at Jim. "I don't know if it's because I'm young or because I'm a girl or because they're all jackasses."

"I just..." Campbell pauses as he climbs up into the van, waiting for me to walk around and hop in before he finishes his sentence. "I get what you meant about people not taking you seriously."

The validation feels nice, even though it doesn't fix the problem. Someday I won't have to prove to sponsors like Jim that I know my business. I'll show up at a meeting and everyone will wait to hear what I'm going to say.

At least I hope so.

CHAPTER

Seventeen

SINCE CAMPBELL GOT HURT, WE'VE WORKED OUT A PRETTY GOOD routine. I've dropped him off at the stadium gym the last two days and then knocked out a couple of hours of work on my covert projects—phone calls with potential sponsors and tweaking the details of each brochure so that they're specific to individual companies. Once Campbell finishes annihilating some muscle group, we meet my dad for lunch and spend the afternoon tackling projects that never get finished when the team is in town. Campbell is willing to do all the tasks I hate—like updating stats on the website and filling our online orders—but I think it's the only thing stopping him from going crazy.

The Beavers have lost three straight games, and even though Campbell couldn't do anything about it, he acts like he's personally responsible.

In the evenings, we either go to Mia's house and work on stuff we can't get done at the stadium, or go home and hang out with my dad and do mundane things. Like laundry. Or just...talk. About baseball and family. And how Campbell worries whether or not Sterling will go away to college and about how his little sisters work so hard on the farm. He loves them all so fiercely and is never embarrassed to let it show.

"You guys are on your own for dinner tonight," Dad says as he flicks off his office light. "I'm meeting with the mayor about the Fall Fun Run."

"Are we hosting again?" I hurry to close the window on my screen. I don't want him to see the brochure I've designed for Chestnut Oil Products. After our lunch with Jim at Advanced Machining, I decided I needed something more substantial, more impressive to convince Mr. Chestnut that sponsoring an expansion of Perry Park is a smart move for his company. I have a mental clock in my head, ticking away the minutes before the visitors from the conglomerate come.

Campbell is sitting on the couch between the copy machine and the watercooler, injured leg resting on the coffee table, a stack of contracts spread out in front of him.

"Yep. Same route. Different start times," Dad says, reaching for his wallet, and pulls out two twenties. "Why don't you try that new pho place near the Kroger?"

Campbell grimaces, but my dad doesn't notice.

I hold back a snort and accept the cash. "Don't worry about us. We'll figure something out."

"Don't stay too long," Dad says, from the doorway. "Everything will still be here tomorrow."

I groan and Campbell gives a half laugh. Then my dad leaves. The A/C kicks on, highlighting how quiet it is. How empty. How very alone we are. Again.

"So," I say only because the silence makes me feel all jumpy. "You're not a big fan of pho?"

"Pho is good. I'm just—" He stacks the papers, squaring them off before putting them into a folder. "Do you ever get tired of eating out?"

"Sure, but I don't have a lot of other options. It's not like someone is going to fix a big home-cooked meal for me, you know?" I shut down my computer and push my chair under the desk.

"You don't cook?"

"Sexist much?" I have to choke back a laugh at the horror on his face.

"That's not what I meant! I wasn't asking *you* to cook for me. It was an honest question."

"Mm-hmm."

"I..." He takes a deep breath and shakes his head. "How about I cook for you?"

I know he's only talking about making food that we both will eat. But something about a guy offering to cook for me feels—to use Mia's favorite word—intimate. Way more than going somewhere and splitting the bill. We'll be alone. In my house. Eating together.

If anyone walked in, what would they think?

Does it even matter? If it's not anything, don't make it into anything. Campbell has barely flirted with me since he saw how Jim Stein acted, and I've barely flirted back.

It doesn't change the fact that sometimes when we're sitting on the couch together, everything is too still. I try not to look over at him, and I feel like he's doing the same. In those moments when I get caught staring, or he does, our gazes sort of *clash*. Those moments feel so real, like he's dragged his finger down my arm or touched the small of my back.

I'd call Mia to come over and hang out with us as a tension-reliever. But she's a very unwilling chaperone on the best days. Tonight she's at her littlest cousin's princess birthday party. Although she might appreciate the rescue.

"What will you cook?" I ask as I grab the keys to the Beaver-mobile.

He shrugs. "Nothing fancy." He pulls his crutches close. "I'll be doing it all on one foot."

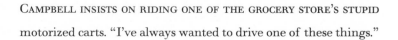

CAMPBELL INSISTS ON RIDING ONE OF THE GROCERY STORE'S STUPID motorized carts. "I've always wanted to drive one of these things."

"Why? They go like three miles per hour." I don't mention that he'll look ridiculous sitting on it—this giant, super-fit guy riding a grandma cart. Okay, maybe it will be worth it to confirm the hysterical visual in my head.

"Have you ever driven one?"

I roll my eyes. "No."

"Exactly. It's the novelty of doing it." He pushes the lever down and the cart suddenly jerks, and then stops, making his head whip forward.

A laugh explodes from me before I can contain it. "A little more powerful than you thought?"

"Way more powerful," he says, a laugh in his voice. "It can go at least eight miles per hour."

We pick up the most random things: a can of cranberry sauce, a bag of grapes, a box of spaghetti. When we get to the cereal aisle where there are no other shoppers, Campbell pushes the cart as fast as it will go. Which is still ridiculously slow.

He stops in front of the bags of dry cereal and starts to stand up from the chair.

"Stop." I put my hand on his shoulder, pushing him down. "If you're going to be injured, be injured. What do you want?"

"The Tutti Fruttis."

The bag is enormous. I haul it down and put it in his basket. "Are you seriously going to eat this much?"

"Maybe. Plus, it's a much better price."

"Are you going to buy five gallons of milk, too?"

His face scrunches in disgust. "Milk on cereal is gross."

"Wait. What?"

"Why would you make perfectly good cereal soggy?" He looks like I've suggested that he kick a puppy.

My mouth hangs open. I'm baffled. "Milk and cereal are like butter and toast. They belong together."

"No." He starts his cart, leaving me behind.

"Now I'm terrified to eat whatever you're going to make."

When we get back to the house—and after Campbell has insisted on carrying in all the groceries by himself on the crutches—he makes the most repulsive-looking sauce I've ever seen. Jelled cranberry sauce, chili sauce, brown sugar, and lemon juice all go into the blender. I preheat the oven and dump the frozen meatballs into an old pie tin. Mom took most of the good pans with her when she left. I didn't miss them until now.

Campbell pours his concoction over the meatballs and throws them in the oven, then starts the noodles.

I sit on the corner of the counter, legs folded so that I'm out of the way, and steal a handful of dry Tutti Fruttis from the bag. "This isn't food. It's candy."

"Are you *complaining?* Toss me one." He tips his head back and opens his mouth. He catches six in a row before I throw one way off the mark and it lands in the noodles.

"Oh no!" I bounce off the counter and grab a ladle, trying to fish it out before it dissolves completely. But the stupid piece of cereal sinks deeper into the pot.

"Well," Campbell says as we watch little chunks of pink loop float to the surface. "If it's good, I'll tell my mom it's a new ingredient."

Setting down the spoon, I turn so my back is against the cabinet, the stove separating us. This is okay. We're two people making some dinner. It's actually kind of fun. "This is your mom's recipe?"

"Yep. She's a good cook." He looks at the timer on the oven. Four minutes left. "We don't eat out very often."

I've always known other families, like Mia's, eat home-cooked food, but I've never felt embarrassed about the fact that we don't. Until now. "I'm sorry. You must think that staying with us is awful."

"No! This has been great. You have been...great." Campbell tightens the loose knob on the drawer pull. "There's a lot of us to feed, so eating out is really expensive."

"You do kind of eat a lot." I wipe my hands on my pants. I don't know why they're suddenly so sweaty. "But with your signing bonus and everything, they could probably afford to eat out more often."

Campbell looks away, moving to the next drawer to tighten that knob too. "My family—well, my dad—won't accept any money from me."

It's like he's sucked the air out of the room. "Oh."

"I paid off the farm's mortgages behind his back. He's so

angry that he still hasn't spoken to me."

"But—"

"It's fine."

"Except that I can tell that it's not."

Campbell sighs, gaze focused off to the side, somewhere between me and the window. "What if I'm one of those players who is prospected to be amazing but is always injured? What if this is the beginning of the end of my career?"

My mouth hangs open for a minute, as I try to find the perfect thing to say. "You're only *seventeen*. You can't possibly believe that this one crazy accident will stop you from doing something amazing."

When he finally looks at me, his blue eyes don't hide any of the frustration he's harboring. "I didn't leave the farm so that I wouldn't have to help. I left so that I could help *more*, in a different way. You know?"

I *do* know. Our situations are different, but they're not really. We both have so much at stake.

The oven buzzes, breaking the moment. Campbell shakes off his emotions and crutches toward the oven. "You ready to try my mom's famous meatballs?"

Despite the scary-seeming ingredients, they're actually delicious.

I don't know what is taking Dad so long with the mayor. Actually, that's not true. Dad can talk to anyone about anything for any length of time. But as Campbell and I clean the kitchen, the light outside wanes. Our conversation fades with it, and there's no ignoring that we're alone.

"I'll get that." I reach to take the container of leftover meatballs from Campbell, and our hands skim. It's the merest contact of skin on skin, but it sends a tingle all the way to my toes.

"I've got it," he says as he crutches forward.

I have to back up so he can swing open the fridge door. He rests his crutches against the cabinets next to me and tucks the food on the empty shelf, illuminating the room, then flashing it back into darkness as the door glides shut.

I flip on the light near the sink. It's a single bulb, dim and dusty, and when I turn back Campbell is right behind me, closing the bag of rolls.

The dim light doesn't hide his expression—the same one from the morning when I caught him in the towel.

My pulse races in my throat. My hand buzzes from the place we touched. "Do you want some ice cream?" The words sound gravelly, rough with the awareness of how little distance is between us.

We both reach for the freezer at the same time, and then laugh at our near collision, but it's strained. Breathy.

I look up at him and it's a mistake. Because he's looking down at me. And I'm frozen. I can't move away, and I don't want to.

His hand is on my waist. My palm is on his chest.

"Ryan." He says just my name, but I hear the request. *Is this okay? Tell me this is okay.* His fingers slide up my spine, easing me closer.

Yes, this is more than okay.

No one is here, I tell myself as I lean in. *No one will ever know.*

What's the worst that could happen?

My mind supplies plenty of answers: *No one will take you seriously. No one will believe you're in this business for the business. If anyone finds out, you'll be another fraternization casualty.*

And he didn't want any distractions.

"Campbell, we can't," I say, swallowing down my want with a swig of bitter reality. I use the hand on his chest to push myself back a step. He lets me go easily, but I see the disappointment on his face. "There are rules."

"I know." He grabs the ice cream and shoves it back in the freezer. "Sorry."

"It's getting late." It's not *that* late. It's the earliest we've been home since we've met, but I need the excuse. And I am tired. Tired enough to make mistakes that I'll regret later. "I'm going to bed."

He doesn't call me on it, gathering up his crutches. "We'll leave for the stadium about nine tomorrow?"

"Yep." The same time as every other day this week.

"Sounds good. Sleep well."

Yeah, right.

CHAPTER

Eighteen

THE NEXT AFTERNOON, RED IS ALONE IN THE TRAINING ROOM when I walk in. He's got a folder and paperwork spread across one of the tables and has pulled his bifocals way down low on his nose, squinting at whatever he sees.

"Hey, Red! Campbell was supposed to come get me when he finished his workout so we could go pick up some lunch." When Red doesn't look up, I lean back, trying to see if there's any light under the door where the ice baths are separated from the rest of the training room. It's dark. "Is he showering?"

"Nope. That boy is in a mood today."

"A mood?" Campbell doesn't really have *moods*. Every now and then his frustration sneaks out, but he's careful to tuck it away. Always polite. Generally optimistic. He's basically Captain

America minus performance-enhancing drugs.

Red finally looks up, eyeing me over his wire frames. He doesn't say anything about my navy pencil skirt, sleeveless white blouse, and neat ponytail, though I see it register on his face. I've been trying to dress more professionally so that *if* someone with money wanders into our office and I have a chance to meet with future "community partners" face-to-face, I'll look legit instead of like one of their kids.

"He's been working out for"—Red squints at his watch—"however long it's been since you dropped him off."

"Three hours?" I know Red's eyesight isn't great and his hearing isn't much better, but this is the first time I've worried about his mind. "There's no way. What could he possibly do for three hours without working his legs?"

Red waves me toward the gym door. "See for yourself."

Doubtful, I march away, assuming Campbell found something to watch on one of the TVs and lost track of time. He reads on his phone a lot and plays his brother in silly online games. Even though there are more comfortable places to do all of that. Like in the chair I've pulled up next to my desk.

As I swing open the glass door, I can hear the repetitive whir of one of the machines.

The rowing machine.

He's dangling his right foot off the side, using only his left leg to propel the sliding seat backwards. His hair is dark with sweat;

his sleeveless dry-fit shirt is soaked through in a neat line down his spine. Triceps, biceps, quad, and what I can see of his back muscles are sharply toned, and while any other day I might have stopped to watch, I'm a little too irritated to really enjoy the sight.

"What are you doing?" I demand, coming to stand beside him.

He gives me a chin-tilt hello but doesn't slow down.

The time on the machine's readout shows forty-two minutes. He's been rowing one-legged for *forty-two minutes.* How can his body do that? How can anyone's body do that? Isn't his quad exploding? I tap the timer on the machine.

"Almost. Done." There's a big gap between words, when he inhales.

"Forty-two...three minutes? Are you crazy?"

When he doesn't answer, I step on the surge protector button, killing the power to the machine.

"Ryan," he snaps. It's the sharpest tone he's ever used with me. He rips his earbuds out, clearly pissed off. "I only had fifteen more minutes."

"What if you slipped? What if you snagged your stitches on the edge? It's sharp." I push my fingers against it to show him, leaving a red line in my skin. "What if I had to haul you back to Arlington—"

"I wasn't going to slip. I don't *slip.*"

"You're not supposed to put any pressure on your foot." I pick up a towel from the wire basket against the wall and throw it at him.

"I wasn't."

"For *three* hours."

He wipes his face, and I get the sense he's composing himself behind the towel.

"I know you're upset that you're not playing, but this"—I wave to the whole gym and then point to the rowing machine—"is not normal. It's my job to take care of you, and I don't want to get into trouble if you hurt yourself."

"Oh." He picks up his water bottle and flicks back the top. "That's what this is about."

"What?"

"You. Your rules. Getting into trouble."

My face scrunches in confusion. "No. It's about *you* not being stupid. You'll be back on the field soon enough. Chill out a little."

Campbell laughs, but it's cold, humorless. "That's funny coming from you."

I stand up straight and fold my arms across my chest. "What's that supposed to mean?"

He says nothing, shakes his head, and swings his legs over the side of the machine. His crutches are leaning against the wall behind me, and I know he's going to have to limp over to them. I could hand them to him, but he's obviously eager to prove that he's Superman.

The space between us is loaded, ready to explode at the next word or breath or look.

How did we get here? To this place where we can be angry at each other over a sentence or two?

I guess when you spend so much time in such close proximity to one person, the nature of your relationship changes faster. There's a scientific term for it—saturation point or critical velocity or both of those combined—and I can't remember what it is, but we've reached it quicker than I knew was possible.

He breaks first, taking a swig of his water before he speaks. "Can you hand me my crutches? Please."

"What did you mean?"

"Nothing." He holds out his hand. "Crutches."

I lick my lips, suddenly nervous to hear his response. "I only turned off the machine because I was worried." I grab the crutches and offer them to him.

"I know. It's just..." He doesn't take them immediately, resting his elbows on his knees, good foot bouncing up and down. "I figured you would understand. I've seen you after your runs. I know how hard you push yourself."

"Not *this* hard."

"I'm not talking about physically." When he looks up at me, his expression is open and a little vulnerable. "You think I haven't heard you typing in the middle of the night? Do you think I don't notice that you have twenty new ideas every time we talk about saving the stadium? How many hours are *you* sleeping, anyway?"

I can't hold his gaze, afraid of what my face is giving away and refusing to let him see it. "Enough." Okay, that's a total lie. I'm getting three or four hours most nights, when my mind shuts off enough to fall asleep.

"I don't blame you. I know *exactly* how bad you want this." He stands and takes my elbows, forcing me to meet his eyes. "I don't want to lose baseball either."

Campbell doesn't explain himself any further. He doesn't have to. I know why he's in the gym, killing himself to get better, faster. We're both terrified of what may happen if we don't work harder than everyone else, if we aren't constantly devoting our time and energy to this thing we love.

For both of us, baseball is so much more than a game.

He takes the crutches from me, but his fingers trail down my forearms first. It's too slow to be unintentional. It's a silent apology. And maybe something more.

It's that something else that jerks me out of the moment. I shouldn't recognize that's what his touch means. I shouldn't have let myself get comfortable with the hand-brushing and shoulder-bumping. And I definitely shouldn't be standing so close, with my pulse thrashing in the base of my throat and him looking down at me with half worry and half want on his face.

This—whatever this is—has gone too far. We shouldn't share any of this. We shouldn't know about each other's drive and passion and fear. I shouldn't feel a jolt of awareness every time his fingers skim mine. We're so far beyond the bounds of what is professional.

None of *this* is in my job description.

I've crossed the line with Sawyer Campbell, but not so far that I can't step back. So I do, creating more space between us, both physically and mentally. "I'm..." I swallow hard, trying to box out whatever I'm feeling and focus on getting back to the professional. "I'm going to go back to my desk. Please have Red call me when you're ready for lunch. I can have something delivered for you."

"Ryan."

I take another step backwards, toward the door and away from him. "I'm sorry I interrupted your workout. I promise this won't happen again."

He calls after me, but I rush out of the gym and let the door swing shut between us.

"So, you left him there?" Mia screeches as I kick off my shoes and flop onto her unmade bed.

After my very ungraceful exit from the training area, I grabbed my laptop and keys and drove straight to Mia's. I sent Dad a quick text saying that she needed me for "girl stuff." He doesn't question anything of that nature, so I may not hear back from him at all.

I put a gray pillow over my face, blocking out the light

streaming in through the windows that wrap around Mia's room. "I didn't know what else to do."

"Running away is usually not the best choice. For anything."

"I wasn't running." My words are muffled by the soft, bumpy texture. I don't know why Mia has a pillow made out of baby blanket material, but this minky-velour stuff is a nice option for face-covering. "Just walking. Fast-ish."

The bed shifts as Mia sits down beside me. "You could have kissed him. That would have been a good choice."

"Not an option."

"Maybe not, but that's what I would have done." She gives a naughty-sounding laugh.

I push the pillow partway to the side and glare up at her. "Not helpful."

"I know, but..." She props herself up on a pillow that's shaped like the back of a chair. Mia has more pillows than anyone could possibly ever use, all test products for her pillow-making business. She'd sewn all of them herself. They're all funky textures and shapes, and seemingly mismatched. And yet somehow her room looks like the cover of a magazine, done in gray, white, silver, and little pops of gold. I keep telling her she should sell her pillows, maybe in an Etsy shop, but she doesn't think she's ready yet.

"Let's pretend that you let something happen between you and Sawyer," she continues once she's comfortable. "What's the worst possible outcome?"

"I get fired."

She shakes her head. "Your dad is only going to fire you if you do something totally gross. Like sneak into the locker room and get naked. You're his right arm. He pretty much can't function without you."

"My mom finds out. And then she sends me to a convent or something."

Mia makes an ugly, teeth-gritting face. "I'm pretty sure convents don't take girls anymore, but it wouldn't surprise me if your mom tried it. That is, *if* she found out. Which she probably wouldn't since she's not around all that often."

"Whispers follow me and no one ever believes that I'm good at the job without some guy standing beside me."

Mia doesn't say anything for a little while, just pats my arm like her abuela does. "This is so sad. You finally really like someone."

I put the pillow back over my face. She's right. I do like Campbell. He's funny and smart and intense and not at all what I expected. He's also completely off-limits.

"It's fine. I can handle him." I sit up and smooth down my ponytail. "I'm just going to—"

"*Handle* him?"

"No." I huff at her villainous smile. "Handle *it*. I meant handle this whole situation."

"Sure you did."

Nineteen

I DON'T GO HOME. I NEED A NIGHT OFF. NOT FROM WORK, BUT FROM Campbell. From sharing a pizza. From debating whether or not Curt Schilling faked his ankle injury during the 2004 American League Championship. From Campbell's proximity while we work on sponsorship presentations.

And even though I'm not great company, Mia does her best to keep my mind free of all things Campbell. She convinces her mom to make cookies, and then they *Shark Tank* me—somehow that's become a verb—asking all the tough questions.

I'm one hundred percent confident that I can face Mr. Chestnut tomorrow without Campbell being there. Sure, his experience with recreational therapy is really compelling, but it's not like he's going to be around forever. And Mr. Chestnut is going to help fund the stadium's addition because he wants to help his community, not because a first-round draft pick talks him into it.

Mia lends me a tank top and a pair of shorts to sleep in. And once I climb into her bed with all its perfect pillows, I fall asleep. It's one of those dreamless sleeps that should be restful but is so heavy that you wake up feeling even more exhausted.

"Let me do your hair today," Mia says when my alarm goes off at seven thirty a.m. She's built a wall of pillows to block out the light streaming in from one of the windows that overlooks the Grotto.

"What's wrong with a ponytail?" I say, thinking of Amerie's perfectly parted, perfectly sleek hair. "A ponytail can look professional."

Mia's pillow blockade collapses onto her head, but when she lifts it, the expression on her face is so pained that I don't even argue.

When I get out of the shower, she's laid out a dress for me that will go with the shoes I wore over here last night. I'd picked out a great skirt and top, but this way I won't have to go home. The knots in my shoulders release, knowing that I don't have to see Campbell. I fully recognize that I am a wimp, but I'm still so grateful that Mia's given me an out.

The sleeveless black dress is skimpier when stretched over her six extra inches of height, but perfectly appropriate on me. Somehow it manages to be formal without looking like something you might wear to a funeral.

Once my hair is done, she smiles at her handiwork. Her eyes meet mine in the mirror.

"You've got this."

I do. I totally have this.

First the office, then to the lunch that will save the stadium and stop my mom from selling to the conglomerate.

THE OFFICE IS BUZZING WHEN I GET IN. WE'VE GOT A TEN A.M. all-hands-on-deck meeting, but everyone is in early, trying to catch up on the stuff they didn't do while the team was out of town. Even though I'm on time, I feel like a slacker rolling in so late.

I peek my head into Dad's office, letting him know that I've arrived. He's on the phone but gives me a little wave. The proofs for the baseball cards are in, and they look amazing. This year we went with a nontraditional layout—sort of a futuristic theme with a digital-looking font. For as old-school as baseball cards are, they're always one of our most successful promotions. And with Campbell's first-round draft card in the stack, we'll get a ton of orders from our online store to boost revenue.

I pick up my phone to text him a picture of his card, but stop myself. I wouldn't do it for anyone else on the team, except maybe Ollie. I've really got to stop treating Campbell like he's something special.

My phone rings. "Buckley Beavers, this is Ryan—"

"Ry, patch me through to your dad," Red says. "It's an emergency."

Dad's call light is still on, but I buzz him anyway. Five seconds later he's marching out of his office and waving for me to follow.

I rush after him, taking the stairs two at a time—which is way harder in heels than in tennis shoes—down to the training room.

"What happened?" I hear Dad say as he pushes through the door.

Campbell is sitting on the vinyl table, elbows on knees, head in hands, blood on his sock.

My stomach rucks into a ball and wedges right under my heart. "What happened?" I echo.

Campbell looks up. And his face—it's distressed, heartbroken. Bereft.

"I stepped backwards off the machine. I didn't think anything of it. I didn't even feel it." He jams his fingers into his hair, not even trying to hide his frustration.

Red pats Campbell's shoulder. "One of his stitches pulled through the skin. I already called the training office at Arlington and they want him there as soon as possible."

Dad turns to me. "How much gas is in the Beavermobile?"

"I—I can't take him." Now my stomach is in my throat. I can't tell my dad about my lunch meeting with Mr. Chestnut. Even though his company doesn't sponsor the team, every major business in our town is assigned to a member of our sales staff.

I'm not trying to convince him to buy ads or promo space, but that doesn't change the technicalities. I'm poaching this business off a member of our staff. It's a fireable offense. Dad *should* fire me. And since I don't even have anything to show for my efforts, I wouldn't exactly blame him. "Not today, Dad. Please."

Not today. Any day but today. I've worked too hard for this.

"I'll take a cab," Campbell offers without looking up. "Or an Uber."

"We don't have cabs in Buckley, and no Uber driver is going to take you all the way to Arlington." My dad's voice is terse, but I have a feeling he's more irritated at me than anyone else.

I turn to Red. "Can you take him?"

He shakes his head. "It's a game day."

"What's the big deal, Ryan?" Dad is looking at me like I've grown a third eye. "Mia can handle promotions. She's done it before. And if you hurry, you can be back by game time."

"Dad..." I look from Campbell to my father and back. "There has to be someone else who can drive him. Steve, maybe?"

And for once in my life, my dad reads my body language or notices my dress, or the effort Mia put into my hair. His eyes narrow, and then he looks at Campbell. "Is there something going on here I should know about?"

"No," Campbell and I answer simultaneously. We might as well have declared our guilt. A flush starts to climb up Dad's neck—fun to know where that bit of my genetics comes from—

and I rush to give him any other explanation.

"I was going to have lunch this afternoon. With a friend," I finish, sounding exactly like I'm hiding something. "I'll have to reschedule."

Campbell grimaces and I don't know if it's because he's in pain or because he knows how huge of a deal this is.

I manage a weak smile. Dad's expression doesn't soften.

"I'll get the van." And I hurry for the door before Dad can say anything else.

I CALL MR. CHESTNUT ON MY WAY TO THE PARKING LOT. HE IS pretty understanding, given the circumstances, and agrees we can reschedule for another day in the future.

In the future. Those three words feel like a death sentence. Mom is coming with the people from the conglomerate in two days. There's no way I can get enough backing to support the events center in time. Not without Chestnut Oil Products.

I hang up as I stop outside the stadium's door, where Campbell crutches out, ankle wrapped in gauze again. He shoves his crutches into the van and slams the door hard enough that the sound hurts my ears.

I don't say anything, but I can feel the pressure building, between us, inside each of us. We're practically combustible.

We make it all the way through Buckley and onto the freeway

before either of us speaks.

"Say it," he says, eyes focused on his hands.

"Say what?"

"I told you so." His long fingers pick at a callus on his opposite palm.

I don't say anything. I'm afraid if I start talking then I'll burst into tears. This sucks for both of us, I recognize that. But my empathy for Campbell and his situation doesn't change the worry and fear I have for my own.

He shoots me a quick glance, then focuses out the window. "I'd feel better if you'd yell at me."

"I'm not really in the mood to make you feel better." It's such a witchy thing to say, but it hits the mark.

Campbell tips his head against the window and closes his eyes. "I'm sorry, Ryan."

Me too, I think, but I keep it inside.

I'm not sure if Campbell falls asleep, but he doesn't move for the rest of the drive.

Three hours alone with my thoughts is not a pleasant place.

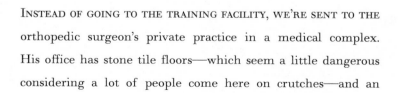

INSTEAD OF GOING TO THE TRAINING FACILITY, WE'RE SENT TO THE orthopedic surgeon's private practice in a medical complex. His office has stone tile floors—which seem a little dangerous considering a lot of people come here on crutches—and an indoor waterfall. The chairs and couches are all large and leather, nearly swallowing me in their plush cushions.

Campbell takes the seat next to me, putting the crutches between us like a buffer.

He doesn't need to protect himself from me. I've had three hours to overthink everything, hate him, hate myself, forgive his stupidity, hate myself some more for not being kinder. There's a part of me that wants to stay mad at him, but I can't. He's so darn remorseful.

"Does it hurt?" I ask as he props his bad ankle on top of his knee and pokes at the gauze.

"Not like it did when it first happened." He fidgets with the screw on his crutches, loosening it, tightening it. It scratches with every turn, and even over the sound of the receptionists' soft discussion, it grates on my nerves.

"Did you call your mom?" Knowing their relationship I can't imagine she wouldn't have called to check on him a half a dozen times.

"No," he says, tightening the screw. "I didn't want to worry her until I knew whether or not there was something to worry about." Loosens screw.

"What about your agent?"

Tightens screw. "If someone else hasn't called him already, then I will later."

When he's halfway through spinning the screw the other

direction, I slap my hand over his. I did it to stop his nervous fidgeting, but then he winds his fingers through mine. The contact
sends a shock up my arm and into my chest, but I don't pull away
from him.

"Ryan," he says, without looking up at me. "I'm *so* sorry."

It's for more than making an annoying noise. It's an apology
for everything. I squeeze his hand in response.

"You think the Yankees are going to get the wild card?" I ask,
tossing out a subject I know we'll be safe discussing.

"No way," he says, rubbing his thumb across the back of my
hand. "They don't have the pitching to get into the playoffs."

We stay that way, hands interlocked, until the nurse calls his
name.

He looks back at me once as he reaches the door that separates
the exam rooms from the waiting area. He's nervous. So am I, but
I give him the dorkiest thumbs-up and he looks a little less grim.

Campbell comes from a churchgoing family. Mia, too. My
family never had time for any religion other than baseball, but
as Sawyer disappears behind the door, I close my eyes and pray.

Ten minutes into the appointment, Mia sends me a text.
Campbell's fidgets must have been contagious, because I use her
message as an excuse to go out to the lobby and pace while I
respond. My shoes click on the stone floor, reverberating all the
way to the vaulted ceiling.

Dash for Cash after the first. Hot dog cannon after second.

Don't forget to put the flowers in the fridge for the Green Thumb Giveaway. I text Mia the rundown of the night's promotions, not because she doesn't know them, but because I need something to do. To shift my mind from the nervous, anxious energy I can't shake.

A hand falls on my shoulder.

I gasp and turn, almost bumping into Campbell.

He's grinning, the giant face-dimpling smile that makes my heart skid to a stop. "Didn't mean to scare you," he says.

"Liar."

And then I realize he's standing next to me on both feet.

"What—"

"It was one stitch." He turns his foot to show me the butterfly bandage on his ankle. "Otherwise it's completely closed up."

"So...you're okay." My heart remembers to do its job and races to catch up with the missed beats.

"I can work out tomorrow and be back on the field the day after."

"Oh my gosh, Campbell! That's amazing."

And then he's pulling me in close, crushing me against him, telling me about how the doctor said he was shocked it had healed so well.

When Campbell releases me, I refuse to let myself feel guilty. This one time that hug was totally appropriate. If our team had won the championship there would have been all sorts of hugging and celebrating. This was basically the same thing.

He holds the door open for me as we leave the building. "Do you think Mr. Chestnut would be able to meet us for dinner?"

THE RIDE BACK TO BUCKLEY IS COMPLETELY DIFFERENT FROM THE ride to Arlington. Campbell is bouncing around the Beavermobile— probably hyped-up on the energy drinks we nabbed during our pit stop at the Bucc-ees gas station—talking on FaceTime to his mom and brother and singing along to some ridiculous country song that he loves.

I'm so happy he's okay, but it doesn't stop that deep, rumbling fear in my gut. I smile. I talk to his mom while I drive. I turn up the radio. But it's all surface. I'm not going to ruin his high with my problems today.

We make great time getting to the stadium. As we pull into the parking lot, Campbell gets a text.

"Is it your mom *again?*"

"No," he shakes his head, eyebrows pulled together as he reads whatever is on his phone. "It's my agent."

That sandwich I ate for lunch grows thorns. "Is everything okay?"

Campbell nods, and his face breaks into its full-wattage grin. "He's on board to help us launch the camp. And he's got some ideas that might help us bring on some other sponsors."

"What?" I say the word on a surprised exhale.

Most of the lights in the stadium tunnels are off, leaving only a dim glow from the yellow security globes attached to the support columns. Campbell tilts his phone toward me so that I can see the details, our heads pressed together as we walk toward the training room. "I emailed him last night. He'll have his assistant contact us with more info."

Last night. After I abandoned him in the weight room. After our argument. After I spent the day hiding at Mia's, trying to find a way to not be attracted to him.

"I can't believe you did this for me."

He puts his arm around my shoulder and pulls me into his side, half-hug style. "I promised to help."

With every word he says, I'm drawn to him, hooked like a fish at the little pond Dad used to take me to when I was a kid. I let myself lean in to Campbell a little, and his other arm falls around me. It would be so easy for this to turn into something else, to come up on my toes and drape my arms around his neck, to let my lips brush against the side of his jaw. I want to see him look at me the way he did that night we were alone in the kitchen. I want. I want. I want.

I can't.

Dad's suspicion before we left the training room today, Amerie's assumption that I was already crushing on him, and Hadley Pearson's comments at Rudy's. If anyone added up that evidence—even though it's all circumstantial—it would be impossible to ignore.

Instead, I say "Thank you" against his chest, hoping he can hear the sincerity in my voice.

Campbell drops a kiss to the top of my head and my whole body melts.

And then I hear a laugh.

Hadley Pearson is standing in the open training room door, attaching one of those long elastic bands they use to stretch a sore shoulder to the doorknob. And behind him is half of the team, all getting ankles and wrists taped or injuries treated. Every one of them looks up as Campbell and I break apart.

"I'll see you later," Sawyer says, but it's not soft enough.

"I'm sure you will." Pearson gives a laugh that sounds like a cackle.

A couple of the guys laugh along, and I see the exchanged looks and raised eyebrows. But it's Ollie's face that kills me. That disappointed stare he wore that day at Rudy's is nothing compared to the shock on his face. If there weren't rumors before, there are now.

I paste on my distant-but-polite smile, ignoring the way my chest caves under the weight of my embarrassment. "Let me know if you need a ride to your next appointment and I'll arrange it."

Campbell nods, and I back away, letting the door swing shut.

"You hear that?" Pearson yells, looking at me through the narrow glass window that flanks the door. "She'll arrange for his next *ride*."

I give him an eyeroll through the all-glass door and turn to go, glad I can't hear whatever else he's saying, but a dull thump draws my attention. Pearson's back is pressed against the window. Campbell's got his forearm wedged under Pearson's chin, and I don't know what he's saying, but it's coming through clenched teeth.

Red is already across the room, eyes wide with shock, hands on the back of Campbell's shirt. Campbell releases Pearson and shakes off Red. Our eyes meet for a second, but I hurry away, pretending I didn't see anything at all.

Twenty

W HEN I SIT DOWN AT MY DESK, I HAVE FOUR TEXTS FROM Campbell. I don't read any of them. I'm not think-ing about the scene in the locker room. I'm not dwelling on it. I refuse to give it space in my already overcrowded head.

I pull down the long roll of uncut baseball card proofs from behind my desk. The players have to sign off on them before we send them to the printer. No mistakes ever again.

"Cards look great," Meredith says when she walks in, stop-ping to lean across the top of my desk to get a closer look. Her light brown hair is half up and a little frizzy from the humidity, and there's a wet spot on the shoulder of her shirt, like she'd spilled something and then wiped it off.

"Thanks. Did you have a good couple of days off?"

Her smile crinkles the corners of her eyes. Meredith's actually a lot younger than she looks, only in her late twenties, but she's got three little kids, and her husband left when she was pregnant with the last one. They'd moved here when he got traded to the Beavers, and she started working for the team. But when her husband's career ended, he left town and didn't come back.

Meredith's mom moved out here to help her, but most of the time Mer still seems worn a little thin. Today's no exception. One more reminder that dating one of our players is a bad idea.

"Any free time is good," she says, smoothing down her hair. "The kids and I repainted their bedroom, which was less of a disaster than you'd imagine."

I laugh, because we've had her kids at the park a couple of times when her sitter canceled or when her mom couldn't take them. They are three little tornadoes. Brown-eyed, pink-cheeked tornadoes, but their cuteness doesn't stop them from being destructive.

"Did *you* do anything fun while the team was on the road?" she asks, giving me a sly look.

"I hung out with Mia and..." I almost say Campbell but finish with "and got a couple of runs in."

She nods but doesn't walk away, like she's waiting for something.

"Is there anything I can help you with?" I offer, not because I don't have enough to do, but because Meredith is always so kind to me. She's helped me out with promo stuff and kids club and other things even when she's equally busy with her job.

"No, but——" Meredith gives a big sigh and pulls out her phone. She finds what she's looking for and pushes it across the counter to me. "Do you have anything you want to tell me about?"

The picture is blurry, like it was hastily snapped before the action ended, but I know what it is without a second look. Campbell's broad back, legs spread wide as he leans against Pearson. It looks violent. It looks angry. It looks bad. Like seconds from fists flying and reports needing to be filed and discussions with the head office.

Meredith takes her phone back and sighs again—she's a world-class sigher. "Ollie sent it to me." She looks down at the picture once more before clearing the screen. "He says Campbell attacked Pearson after Pearson said something *lewd* about you."

Ollie sent the picture to Meredith. That traitor.

"Did you hear what Pearson said? Is this something I need to worry about?" When I don't answer, she lowers her voice and whispers, "Is this something your dad is going to need to know about?"

"No." I am clearly the master of hasty denials. I wave Meredith behind my desk, so we can talk without anyone getting too close. "Campbell's been staying at my house."

Her eyes grow wide with shock. "Ry——"

"It's not like that. Campbell's dad and my dad played baseball together in college. When Campbell got hurt, Dad sort of adopted him."

"And?" She nudges the conversation along gently.

"And Campbell and I are friends." I fumble for an explanation. "He's got two little sisters and doesn't put up with anyone saying gross stuff about them. I think, maybe, he's sort of protective of me in the same way."

Meredith gives a relieved half laugh. "Thank goodness for that! I was afraid you and Pearson had a *thing*. And I was thinking, *Dear God in Heaven, has that girl lost her mind?*" She shakes her hands at the sky like she's calling for divine intervention. "Pearson is a good-enough-looking guy, but good Glory Almighty, he is awful. Every time he opens his mouth I have to hold down my hands for fear I'm going to punch him. And when I saw that picture, I thought maybe someone had finally had enough and hauled off and done it." She tilts her head like she's sharing a secret. "I would have thanked Campbell for it, too."

I smile, but it feels shaky. "You're not going to report this?"

She doesn't notice my nervousness, already slinging her giant purse over her shoulder and moving away from my desk. "A dustup in the training room?" She waves it off with her free hand. "We've got ten every season. Your dad doesn't bother with them unless blood is drawn or it's in public."

I drop, boneless, into my chair as soon as she walks away.

Relieved. Sick. Angry. A text makes my phone buzz, but it's from Mia, asking if I want her to come in early.

Then another text comes in and my phone opens it automatically. It's from Ollie: *How long have you and Campbell been hooking up?*

And below that is a screenshot of the Globe Life Park Kiss Cam.

I STAY BUSY PREPPING FOR THE GAME, BUT IT DOESN'T HELP. THE nervousness builds inside my chest like a storm on the horizon. It's a dark feeling, weighty with threats of a hurricane.

Before batting practice starts, I jog down to the tunnel that leads to the dugout and tape the baseball card proofs to the wall. The guys can read over the information and sign off that it's accurate, and I won't have to worry about any errors this year.

I'm standing high on my toes to tape a little message above the proofs, explaining what I want the players to do, but the tape won't stick to the cement.

"Here." Someone takes it out of my hand and presses it to the spot I was reaching for.

There's a sharp tug in my chest, and I know who it is without looking. I turn slowly and look up into Campbell's face. He's not smiling. His eyes catch mine and hold for a second. It's such a short, cold evaluation before he turns his face away, focusing on the tunnel floor.

Meredith said he wasn't going to be in any trouble from the Rangers, but that doesn't mean the team manager won't be pissed off. Or his teammates. Was Pearson just the first one to give him crap about me? Or do they all think something is going on? Did Ollie send the screenshot of the Kiss Cam to *everyone?*

Questions fill my mouth, and my tongue can't decide which to ask first. "What—"

"Tape." He nods to the roll in my left hand.

The interruption feels like a slap, the sting traveling all the way to my eyes. I blink away the hurt and tear off a strip of duct tape. He doesn't touch me when he takes it from my fingertips, smoothing down the corners.

"Thanks." The word is barely audible, trapped behind the knot in my throat.

"Sure." And with that, he walks into the dugout.

It's like I mean nothing to him.

And I realize that's exactly how it's supposed to be.

CHAPTER

Twenty-One

T HE FIELD OF DREAMS TEAM IS ALL LINED UP TO RUN ONTO THE diamond before the national anthem. They're a T-ball team of five-year-olds in orange and gray Orioles uniforms. Not one of their hats fits quite right, their pants bag around their ankles, and every one of them is wearing eye black stickers even though it's 8:05 p.m.

They're basically the cutest little munchkins I've ever seen.

"Okay, guys," I say as I squat down in front of them. "What are we going to do after the song ends?"

"Run to you!"

"Right! And where am I going to be?"

As a group, they turn and point to the gate across the field, near the other team's dugout. Their parents will be waiting for them in the holding area beyond that, and then they can all return to their seats.

"Are you ready for this?"

"Yes!" They dissolve into some sort of contorting that I assume is the five-year-old equivalent of dancing.

I line them up by their numbers so that they'll be in the right order when the announcer says their names. "Okay! Who's in front of you?"

They yell a jumble of names.

"Who's behind you?"

They spin around looking for the person next in line.

"Can you remember that?"

"Yes."

The answer should actually be no, because I've done this a million times, and half of these kids can't even remember their *own* last names, but I still try to keep the chaos as organized as possible.

The littlest one, Leon, is a head shorter than the next closest one in size, but he makes up for smallness with energy. His hand is a little sticky as he holds tight to me, but I don't mind. Once I get him calm, all the others will chill out and stay in line behind me for what seems like an eternity. Or five minutes.

"What's that?" Leon asks, pointing to the scoreboard.

"That's how we know who's winning."

"What's that?"

"That's the pitcher's mound. Don't you have one of those when you play?"

He shrugs. I'm not sure baseball is going to be Leon's game.

"Who's that?" He points into the dugout.

My throat grows a little tight when I see who he's pointing to. "That's the catcher, Nathan Olivera."

"Hi, Nathan!" He waves frantically.

"We call him Ollie."

"Hi, Ollie!"

Without fail, Ollie turns and his face breaks into a huge grin. He jogs over to us, metal cleats crunching on the cement, and offers Leon a fist bump. "Hey! Are you going to be my buddy for the anthem?"

Leon nods so hard I'm afraid his little head is going to snap off his toothpick neck.

"That's awesome." Ollie crouches down in front of him so they're right at eye level. "What's your name?"

Leon doesn't answer. His eyes are wide, like he's crossed from excited into terrified.

Is it possible to be furious at someone and grateful for them at the same time? I know Ollie will take care of Leon, but that doesn't stop me from wanting to smack him in his big, traitorous mouth.

"Ollie, this is my friend Leon. Leon's really happy to be here tonight." I turn the little boy so he's looking into my eyes. "Ollie's going to hold your hand all the way to home plate and then you'll run, run, run to me when the song is over. Right?"

Ollie tucks his catcher's mitt under his arm and takes Leon's other hand. Over the little boy's head, Ollie lifts his eyebrows at me in an unspoken question. I read it as: *Are we okay?* Or maybe: *Can we talk?*

My answer either way: *Not now.*

I give him a flat look in response, and get the rest of tonight's starters lined up next to their assigned kids. Everyone jogs to their positions when the soundtrack from the *Field of Dreams* starts.

Once they're all in place and the announcer starts the rundown, I break into a sprint through the stadium tunnels and out through the other team's dugout door. The last few bars of the national anthem fade, and the T-ball team puts their hats back on. I wave for them to come to me.

Eight of them remember my directions and head my way. One stands next to home plate, glommed on to Ollie like a handful of half-chewed bubblegum.

"Leon," I yell, but he doesn't move. I'm not supposed to go onto the field unless it's between innings, but he's got to get off.

Ollie solves the problem, sweeping the little boy into his arms and jogging across the field to me. We have an awkward handoff, and Ollie smiles at me like he's not Benedict Arnold.

I carry Leon to his very apologetic mother. She hugs me around her little boy and I hug her back, taking in the smell of summer and popcorn and the red dirt that Leon managed to get all over him.

There's nothing like this. Nothing like making those little kids happy, and hearing the ball hit Ollie's glove at ninety-four miles per hour, and the crowd's applause as the team is announced.

Then Mia walks toward me, frown on her face.

"What's wrong?" The ticket office has been having problems

with the computer system, and it takes forever to reboot. If that happens, we charge everyone general admission and let them sit wherever they want. Then people argue over who's supposed to sit where. It's a huge pain. "Do you need my help?"

"No. I'm here to take over for you." Mia touches my arm like she's trying to calm me down. Like I'm her version of Leon. "Your mom's here. And she wants to see you."

I grip Mia's hand like I need it to stay upright. "Do you think she knows about the Kiss Cam?"

"How could she possibly know about that?"

"Ollie." I show Mia the text and the picture.

She doesn't try to smooth it over. "Oh. That does look bad."

The shot must have been taken the instant after Campbell kissed me, but you can't tell from the angle because our faces are so close together.

"But I don't think that's why she's here. She's in the owner's booth with three men. They're all in dress shirts and pants. Very business." Mia grimaces like she's sorry to say those words out loud.

My mom hasn't brought men to the ballpark because they're her friends. This has to be the ownership group. "I didn't think she'd bring them to a game. Maybe for a meeting. Or a tour. I thought I had another day." I press my fingers to the middle of my forehead, a headache blooming between my eyebrows. "Tell her I'm not coming."

Mia tips her head to the side, looking at me with pity.

"We've got the Dugout Dance-Off next, and I haven't pulled contestants."

"I can do that."

I know Mia can, but I need an excuse. I'm not ready to face the people responsible for my nightmares.

———————

LAST YEAR, ONE OF OUR SPONSORS PROPOSED TO HIS LONGTIME girlfriend in his company's suite. It was the first time in my memory that we'd served any alcohol other than beer in the ballpark. They shook a bottle of champagne and opened it, leaving a sticky mess for me to clean up.

Mess aside, the whole thing was awesome. All their friends and family were clapping and cheering and crying when she said yes. I know that, too, because I helped film it.

No one cheers when I open the door to the owner's suite, but something lingers in the air that reminds me of the night of the proposal.

My mom's sitting sideways across her chair. One hand, holding a glass of white wine, rests delicately across the chair's back. She must have brought the goblet with her, because we don't have anything that fancy in the stadium.

She's cut her hair into a perfectly sleek bob that looks like it was professionally blow-dried. And she's wearing a navy sheath dress, a coil of pearls, and nude stilettos. Who wears pearls and stilettos to a ballpark?

Only people who are expecting something big to happen. Like the sponsor's girlfriend. And, apparently, my mom.

She looks up when the door closes behind me, and she smiles like she hasn't seen me in forever. Something lodges behind my breastbone, like a lump of hot dog I didn't chew all the way, and I realize how much I miss seeing her every day.

Mom crosses the room in two quick steps and throws her arms tight around me. I want to sink in, let her be my mom for a few minutes, but I know she's not here for long hugs and longer talks. She's here to destroy my dreams.

"I have some people I want you to meet," she says as she takes my hand and leads me across the room to the three men, who have all come to their feet. Two of them are older, brothers if I had to guess, with salt-and-pepper hair and strong widow's peaks. She introduces them to me as Bryan and Bill Faulkner, owners of Black Keys Entertainment.

The little handful of nachos I snarfed earlier feels like glass in my stomach the moment I hear the company's name. I know all about Black Keys Entertainment. They've purchased four teams in the last five years and moved three of them to new locations.

I fight down my nerves and manage some politeness. "It's nice to meet you."

"Your mom says you're the heart and soul of this organization," one of the Faulkners says, but I'm not sure which first name applies to him.

"She says you're the grease that keeps the machine running."

The other Faulkner wears thin wire-rimmed glasses and nudges them up his nose as he talks.

The words are supposed to be complimentary, but I think about Meredith losing her job, and our seasonal staffers, and Dad. "*Everyone* here works really hard."

The Faulkners smile at each other and at my mom like I said the perfect thing, but I couldn't think of anything else that wouldn't sound combative and unprofessional. My heart wants me to tell them to leave the park and not come back, but my brain reminds me that minor league baseball is a small business. Team owners and front office staffs know each other. Anything awful I might say would spread, and if we lose the Beavers—

I don't even finish that thought.

Mom introduces me to the third man. He's younger, maybe Mom's age, with the build of an athlete and a shaved head covered in thick black stubble and a matching goatee. I'd bet the Beavermobile he's a former player.

"And this is Demarcus Jamison," she says, maneuvering me closer. "He's the VP of Operations for Black Keys."

"It's nice to meet you, Ryan. Your mom says you plan to work in baseball forever."

"Yes, sir. I hope to run the Beavers someday."

"Good. It's easier to know where you're going if you've got a destination." He takes a quick swig from his bottled beer. Something about that makes me like him better than the wine drinkers. Or maybe it's that he didn't look at my mom like he's only talking to me for her benefit. "Have you ever considered interning with another team for a summer so you can get an idea of how other organizations are run?"

"No, sir. I've got a job here."

Mr. Jamison grins at me like that was a good answer too, and the sharp pain eases a little. "If you ever change your mind, I know a couple of teams who'd love to have someone on staff with a little experience instead of coming to them fresh out of college."

"You should think about it," Mom says, nodding at me like this is the best idea she's ever heard.

While I want to give her a big old "Nope," I do the polite thing and accept the business card he offers. "Thank you," I say, stuffing the black and gold rectangle in my back pocket. "But if y'all don't mind, I've got promotions to run."

They all laugh like I'm a kid who's done something cute, and Mom escorts me to the door, her arm slung around my shoulders.

She follows me into the hall and shuts the door behind her. "See. They're not so bad."

I look at her like she's grown horns, and honestly, if she turned into a demon right now it wouldn't surprise me that much. "Mom, I'm sure they're not bad people, but you cannot sell the team to them." I'm trying to keep my voice to a low whisper, but it rises on the last word.

Mom hushes me, but I ignore her. "Black Keys buys teams,

tears them apart, sells their assets and—"

"Not tonight." She cuts me off, then checks over her shoulder to be sure the heavy door is still closed. "They're leaving soon, but I'll be back Sunday, and I'll listen to anything you have to say."

"You swear?"

She cups my face like she used to when I was small, looking right into my eyes. "Yes. I'll hear you out before I make any decisions."

Then she yanks me into a fierce hug and kisses me hard on the cheek. "I miss you so much, Ry." When she pulls back, there are real tears in her eyes. "I miss late-night grocery store runs, and falling asleep on the couch, and knowing that you're never more than one room away."

Her words cut deep. They poke at a place that I'd forgotten hurts. "Whatever."

One tear trickles down her cheek, and she swipes it away before it ruins her flawless makeup. "Call you later?"

"If you want." I turn and walk away.

"Oh! I heard all about Sawyer Campbell."

As fear traces a cold finger across the back of my neck, I face her. "What about him?"

She smiles, but there isn't anything devious underneath it, like when she knows I'm hiding something. "I want to tell him hello after the game. Have him brought up to the press box."

Twenty-Two

T HROUGHOUT THE REST OF THE GAME, I CAN BARELY FOCUS.
I can't help but wonder what the men from Black Keys
Entertainment think as they watch our promotions, when they
hear the inflated attendance number and know that tonight's
sales were abysmal and notice that there is space on our outfield
fence for more signage.

Do they tally all the flaws and count them as reasons not to
buy the team? Or do they think they can get the Beavers at a
bargain price?

I manage the rest of the promotions without any problems, but
when Meredith gives me the names for the postgame press conference, I can't do it. "Will you get the guys tonight?" I ask Mia as
we maneuver the adult-size tricycles into the promo storage closet.

She dings the bell on the one she's pedaling in, her legs bent at impossible angles, but doesn't answer.

"They want Ollie and Dominguez," I say, moving on to the sausage costumes. "And my mom wants to meet Campbell. You might as well get him, too."

Mia sees right through me. "Won't they think something is up if you're not the one to get them?"

"Yes. No. I don't know." I drop onto the other trike, which rolls and almost drops me onto the cement floor. A bruised tailbone would really finish off this day. "What if Ollie showed that picture to the whole team? What if it's only a matter of time before it gets back to my dad? What do I say to Campbell?"

She throws a stinky chef's hat at me. It belongs to the Italian sausage, though nothing about it ever looked particularly Italian to me.

"Don't say anything. Just do your job." She shrugs. "All this crap will sort itself out because you haven't broken any rules and you haven't done anything wrong."

But I've wanted to.

"Plus, I'll come with you. Like your bouncer."

The image of Mia in a black suit with an earpiece is almost enough to make me laugh. "You're not scary enough."

"I've got an older brother. I know how to be scary."

I CALL THE GUYS OUT, INCLUDING CAMPBELL, AND NO ONE HECKLES me. I don't know if they're worried that Campbell will shove them through a window or if they're high on their victory and aren't thinking about it.

"Ollie and Dominguez, you're wanted for the press conference. Campbell, you're wanted in the owner's booth."

Ollie's eyes shoot in Campbell's direction as soon as they're out of the locker room, and I realize it's probably because he's expecting someone to get chewed out. Campbell doesn't even look at me. He's cold, stoic, as he pulls out his phone on the way to the elevator.

I know he's faking. We all do. There's no service under the stadium.

When the doors pop open, I wait outside, letting Campbell and Dominguez get in first. They both slump against the back wall. Mia follows Ollie in, but instead of turning and facing the door like a normal person, she stands toe-to-toe with him and says something in Spanish. Dominguez's head whips toward them, face shocked. He's from Puerto Rico, so I'm guessing he understands every word Mia's whispering.

And it doesn't take a translator to know it's not nice. She's got her finger right below Ollie's chin. At first, Ollie looks irritated, but the longer she talks—and when he manages to get in a one-word response—his faces morphs to humor.

She raises her hand like she's going to slap him, but Ollie

catches her wrist before she lets it fly. He says a couple of quick sentences, holding on to her arm, and Mia's bouncer posture melts.

I have no idea what's happening and wish for the first time since I left Señorita Smith's second-year Spanish class that I'd studied a little harder.

The doors finally slide open, revealing the press box beyond and the reporters waiting, but Mia doesn't let Dominguez out until she hisses a few words in his direction that I think mean "Keep your mouth shut." He holds both palms up like he's warding off an attack.

"Bye, Mia," Ollie says, lifting his eyebrows at her like he's got a secret.

"Have a good night." Her grin is a little sassier than usual. "Sweet dreams."

I follow her out of the elevator. "What did you say to Ollie?"

"She said"—Campbell's mouth is close to my ear—"that she'd cut off his balls and feed them to him if he ever causes problems for you again."

My mouth drops open.

Mia gives a half laugh. "You catch the rest, Campbell?"

He looks between us and then checks to see how close the rest of the crowd is standing. "I got the gist of it."

She gives him a light pat on the shoulder before she steps back into the elevator. "Same goes for you."

"Noted."

Campbell's eyes find mine, and the temperature in the room jumps up a million degrees. "Am I in trouble?" he asks.

"Sawyer Campbell!" My mom rushes across the press box to us. She has both palms pressed to her cheeks as she looks into his face. "You look exactly like your momma."

Mom puts her hands out like she wants to pull him into a hug, but stops and lets them fall to her sides. "You won't remember me at all, but I held you and your brother when you were tiny babies. In fact, you were the first newborn baby I *ever* held.

"I can't believe you're here and so *big*," she continues, laughing at herself. "It is such a pleasure to see you again."

"You too, ma'am."

"You must let me take you to dinner tonight. I'm sure you're hungry." She loops her arm through mine and tucks me close to her side. "Boys like you are always hungry. Ryan, do you think we can get your dad to let you leave early so we can eat someplace healthy?"

"That's not necessary, Ms. Russell. I'm—"

"Oh! It's so late." She looks at her sparkly watch. "Is there anything nice still open?"

Is she delirious? This is Buckley. "We've got two choices: What-A-Burger or Taco Bell. Unless you want to make something." I throw it out there because the last time she came to the house was to make frosting for my birthday cake in February. She baked the cake in her little apartment in downtown Houston but said the frosting would have melted by the time she drove it out to Buckley. That was back in the day when she and Dad were still trying to make their divorce *seem* amicable.

"Well..." She hesitates, looking over to where my dad's talking to one of our sponsors. "I guess I could pick up a few things on my way."

Campbell and I exchange a look because we both know there's *nothing* at the house.

"Let your dad know our plans." She gives me a significant look, which I take as code for *Tell your dad not to act like a jerk when he finds me in the kitchen.*

"Does your mom still make that delicious tortellini soup?" Mom asks Campbell. "I haven't made it in ages, but I'll give it a shot."

"That sounds great?" Campbell says it like a question but directs it at me.

I have no response. The last thing I want right now is to be caught anywhere in Campbell's proximity.

Mom's already moving toward the back stairs, and I imagine she's compiling a grocery list as she goes. "You'll have to ride over with Ryan in the Beavermobile because I've got training equipment all over my car. See you at the house in twenty!"

I RUN BACK TO THE OFFICE AND TALK TO MY DAD. HE TELLS ME HE has some work to do and will probably be really late. Code for *Don't expect me to come home while she's still there.* Then I jog down to the stadium tunnels to find Mia and make sure that everything's ready for tomorrow. The closet is all locked up. One of the stadium janitors tells me she's in the batting cages.

Why?

Dad lets her use the cages all the time to work on her swing for softball, but she's always texted me first.

What surprises me even more is that she's not alone. She's pitching to Ollie instead of letting the machine do it.

"Hey!" I yell through the nets. "Everything okay?"

"Yep." She tosses one more at him then faces me. "We've come to an understanding."

"Have we?" Ollie asks, face mischievous.

Mia throws a pitch so far inside that it's actually behind him. Ollie jumps out of the way so he doesn't get beaned, but he's not mad. He's laughing, and Mia's smirking like she's proud of herself.

Ollie lowers his bat and comes closer to where I'm standing. "Mia has made things *very* clear. I didn't mean to upset you." He looks back toward Mia, and she makes a circle with her hand like she's telling him to keep going. "Look, Campbell's a nice kid. But I worry about you. You've never gotten all..."

"Starstruck," Mia supplies.

He gives her a dirty look, but continues, "Or whatever you want to call it, by any of the other guys, and I'd hate to see you get hurt by one who's going to move up so fast." Ollie's eyebrows arch, chin tucked down, looking at me like he's a mentor. Or Yoda. Or the big brother I don't have. "You know that, right? I'll be amazed if he's still here at the end of the month. The Rangers have plans for him."

I know all this, but the reminder stings. Like I've taken one of Mia's inside pitches to the ribs. "Right. Of course."

"Good." He backpedals to his place and points his bat at Mia. "This one's coming back at you."

She laughs and puts a little heat on her next toss.

"Have fun," I say, miming for Mia to call me later.

"Oh, I will." Mia gives me a grin that I recognize.

When her next pitch is head high, I have a feeling poor Ollie has no idea what he's in for.

THERE'S A SHADOWY FIGURE SITTING ON THE VAN'S BUMPER WHEN I walk out to the staff parking lot. Last year we had a rabid fan sneak through the sliding gate and wait for one of the major-leaguers who was rehabbing with us. She squatted on the ground next to his car and jumped out at him, wearing only a tiny bikini. Luckily there were plenty of other people in the lot to save him (and call the cops) when her attraction flashed to anger the instant he turned her down.

Until this moment, it was one of my favorite stories to tell when people ask about the wild stuff I see at work. But now, alone in the parking lot with only three other cars, I'm scared. I clench my key between my knuckles, dial 911 without pressing Send, and slink backwards toward the building.

"Ryan." It's a whisper–yell, but it's a voice I recognize.

Campbell's shadow uncurls to his full height—no crutches— and I laugh out loud, relieved.

And then I remember I'm not supposed to be happy to see him. The situation with Ollie may have blown over, but it served as a perfect reminder of how quickly rumors spread and that everything I'm working for could still collapse.

I check the parking lot again, this time looking for anyone who might witness this late-night meeting. No one has appeared, but I check over my shoulder, expecting to see Pearson grinning like a monster in a pool of darkness.

"Hi," I say, brusquely, clicking the unlock button so that he can climb in before anyone notices.

As he puts his seat belt on, I'm tempted to tell him to duck down, but that's maybe a little ridiculous. And impossible.

"Your mom seems nice," Campbell says, breaking the silence.

I'm not playing this game. "What did everyone say? You know, after you *slammed Pearson against a window.*"

Campbell cringes like he was on the receiving end of actual violence. "I can explain—"

"What could he have possibly said that made you *that* mad?"

"Don't ask."

Now I'm dying to know, but it doesn't really matter. "This is exactly what I was afraid of. He doesn't respect me. I've probably lost the entire team's respect over one stupid hug and—"

"Pearson will never respect you. No matter what you do. He's the sort of guy who only sees women as toys. Or targets." Campbell's hand clenches into a fist. "If I hadn't been standing closest to him, Red would have done the same thing. Or Ollie. Once he found out what Pearson said."

"Oh," I say, feelings jumbled. Mad. Sad. Angry.

"Everyone else likes you. Everyone else thinks you're amazing at what you do." He relaxes back in the chair. "But you're working with *guys*. No matter how hard you work, no matter how smart you are, there are always going to be a few like Pearson and Jim Stein. I wish there weren't, but..." His shoulders climb up and drop, a giant *I can't punch them all* shrug.

But this is reality. As bad as it all sucks, I'm still a girl, fighting for a position in a male-dominated profession. Was there ever a point when I imagined it *wouldn't* be a fight? Maybe someday, but not today.

"I'm sorry it happened," Campbell says as we pull into the garage. "But I'm not sorry for what I did."

I lead him into the house without saying anything else. As soon as I open the door, I hear my mom mumble to herself, so I know she's upset about something.

"Hey, Mom!" I say brightly, trying to overcompensate for the friction between us—both me and mom, and me and Campbell. "We're here."

"Great! I've got the soup started and a salad under way, but I didn't realize you're out of butter." She gives me a disappointed look. "Ryan, why don't you take Sawyer into the living room and make him feel at home?"

Do I tell her that for the last ten days this has been his home? Nope. I don't. That's one battle I'm going to retreat from tonight.

Campbell drops into what I've come to recognize as his corner on the couch. He doesn't even have to adjust the ottoman because it's exactly the right distance for his feet. I toss the remote at him, and he automatically turns it to *SportsCenter*. Somehow this has become our thing.

He pulls out his phone and sends me a message: *Does your mom know I've been staying here?*

No, I mouth, but then I notice the other texts from him that I'd ignored earlier in the day.

I'm sorry.

But Pearson deserved so much worse.

Please don't be mad.

Hello?

My breath catches at the sweetness of it all, but I forward him the Kiss Cam picture from Ollie.

Campbell responds with a word that would have earned him a mouthful of soap at home.

Exactly.

"Put your phones away! You two should get to know each other." Mom leans over the edge of the couch between us. "How's your brother? How are your sisters? I haven't talked to your mom in ages."

"You could call her now." His thumb hits something on his phone and we hear it ring. "Here's your chance."

"Oh, don't wake her up!"

"Marie?"

"Brenda!"

Then the two women are speaking over each other in giddy half sentences. Mom takes the phone out of Campbell's hand and is laughing and crying. She motions for me to finish dinner while she slips into the office to continue her conversation without ESPN in the background.

As soon as I hear the office door shut, I head to the kitchen with Campbell right behind me. "Black Keys Entertainment was at the game tonight." I don't even want to say it out loud because that makes the likelihood of losing the team and the stadium that much more real.

"Did you talk to your mom?" He picks up the knife and finishes dicing the onion for the soup.

"She says she'll be back on Sunday. We can hash it all out then."

"Do you want me to leave? So you can talk about it now?"

"That'll make her more mad."

We work in silence. At first, it's strained, but it gets more comfortable as Campbell tosses stuff into the soup pot while I finish the salad. We've gotten good at this. Working together. Being together. I push any ideas of doing this again out of my head—especially when he moves behind me to rinse the cabbage and his hand brushes along my back.

Every nerve ending is perfectly aware of where his fingers touched, of how long they lingered. How it was barely short enough to not mean anything, but still felt intentional.

I plunk a ladle into the pot, and he moves to stand beside me where the counters meet at an angle. "Looks like it's almost done."

"Since this is apparently your mom's soup, I guess you should taste test."

He's leaning against the drawer where the spoons are. He could slide to the side, but instead he moves a step toward me so that we're almost chest-to-chest. I tilt my head back to look up at him, and he's smirking like he knows exactly what he's doing. He thinks he's being funny.

"Excuse me." My right arm is against his side on the drawer pull. I could hang on to my anger and huff at him. I could pretend to still be mad about what happened with Pearson, but I suck at holding a grudge. And with him looking down at me, standing so close that I can smell the fabric softener and Wint-O-Green mints on him, it's really, really hard. I could step away, and ask him to move, but I don't. I open the drawer and it bumps into him. I shouldn't be flirting after everything that went down today, but a little banter isn't bad. Friends banter.

"Am I in your way?" he asks, but stays in the same spot.

"Just a little." I use my left elbow and box him out like a basketball star.

Campbell gives this laugh, deep in the back of his throat, that makes the skin on my chest prickle. He takes back his spot in the counter's corner.

I give the soup another swirl, then scoop up a spoonful and blow on it before I raise it up to his chin level. "Careful," I say, cupping my other hand under the spoon as I offer it to him. "It's hot."

His eyes don't leave mine as he swallows the bite, and something hotter than the soup fires up my belly.

"Not bad." He reaches behind me, grazing my shoulder with his arm as he grabs the salt. Campbell holds the shaker a little to one side, not quite offering it to me, so I'll have to come even closer to take it. "Needs salt."

This is dangerous and we both know it. If my mom came in now, if she saw the way we're standing, so close that I'm practically pinned between him and the counter, she'd know we're more than acquaintances. But I think something about that raises the stakes for Campbell, like this is another extension of his competitiveness. And having him this close, smelling so good, pushes the mute button on that nagging voice in my head.

"You're ridiculous." The words come out with a breathy laugh. "Give me the salt."

"Answer a question first."

Whatever game we were playing has ended. I can tell from the intensity on his face, the way the corners of his mouth are flat instead of turned up, and I'm a little afraid of what he might ask.

"Okay."

"If I..." He pauses, his arm lowering to hand me the salt even though he hasn't asked anything yet. "If I was with another team, could things be different between us?"

I turn to face the soup. I know what he's asking without saying it completely. *Could we be together?*

My gut-punch response is yes, and that reaction scares me. I *know* better. Baseball and relationships do not mix well. Even if I set aside my worries about the fraternization policy, about people thinking I'm using Campbell for status, I can't forget the disasters I've witnessed. Meredith's marriage. My parents' situation.

And yet I can imagine what it might be like to be with Campbell. Busy days at the ballpark. Cozy nights snuggled up on the couch, watching ESPN, sharing dinner out of the same takeout box when he's in town, and taking trips to visit him when he's not.

I shouldn't picture us together. I should say no. Clear and definite. End whatever this is completely, once and for all. But that feels wrong, too.

Instead, I whisper, "Maybe."

"Ryan—"

Whatever he is about to say is cut off by the sound of my mom's voice moving toward us.

"Of course." Her heels click on the tile in the hallway. "I'll tell him."

When she enters the kitchen, I'm salting the soup and Campbell is supervising. Mom is still smiling down at the phone.

"Definitely! We'll have to get together when you're here. Send me your itinerary and we'll send someone to pick you up from the airport. It's no hassle, I promise. I can't wait to see you!"

She hands the phone off to Campbell, and he leaves the kitchen to tell his mom good night. I focus on stirring the soup, but I can feel my mom watching me.

I don't look up. She leans one hip against the counter and taps her fingers on the granite in a quick pattern.

"Funny the things you learn from old friends," Mom whispers, her Ice Witch voice on at full frost.

"Oh yeah?"

"I had no idea you drove Sawyer all the way to Arlington." She takes the ladle out of my hand and sets it down with a thump. "Was that your dad's idea?"

"Umm…" *What is the right answer?*

"And you and Sawyer had such a *fun* time staying at the game after." Her words sound fine, even friendly to someone who doesn't know her, but they chill me like the rare ice storms that blow through Buckley every couple of winters.

"We weren't going to make it back in time for the Beavers game anyway, so we figured we'd stay." I give her a big grin, pretending I've missed her tone.

"But it wasn't too late to make a three-hour drive in the dark from a major metropolis?"

Campbell edges into the kitchen, and the happiness on his face morphs into worry. "That was my idea, Ms. Russell. I thought that since Ryan had never been to a Rangers game and I had such good tickets, it might be nice to stay."

"Of course." Mom musters a smile for him, but it's stiff. More cadaver than kind. "Looks like dinner is done. Why don't we eat before it gets cold?"

We sit down to what has to be the most uncomfortable meal in the history of the world. Mom's playing her role well—polite hostess, light small talk—but the undercurrent of anger, of conversations unspoken, floats around the table like moths caught in the stadium lights.

She doesn't offer dessert when we're finished with the soup and salad, even though there's a bag with store-bought brownies next to the fridge. "It sure is getting late. Ryan, why don't you and I take Sawyer home? Who'd you end up staying with, anyway?"

Campbell's eyes flit to mine—the first time he's really looked at me throughout the entire meal—and beg me to field that question. All of his things are in the guest bedroom.

I choke down my last bite of baguette. "He's living in the Rodrigueses' pool house, but he stayed with us for the first few days after his injury." *Please forgive me, Ms. Vivi. Mia, please cover for me.* "He's still got some stuff here."

"Oh." Mom stands and begins clearing the table.

Campbell excuses himself and disappears into his room as Mom drops her dishes in the sink a little harder than necessary.

I bring a second pile to the counter, and she rounds on me. "No one thought it would be a little inappropriate to have him here. Alone. With you?"

Her voice is soft, but probably not soft enough.

"Mom—"

"Let's take him to the Rodrigueses'." She turns back to the sink. "We will discuss this later."

I MADE A PIT STOP IN THE BATHROOM AND SENT AN EMERGENCY TEXT to Mia. She must have gotten the message because Ms. Vivi didn't look surprised when she opened her door and found Campbell and his bags on her doorstep.

Mom doesn't speak on our drive back home. Her silence means her thoughts are distilling, getting sharper and more potent. She'll drop them like firebombs on Dad as soon as she explodes into the kitchen.

I feel bad for Dad. He has no idea that he's about to be at the epicenter of Mom's nuclear detonation. He's standing next to the sink, soup bowl in hand, shoveling spoonfuls of leftovers into his mouth when she blows into the room. I'm a step behind Mom, and I see the shock on his face.

"Marie—"

"You let Ryan drive to Arlington and back? In the dark? With a boy she barely knows?" She raises her hands to the side of her head like her brain is about to implode. "She's *seventeen*. The liability—"

"First, she's on the insurance. Second, she was the only person available to go on a game day." He pauses, looking at me for backup. "And third, that boy was Sawyer *Campbell*. He's Mike and Brenda's son."

"To Arlington. The traffic is insane. The roads between—"

"You act like Ryan is some irresponsible—"

"You're her *father*. Not some overgrown roommate. It's your job to take care of her. I mean, look around. There's no food in this house!"

They're talking about me, but I'm not a participant in this conversation. And for the first time in a long while, I'm too tired to try to diffuse the tension, to remind them that I'm here, and that it's totally inappropriate for them to fight like this in front of me.

My energy is tapped out. Like the kegs at the stadium that don't even have enough left in the tank to sputter foam. I slip around the island, staying close to the wall, and disappear into my bedroom.

I fall into bed fully clothed, put my headphones on, crank up my music, and try to go to sleep.

My phone buzzes once and I glance at the screen, thinking that one of my parents has noticed my absence, but the message is from Campbell.

Mia and Ms. Vivi must work fast. The pool house was ready for me.

Then: *It's too quiet here. I liked your noise.*

I try to come up with the perfect comeback, but I fall asleep before I send it.

CHAPTER
Twenty–Three

I DIDN'T SEE CAMPBELL AT ALL YESTERDAY. MIA DROVE HIM TO THE field. Ollie drove him back to Mia's. It's like we had some sort of unspoken agreement to pretend that the other person doesn't exist. I'm not positive, but I think it's partially because he's not trying to stir up any more trouble with Pearson, and because today's his first game back. It needs to be huge, proving that his injury hasn't slowed him down at all.

Dad had already left for the office when I got home from my run. Weird, but not unheard of, so I pick him up a sausage kolache and some hash browns on my way to the stadium.

All the lights in the main office are off, except for Dad's. His door is cracked open, and he's sitting behind the dark wood desk that's a lower version of mine. Piles of paper are spread across the surface—this is nothing new—but the look on his face is something I haven't seen before. He's rubbing his chin as he reads whatever is in the folder in front of him, and his skin is pale underneath his ballpark tan.

He looks scared or sick or both.

"Dad?" I say softly, peeking my head into the room. "Are you okay?"

His eyes find mine, and he doesn't say anything for a minute, like he's really studying me. A slow, sad smile spreads across his face, and he waves at me to come in.

I drop the bags of breakfast on his desk, but he doesn't even look at them.

"Are you happy, Ryan? Do you like working here?"

"What?"

"Do you feel like this business..." He lets the sentence stretch for a few seconds. "Has it stopped you from doing *anything* you've wanted? Like being in clubs at school or spending more time with the cross-country team?" His smirk is a forced thing. "Or having a boyfriend?"

Did he hear about the training room disaster? Did he wonder why Campbell was gone when he got home? I open my mouth to explain, but Dad gives a snort–laugh.

"Your mother says I've stolen your childhood. That I'm violating child labor laws. That you're not experiencing high school like a normal kid should."

"That's ridiculous." Anger makes my eyes burn. "I *love* the Buckley Beavers."

"I know that. I've never questioned your dedication." He swallows like he's gagging down regrets. "But if you wanted to leave today and never look back, I wouldn't be upset with you. Don't keep working for the team out of loyalty to me."

"Dad." My voice is more watery than I intend it to be. "Would you be asking me these same questions if we owned a watermelon farm like the Campbells?"

He shakes his head. "That's different."

"But it's not. I listened to you and Sawyer talk about what it's like growing watermelons. It's hot, miserable, backbreaking work. Some seasons are successful, and some are failures, but the Campbells have owned that farm for—"

"More than a hundred years," he finishes for me.

"And they love it. If Sawyer wasn't playing baseball, he'd be back in Georgia working for his family." I lick my lips, suddenly nervous to voice my dreams out loud. Maybe I've picked up some of the players' superstitions. "I've always wanted to follow in your footsteps. To run this team. I can't imagine being anywhere else."

Dad fidgets with the pen for a second, eyes focused somewhere beyond it. "Then if you're absolutely positive—"

"Absolutely positive."

"I'm glad I have you, Ry."

I hurry around his desk and give him a half hug, cheek pressed against the top of his head. "You couldn't do it without me."

He laughs. "I really couldn't."

I DEVOUR A FOOTLONG AS A SACRIFICE TO THE GODS OF BASEBALL ON Campbell's behalf, but they must not accept my offering. He strikes out twice, pops out, and walks.

We'd originally planned to meet up at Mia's after the game and go over my presentation, but he texts me that he's going to bed early. I can't blame him.

The lights in the pool house snap off pretty soon after I get to Mia's house, so I don't check on him. I'm sure he's beating himself up over his performance.

Mia and I work late, finding an argument for every possible reason my mom wants to sell the team—using the sound of the waterfall in the Grotto to cover our conversations. When I get home the TV is off, so I figure Dad has gone to bed. He knew I was at Mia's and had no reason to worry.

But then I see a shape on the sectional that isn't one of the throw pillows that Mom used to have littered around.

"Dad?" I whisper, edging closer. The front porch light throws a patch of brightness that illuminates the coffee table well enough to make out a small glass and a half-empty bottle of brandy. He's had the bottle for as long as I can remember. The only time I've ever seen it out was the night Mom left.

"Hey, sweetie." He looks over the back of the couch at me. "How was your night with Mia?"

"Good. We went swimming for a little while. It was nice out."

He returns to his bottle and puts the cork back in the top, hammering it down with the bottom of his fist. "I'm glad. The Rodrigueses are good people."

"They are." I swallow hard, as if I'd swigged down a shot. "Why are you sitting in the dark?"

"Just tired."

I nod, even though he can't see me. "Everything okay?"

"Yeah." He turns halfway on the couch and puts his hand over mine. It's big and warm, still callused from years of holding a baseball. "Nothing for you to worry about. We can talk more in the morning."

That imaginary shot makes my eyes burn. I'm not sure what's made my dad bring out the good stuff, but I'm guessing that it has something to do with Mom and the fight last night. I don't blame him. We know a lot of people who drink too much to forget bad relationships. Actually, there are a lot who work for the team.

"If you're really okay—"

"I'm fine, Ry." He hurries to say, "Thank you."

I lean over and give him a hug that's half stranglehold. He laughs and pats my arms where they lie across his neck. "Get some sleep, okay?"

"I'll head there soon."

He doesn't move as I walk away.

The green charge light of my laptop draws my attention as soon as I open my bedroom door. I'm exhausted and sunburned, but tomorrow is the day. I'm meeting my mom at ten a.m. at the stadium. The promise of a second meeting with Advanced Machining isn't as strong as having a signed contract in hand. Is the *potential* of bringing them or Chestnut Oil on as sponsors going to be enough to convince her? Will the truth about what Black Keys has done to teams like the Beavers be enough to change her mind?

Sitting down at my desk, I open the file and search through it for any mistake, for any place I can make it stronger. I mouth the words I've scripted for myself over and over, until I don't stutter over a single one.

This will work.

It has to.

Twenty-Four

I PICK UP BREAKFAST BURRITOS AND LEAVE THREE IN THE FRIDGE for Dad. I can't eat mine, no matter how good the bacon smells. My stomach is tied in a million knots, and every time I think about meeting with Mom a new one forms.

Even my extra-long shower, including the deep-conditioning treatment with "soothing lavender," doesn't help. My hands shake as I flat-iron my hair and put on mascara and slip on the red, blue, and gray silk shirt that I've paired with a charcoal skirt. I intentionally picked colors that wouldn't clash with my PowerPoint background, and then I wonder if that's stupid and change twice before I switch back to the first outfit.

When my phone buzzes on my nightstand, I almost break my ankle in my new peep-toe wedges to get it.

It's just Sawyer.

Not *just.* But it's not my mom. And that's a huge relief, though I can't say why.

Wanted to wish you good luck. You'll kill it.

My lips curve as I imagine him sending that message.

Fingers crossed. I send back.

He responds with a gif of a nasty pair of feet with the toes crossed. It makes me laugh.

The main office is empty when I walk in, flicking on all the lights as I move down the box-filled hall to the conference room. We've got leftover promo items and T-shirts, stuff we'll give away at the end of the season, mixed in with last year's baseball cards and random things people can order from our website. It makes it easy to fill orders but doesn't look great.

Nothing I can do about that now. I start the conference room's coffee machine, pouring in mom's favorite dark roast so it will brew while I set up the projector at the far end of the heavy wood table. The glossy portfolio I've created for the Perry Park Events Center is squared up in front of the first chair.

The largest church in our area is hosting their noon worship service on the field. We gave them free admission to the game that will start as soon as they're done praying and whatnot. Apparently, there's something biblically inappropriate about charging to come to church, but we set up a big food tent for their congregation and charged for their post-service mix and mingle. We presold twenty-five hundred food vouchers, so it should be a reasonable day for revenue, even if we don't have a ton of people in the seats. The catering crew is out there now, but I only scheduled forty-five minutes with my mom.

And she's ten minutes late.

I call her phone. It goes straight to voice mail.

I send her a text. *In the car?*

No response.

Fifteen minutes later, Meredith pokes her head in the conference room door. "Don't you look pretty! What's the occasion?"

I hurry to close the PowerPoint presentation and Meredith's eyebrows pop up. "I have a meeting with my mom. Some ideas about the park I wanted to run past her."

"Oh. That's good." She squints at me. "Aren't you going to share it with your dad?"

I'd hoped that if this convinced Mom to keep her ownership, it would be good enough to show him. "Eventually."

Mer nods. "Well, okay. Any chance you'll be done in the next twenty minutes or so? We really need some help out there." She thumbs toward the park.

I check my phone again. No message. "I'll call her. This will only take me a few minutes." Eighteen, actually. I timed it before I went to bed last night, practicing talking slowly and clearly, and leaving a few minutes for questions at the end.

My phone rings and I sigh when Mom's name pops up. "This is her."

"Okay. See you in a minute." Mer shuts the door and I answer the phone.

"Hey, Ry! I got stuck with some paperwork that I couldn't get out of, but I'll be there by game time."

"Mom, you're a personal trainer. What possibly couldn't have waited until Monday?"

She's silent for a few heartbeats, and I realize I've probably ticked her off with my tone.

"We can talk after the game."

"No. Let's do this now." It won't be as powerful without the slides, but I think my speech is strong enough. I can show her the portfolio when she gets here. "I wanted to tell you what I've uncovered about Black Keys Entertainment and then discuss some options we can use to increase off-season revenue for Perry Park."

"Ry—"

I talk over her. "While Black Keys is a reputable group that owns multiple money-churning organizations, they take over teams and—"

"We'll talk about this in person."

"Just hear me out."

"I'm on speakerphone in my car. The connection isn't great. And I'd rather have this conversation face-to-face."

I swallow hard. "Please, Mom."

"I'll see you shortly."

And then she hangs up. I look down at my phone, expecting her to call me back, to tell me the call dropped. But my phone doesn't ring.

At ten forty-five my phone buzzes. It's a text from Campbell. *How did it go?*

It didn't.

I MUSCLE MY WAY THROUGH PREGAME, CARRYING ON LIKE DAD DOES. Pretending that Mom's words didn't bother me.

Pearson makes a big deal of checking me out when I set him up with his Field of Dreams buddy. "Dressing up for somebody special?" He wags his eyebrows suggestively.

Before I can respond, our right fielder, Brandon Johnson, steps on Pearson's heel. Brandon apologizes, but when he winks at me as they jog onto the field, I know the incident was no accident, and I give him a grateful smile in return. I don't know him well, but I make a mental note to thank him later.

Despite everything my mom says about the benefits of dressing professionally, the wedge sandals and fitted skirt are not as functional as my shorts and sneakers, even if they look better.

I'm going to burn this outfit in Mia's fire pit later.

When Mia comes to help me after she's finished her ticket

office duties, I've shaken off my grouchiness. Mostly. Unless I think about it too much.

"Hey, sexy." She slaps me on the butt as she walks past.

I'm trying to roll one of three giant tires off its cart and over to the gate beside the dugout, where the contestants will try to get them to third base and back the fastest. The tires are *heavy*, but we've had guys carry them the whole way. Some try my method, propping it up on its side and attempting to control the way it rolls. But in my outfit, any manhandling is a total joke. I really should have changed.

Mia tips the second tire on its side. "How'd the meeting with your mom go?"

"It didn't." I blow at a strand of hair that has slipped into my face. "Mom was running late, so we're going to get together tonight."

Mia stops midroll. "But it's Sunday."

Sunday. Dinner at the Rodrigueses' house. "Oh. Yeah." I lean the tire against the fence and walk back for the third one. "I don't know if I can make it."

"Your mom will be there." She offers me the pen out of her hair, but mine won't stay twisted up without eighty-five bobby pins. "My mom invited yours and maybe some other people."

Mom and Ms. Vivi used to be really close before the divorce, so I guess I shouldn't be surprised. But suspicion tingles across my skin. "Mia? What are you not telling me?"

Her face breaks into a grin. "Okay, fine. Campbell will be there, obviously. And I invited Ollie. Because we're friends now."

"Reeeally?" I elbow her in the side. "You're *friends*. How do your parents feel about your friends? Especially friends who are a little too old for you?"

"First of all, he's only a couple of months older than my brother, and I dated all of Marc's friends. Second, my parents like all of my friends. Even the rotten ones like you. And third, it's not like there's anything happening between us. We're. Just. Friends."

"I'm going to pretend I'm not offended by being called a rotten friend." Because she doesn't mean it, even if it is true some of the time. "And with you, they *all* start as friends."

"I'm going to pretend I'm not offended by what you're suggesting," she counters, trying to look like she's tough and scary, but sucking at it. "And would you have a problem with him being something other than a friend?"

"Ollie?"

Mia shrugs and glances at her feet.

There's so much in her body language that it catches me off guard. "You *like* like him."

"Is there a reason that I shouldn't?"

Besides the whole fraternization business, which wouldn't stop Mia anyway, there really isn't. Ollie's kind and funny and goofy. He's from Beaumont, so after the season he'd be close enough that they could keep…whatever…going on between them. Still, I don't answer right away. And my reason for that is selfish. If Mia and Ollie get caught, Mia would get fired. Then I'd lose the little time I get to spend with her.

"If he's secretly a dirtbag, you should tell me. Right now."

"He's not," I say, quickly. "I'm a little jealous."

She turns to face me, cartoon eyes enormous. "*You* like Ollie? I thought you and Campbell were—" She presses her pointer fingers together as if that sign should make any kind of sense to me.

"No. I mean, I'm jealous that Ollie would have you and I wouldn't."

Mia laughs and takes my hand. "Getting a little ahead of yourself, Ry? Nothing's happened between Ollie and me."

Yet.

CHAPTER

Twenty–Five

I 'D BE LYING IF I SAID CAMPBELL'S SECOND GAME BACK WAS ANY better than his first. He struck out looking. Twice. Then he swung at what should have been a meat pitch and missed. Badly.

When he walked into the dugout and threw his helmet against the wall, I was a *little* surprised at his temper. But not completely. He didn't reach this level by being easy on himself. My explosions are more...implosions. Waking up in the night panicking that we'll lose the team and the stadium. Eating my emotions. Running until I make myself sick.

Throwing a helmet against a wall or breaking a bat across my knee might actually be a little healthier.

My mom shows up during the seventh inning and waves at me before she disappears into the owner's booth. I'm dying to pull her aside and talk to her, but I've got to get through all the promotions first.

I try to catch her at the end of the game. She's wearing a polka-dotted sundress and a pair of strappy espadrilles, chatting up the family who rented the booth next to ours. She kisses my cheek and plays the part of Sparkly Personality Owner Lady, introducing me to people who have lived in my hometown for my entire life.

"I'll see you at the Rodrigueses'," she promises, giving me a little push out the door.

I finish up my postgame duties, grateful that the one o'clock start left me with plenty of time to talk to my mom after dinner. Dad doesn't give me any extra assignments. Meredith has already left, happy to get home to her kids early. Even my mom has finished schmoozing people.

It's not until I'm in the van when my phone starts pinging with a group message from both Mia and Ollie.

Mia: *Ollie didn't bring Campbell home*

Ollie: *He lives at your house. Didn't know I was supposed to*

Mia: *Grab Campbell if you're still there*

Ollie: *Do that. He'll like it*

Mia: *You are disgusting*

Ollie: *I didn't say *where* she was supposed to grab him. That's your dirty mind at work*

I can't help but snicker at their back-and-forth.

Campbell isn't in the training room or locker room. I stuck my head in enough to see that the lights were off. The gym is empty. There's only one other place he could be, and once I think about it, I realize it's the only place he would go.

The dull thump of a ball hitting the cinder block behind the net reaches my ears before I enter the batting cages. He's still in his baseball pants and undershirt but has stripped off his jersey and hat. Between pitches, he wipes the sweat off his forehead with his sleeve.

He really does have a beautiful swing. The clean twist of his hips, the follow-through and long extension of his arms, the power his shoulders add. He crushes the next ball, sending it into the ceiling at the far end of the cage. Home run ball, for sure.

"Hey there, Slugger." I imagined saying that would seem one part sexy and a thousand parts hilarious, but his eyes barely flick in my direction. My smile dies. "So. Everyone is already at the Rodrigueses'. How long are you going to be?"

"Road trip tomorrow."

He's upset. I would have to be pretty stupid not to notice. The sweat. The number of baseballs rolling around at the far end of the cage. The grunt as he blasts the next one so hard that he actually loses his balance and catches himself on the bat.

"I'm gathering you want to get in some practice." I hook my fingers through the net above my head and lean a little closer, aiming for a light attitude to counteract the darkness I can see swirling around him. "Do you want me to tell Mia that we will be there in thirty minutes? Forty-five if you decide to shower here?"

"You should go." He switches sides of the plate, so his back is to me. "Don't wait for me."

"Right, but there's the whole matter of you needing a ride."

He settles into his stance. Works his wrists in a little circle. Blasts the ball when the pitch comes. "I'll walk."

"You've got to be up early for your road trip tomorrow, and it's at least three miles to Mia's house."

"I can run that far." Stance. Circle. Smash.

I kick my toe against the heavy black plastic that lines the bottom of the net, making the whole thing shake. His frustration is getting to me. "I'll wait."

He huffs and steps out of the batter's box, hitting the button on the wall to stop the machine, then slouches over to me. "I don't want you to wait."

But then he winds his fingers through mine with the net between us, sending me every sort of signal. He's angry, but not at me. He's in a bad mood, but I'm not making it worse. Do I pull my hand free or leave it there as a sign of moral support?

Am I overthinking this again?

"I'm not going to be good company until I work this out." His tone is polite, but still clipped. Instead of that southern drawl that's as warm as my favorite sweatshirt, he's enunciating and biting off the ends of his words.

"You had a bad game," I say, looking into his eyes and giving his hand a squeeze. "You'll bounce back."

"This is not about a bad game." He pulls free of the net, and of me, then switches his bat to his left hand. "My agent called."

My heart makes a sudden jump against my ribs, pressing into my bones likes it's dreading whatever Campbell's about to say.

"The Rangers called Reynolds up to Triple-A." He gives me a smile that looks like a grimace. "They promoted him over me."

Reynolds had filled Campbell's position while he was on the disabled list. And he'd done a pretty good job. "You've been injured. What do you expect?"

"Exactly." He bumps the head of his bat against the patch of turf that runs along the side of the cage. "And if I'd played better yesterday and today, they would have pulled me up instead."

Oh. No. "You don't know that for sure. It might have been in the works before—"

"Jay knew. He told me to pull my act together." Campbell walks back to the batter's box, punching the button harder than necessary to start the machine. "So that's what I'm doing. This is me, pulling it together."

Stance. Circle. Smash. "Campbell..." I can't think of anything else that will comfort him.

"Isn't your mom waiting?" He asks between swings. "Get out of here. Go talk to her." He lets one pitch sail by him and looks over his shoulder at me. "It doesn't make sense for us both to lose what we're working for."

I hesitate, trying to force the right words across my clumsy tongue. Finally, I say, "Call me if you decide you don't want to walk."

"I won't."

The words ring with finality, like a door slamming. I don't know what to call this thing between us, but whatever it is— *was*—it feels broken. I walk slowly to the door, expecting him to call after me and fix it.

He never does.

WHEN I GET TO MIA'S HOUSE, SHE'S OUT AT THE POOLSIDE TABLE tossing grapes into Ollie's mouth. They both yell my name like they're happy to see me and I'm not the wobbly third wheel on what looks a lot like a date. I guess since her dad is at the grill a few yards away, I may actually be alleviating some of the awkwardness.

"Where's Campbell?" Mia asks.

"Taking extra BP. He'll be along. Eventually."

Mia doesn't miss my monotone, but knows better than to ask about what happened in front of Ollie.

"Can I borrow something to wear?" I ask, waving to my outfit. "I'll let you burn these if you want." I pull off my shoes.

"Don't tempt him. He might actually try it." Mia kicks my

shoes under the table. "Come on. I'll find you some clothes."

"I guess I'll just wait here and pretend I don't know you're talking about me," Ollie says, a naughty grin stretching across his face.

"Please. We have better things to talk about." Mia throws a lime slice at his head, but the irritation on her face is fake. And as we walk away, I catch her checking over her shoulder to see if Ollie's watching us walk away. He is.

The moms are hovering over the kitchen island, snacking on chips and salsa. Their voices fall silent as soon as we push open the door, so I know they're discussing us.

"What's going on?" Mia snags a handful of chips and dips one into the salsa.

"You have your own food outside." Ms. Vivi slaps her hand away.

My mom gives me a closed-lip grin that looks completely fake. "Just chatting. Catching up."

Code for talking about the divorce. I've walked into enough of these conversations to know this is one of those times that Mom doesn't want me to hear her slam Dad.

"Sure." I withhold my eyeroll. "I've got to get out of these clothes."

"But you look so cute." Mom's nose wrinkles. "A little rumpled, but cute."

"I don't need to be so dressed up when everyone else is

comfortable." Let her take that however she wants. She's still wearing her shoes in Ms. Vivi's house. Everyone else is barefoot.

Mia flops onto her bed as soon as we walk into her room. "There's a pair of black shorts on top of my dresser. Grab whatever shirt you want."

"What's up with you?" I ask as I'm changing.

"Oh. You know."

I pull a red tank over my head. "Do I?"

"It was a long day."

"Shorter than yesterday."

One of Mia's wrists is draped across her forehead, and she's smiling up at the ceiling. "I may have been texting someone until three forty this morning."

I drop down next to her feet. "You may have failed to mention that earlier."

"Sorry. The crisis with your mom seemed more important." She kicks a pillow in my direction, but it doesn't come close to hitting me. "Have you resolved anything yet?"

"No. She promised we would talk later, but I don't want to think about it until it's actually later. Plus, Sawyer's being all pissy."

"Hmm." Her eyes are closed, and she looks half asleep.

I push her with my foot. "'Hmm,' what?"

"You never call him Sawyer." Peeling her eyelids open seems to be a struggle. "It's cute the way you say it. Saw-yer."

"How else would you say it?"

"Soy-yer."

I want to do anything except discuss Campbell. "Go to sleep. You're delusional."

She holds out her hands. "Help me up. Let's go make this a party."

When we get back to the poolside, she pumps up the music. We have to shout over the thump of the outdoor speakers, but that only makes it seem more festive. The adults leave us pretty much alone, except when they call us in to eat.

At some point, Mia starts dancing and convinces Ollie to join her. And—surprise, surprise—he's actually a great dancer. They do some complicated salsa arm trick. They offer to teach me, but my brain is splitting time between the conversation I'm going to have with my mom and the fact that Sawyer hasn't texted or arrived.

Finally, Ms. Vivi pulls out a gorgeous bundt cake, and I know my mom is going to bow out rather than stay for a slice. I can't remember which diet she's on now, but she doesn't do carbs.

I hug Mia and Ms. Vivi twice. Ollie and Mr. Rodrigues give me a high-five as I follow my mom out the kitchen door.

"Do you want to go to the stadium?" I ask as my mom fishes through her purse for keys.

"I could really use a cup of coffee before I drive home. What's open?"

"At nine on a Sunday night? Not much."

"What about that little snow cone shack? They serve frozen coffee, don't they?"

Picnic tables in a public parking lot aren't exactly what I'd hoped for, but since I'm getting the sense that Mom doesn't want to listen to me, I'll take what I can get. "Yep."

Mom extracts her keys from the abyss of her purse and gets into the car. "You want a snow cone? Tiger's Blood still your favorite?"

I'm surprised she remembers. I haven't been to the snow cone shack for years. "No thanks. I'm full."

It's a short drive, and I barely have time to mentally review my presentation before I park the Beavermobile.

Mom's carrying two drinks as she sways on her espadrilles over to the picnic table closest to the van. Strings of large outdoor lights illuminate a raised wooden platform and six picnic tables, separating the eating area from the all-gravel parking lot.

She sets an iced coffee in front of me. I push it aside, pull out the portfolio—grateful it didn't get crunched in my bag—and slide it to her.

"What is all of this?" She squints in the dim light.

"Let's talk about Black Keys Entertainment." I turn to the second page for her, where I've laid out all the details of their acquisitions and relocations. I tried to make it as fair and as honest as possible, but they *are* in the business of making a lot of money, and they don't particularly care who they run over to make it happen.

Her eyes scan the bullet points, falling on the bolded fonts—catching her attention like I'd hoped it would—and stuttering over the italics.

The following pages are full of my plans: the lists of companies and individuals I've already contacted who have given verbal agreement to support the expansion of Perry Park, the draft of the contract with Chestnut Oil Products for the events center naming rights. The tentative contract Sawyer's agent drew up that will tie him to the special needs camps. So much work, sleepless nights, poring over websites and spreadsheets and trade magazines.

"This is really impressive, Ryan." She doesn't look up at me as she says it, but I can hear the surprise in her tone.

"I want to point out some of the details—"

"Ryan." She closes the portfolio, laying her hand over the cover. "I know you love the Beavers. And I know you *think* you love working for the team."

"I do, Mom, and if this doesn't prove why it's important to keep your shares, then—"

"I sold them."

Her words don't register for a few long seconds. It's like when Mia's abuela speaks to me in Spanish—I have to translate what she says word by word.

"You...you *what?*" The last word is loud, and the people nearest look over before returning to their conversation. I realize this

is why she wanted to talk in public, so that I wouldn't have a
meltdown in front of witnesses.

"I signed the agreement yesterday. It's been in the process
for months, but I wanted them to come up in price a little bit."
She puts her hand on mine, and her fingers are frigid from holding her coffee. "But after everything with your dad the other
night—"

"No." I pull my hand from under hers. She doesn't get to
touch me. She doesn't have the right to try and soothe me. "You
sold my team?"

"There are a lot of elements in play. Things you don't
understand."

"What is there to understand?" My voice goes up several
octaves, and I have to swallow to bring it back into normal range.
"I asked you to wait. To listen to what I said. But you—"

"Your dad hasn't been managing things well. The Beavers are
only two bad seasons from bankruptcy."

"Don't make this about him. About what *could* happen. You."
I point at her. "You sold my dreams. My future. Everything I'd
hoped for." I shove the portfolio toward her, but it bumps her
coffee, which tips over and splatters her dress. "You promised me
you'd listen. You *lied.*"

She tries to mop up the mess with brown paper napkins, but
it's no use. "Ryan, please calm down."

"No." I stand up from the picnic table too fast, and the

sun-splintered wood scrapes across the back of my legs. "This is about you. Everything is always about you. You're so sure that you're right and everyone else is wrong. You haven't even considered that the life you lived with Dad—the one you thought was such a huge mistake—is actually the life I want. It's all I've ever wanted."

"This is about saving you from *every* unhappiness." Mom gives up dabbing the front of her dress. "Do you think I didn't notice the way you look at Sawyer?"

She pushes her phone toward me. It's the picture from the Kiss Cam. His face is partially blocking mine, but his expression is far too revealing. If he looks at me like that, how do I look at him?

"Good mothers protect their children from heartache," she continues, snatching her phone out of my hand. "And I can see you're well on the way to finding yours."

"Good mothers?" I laugh, but tears trickle down my chin. "Do you think you're one? Good mothers don't destroy everything their child wants."

I step over the bench and half walk, half jog to the Beaver-mobile.

"Ryan!" she calls after me. I don't stop. I only look back when I've got the van door open, and I see her struggling over the uneven gravel toward me. Everyone at the surrounding tables has turned to watch her go.

"Don't call me. Don't text me." I climb inside. "I don't want to see you again."

I slam the door as she gets close, and she has to jump back to avoid getting hit. The parking lot lights gleam on her tear-streaked face, but she doesn't come after me. When I look in the rearview mirror, she's standing in the same spot. I think she's sobbing.

But my heart is too broken to care.

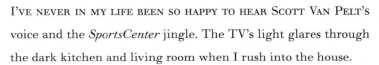

I'VE NEVER IN MY LIFE BEEN SO HAPPY TO HEAR SCOTT VAN PELT'S voice and the *SportsCenter* jingle. The TV's light glares through the dark kitchen and living room when I rush into the house.

Dad's standing behind the couch. Not sitting. Not sprawled in his regular spot, feet on the coffee table. He's waiting for me.

He doesn't say anything, just opens his arms and I fall into them, crying against the team logo on his polo shirt.

"It's going to be okay," he whispers, rubbing my back in small circles. "We're going to figure this out *together*."

Mom must have called him and given him the heads-up that I was on my way home. "You knew. Last night, you knew, and you didn't say anything."

"She asked me not to. She wanted to tell you in person."

It shouldn't surprise me. Dad's the one who keeps his promises—every promise. He wanted to work things out with Mom. He was willing to go to marriage counseling. But she didn't even try. Why was I stupid enough to believe that she'd wait to talk to me before she made her decision?

"What can we do, Dad? Is there any way to block her?"

He takes a big breath, and I hear it catch in the back of his throat. "I haven't seen the contract yet. I don't know all the details. But they only own half the team, and I'm still the managing partner, so we have to come to decisions mutually."

"But won't they try to force you out?" Black Keys has done it before, replacing staff with their people, stripping the original owners of any support system within their organization, making it so miserable that the owners give up.

Dad chuckles. "Has anyone ever forced me to do *anything?*"

I try to smile, but it trembles.

He gives me a bone-crushing hug, the kind that used to make me giggle as a little girl. "Try to get some sleep. We'll figure out the rest of this in the morning."

The mention of sleep reminds me how truly exhausted I am. But it's about more than being tired. I hurt. Everything hurts. Like I've stepped in the way of Campbell's swing.

I don't even turn on my light when I walk into my room. I kick off my shoes and fall into bed.

Twenty - Six

E VEN THOUGH I'M EXHAUSTED, I WAKE UP AT FIVE A.M. I TRY TO fall back asleep, but I'm haunted by flickering images of *Gone with the Wind*. I'd somehow dreamed myself to Tara, complete with thick southern accents and torrid love affairs. The last scene of the movie is ugly—Rhett bails, leaving Scarlett to face the mess of her life alone. I don't even want to analyze the metaphor behind this nightmare. I'll leave that crap to my English teachers.

My biggest issue is that I can't pin down exactly what happens in that last scene besides some serious tension between Scarlett and Rhett. I remember *his* line: *Frankly, my dear, I don't give a damn*. I know she says something almost equally famous, but I have no idea what it is. After fifteen minutes of trying to figure it out, I grab my phone and Google.

A dozen memes come up, most of them with cartoons of women holding martini glasses, but the video clip is there, too.

Oh, I can't think about that today, Scarlett says as she stares out the front door of their enormous mansion, watching Rhett disappear into the fog. *I'll just go crazy if I do. I'll think about it tomorrow. After all, tomorrow is another day.*

There are a lot of theories about what Scarlett meant with that line, standing there watching Rhett's shadow blend in to the mossy cypress trees lining their front drive. I make a mental note to ask Sawyer about foggy Georgia mornings and if that was the director's idea for cinematic effect. But other than the scenery feeling wrong to me, that whole bit about "thinking about it tomorrow" seems out of character for Scarlett. Scarlett O'Hara was a *boss.* She worked people; she worked situations; she was problematic, for sure, but she got stuff done.

She may not have been able to manipulate Rhett with her tears, but I'd bet the wheels in her head were spinning well before he left their property. I bet she was taking stock of what she had left and how she could bend the situation in her favor.

And I'm going to do the same.

I only wait half an hour before I text Dad, telling him I'm going on my run. I know that being alone with the pavement and the sunrise will help me figure out what my plan should be.

Seven miles later, I come home sweaty and discouraged. Not only because my split times sucked, but my brain didn't magically clear. The answer didn't fall from the sky. I can't see any way out of this mess.

I drop my shoes off in the laundry room and head straight to my shower, where I stand under the cold water until I stop sweating and start to shiver. Then I turn up the heat and decide to stay in a little longer and deep-condition my hair. Again.

People always say they get their brilliant ideas in the shower. I'm going to wait around for mine.

But nothing comes.

When I leave the bathroom with the mirror completely steamed over, I catch the delectable fragrance of bacon.

"Dad?"

"In here."

With my towel still wrapped around my head, I walk into the kitchen to find my dad frying bacon, his iPad open on the counter next to him.

I hover over his shoulder, watching the bacon sizzle in the bottom of a stainless-steel pan. "Are you making breakfast?"

"Yep. Figured I'd try."

There are eggs, shredded cheese, a half gallon of milk, some pre-diced vegetables, a bag of frozen hash browns, and tortillas. "Everything to make breakfast burritos."

Dad squints at his bacon tutorial, then raises a piece of bacon up to the light. "Does this look done to you?"

"Is it supposed to be orange like that?" I wrinkle my nose at it.

He shrugs and puts the slice on a paper towel–covered plate.

"I'm going to go brush out my hair. I'll be back in a second."
My phone is on the bathroom counter. There are a dozen missed calls from my mom and several texts from Mia, but nothing from Campbell. My thumb hovers over his name—I'm aching to tell him everything that went down with my mom last night. Instead, I send *Hope you made it home okay.*

Three little dots appear, phasing from dark to light, and then they disappear. No message comes through. I wait, expecting the dots to start again, embarrassingly desperate to hear *something* from him.

After five minutes, disappointment settles heavy on my shoulders, and I set my phone down. If Campbell wanted to know what happened with my mom last night, he'd text me. And since he didn't, I guess that means he doesn't give a damn.

GALVANIZED BY A GOOD, ONLY SLIGHTLY BURNT BREAKFAST, DAD AND I head to the park at the same time. We run through our morning routine as if nothing has changed, because we don't know what we're facing.

Our afternoon staff meeting takes a turn when Dad doesn't start with a joke. Instead, he clears his throat and shifts his weight a little. "I'm sure there have been rumors, but I want to give you the information I have before you hear about it somewhere else.

My business partner"—Dad doesn't say "my ex-wife," though at least half of the staff knows exactly who that business partner is—"has sold her shares of the team to the Black Keys Entertainment group. I'm not sure what that's going to mean for us or how it's going to affect day-to-day operations. I do hope you'll come to me with any questions or concerns. And please know that if..." Dad clears his throat again. I don't think I've ever seen him struggle to find the right words. "If any of you chooses to leave the Beavers or seek new opportunities elsewhere, I'd be happy to provide recommendations."

Meredith's face goes pale. A couple of hands fly to cover mouths. Sucky Salesman Steve doesn't hide his conniving glare. I guess he'll have to figure out how to *not* work very hard for another baseball team.

The room clears out, voices subdued as our staff whispers about what it means and what they've already heard or guessed. I'm sitting on one of the worktables against the back wall, and Mia's sitting backwards in the chair beside me.

"So," she says once the door closes after the last staffer flees. "What are you going to do?"

"I don't know," I say honestly, looking at the top of my knees. "Dad's got a two p.m. conference call, and he'll have a better idea of what Black Keys plans for us then."

"You gonna bust in on the meeting?"

I shake my head. I know it will be better if Dad can assess

what Black Keys plans, and then we can work on counter-measures and evasive maneuvers and some other military-lingo stuff. "Black Keys always sends out a press release when they purchase a new team, and Dad didn't want the staff to find out from the newspaper before they heard it from him directly."

"What about Campbell?"

"What about him?"

Mia gives me her patient look, which honestly isn't very patient. I tell her about my conversation with Campbell in the batting cages, and she clutches her chest like she's been stabbed through the heart.

"Did you tell him about this?" She waves around the room, even though it's totally empty now.

"I shouldn't give him another thing to worry about." She opens her mouth to counter, but I stop her. "You've been through slumps before." I kick the table leg in frustration. "And it's not like he can do anything to change what my mom has already done."

"You're right, but he's going to be mad if you don't say anything."

"I don't know about that." I try to shift the conversation to her. "Tell me about Ollie."

"What about him?" I can see her trying to keep the happiness off her face.

I lift my eyebrows at her.

"He's fun."

"Like, summer fun or...?" I leave it hanging.

"Summer fun for sure." But she doesn't look at me when she says it. I don't push. She stinks at secrets, and I know she won't be able to keep what she's thinking inside for very long.

OUR PROMOTION SCHEDULE IS SET FOR THE REST OF THE YEAR AND we have a lot of good things happening. Maybe *that* is what I can work on—at least so that I feel like I'm doing something—filling up any empty nights with promotions that won't cost us much but will drive up attendance.

Mia and I search best/funniest/strangest game promotions as we take the long way back to the office and find a few that we haven't done and haven't considered: hairiest back competition (gross), speed dating (awkward), and Netflix and Chill on the Field (which I can almost guarantee my dad isn't going to go for unless we can find an ice cream sponsor).

I stop by my desk and check the glowing buttons on my receptionist phone. Dad's isn't lit, which means he's either off the call or using his cell. His door is shut, so I tap softly.

"Come in."

Mia gives me a thumbs-up and heads over to my desk to take calls while I chat with him.

"Hey," I say, shutting the door behind me. "How'd it go?"

He's holding one of the mini-bats in his left hand and rolling it across the desk like he's pressing flat imaginary pizza dough. "They're coming here on Saturday."

"That's in five days."

"They want to get a jump on things, so new elements are in play for next season." He's talking to me, but his focus is somewhere else. "My lawyer is going over the contract right now, but I know your mom. She's got things locked up tight."

Dad's never said it out loud, but I'm pretty sure he got screwed in the divorce. I drop into the chair across from his desk. "What do we do now?"

"Prepare financial reports and sponsorship portfolios, run Meredith into the ground putting a good spin on the sale." He doesn't sound defeated, more like he's gearing up.

"I've got the templates for the portfolios from last year. I can work on those today." We lay out all the details—the number of exposures from each sponsor's contract, photos, testimonials, whatever it takes to convince a sponsor that their money was well spent. It's usually months of work, and I've got a few days to make it happen.

Dad looks up, really seeing me for the first time, and he smiles. "Your mom called right after I got off the phone with Mr. Jamison. She's really upset by the way you left last night."

I make a noncommittal noise and leave it to his interpretation.

"She said to ask you about some presentation you prepared?"

"Yeah." I hesitate, feeling a little guilty about going behind Dad's back, working on new ideas without his go-ahead. The truth is, he loves the Beavers' traditional promotions even more than I do, and it takes a lot to convince him to try new things. I'd hoped that my plans for an addition to the stadium, the camps, the extra events, would sway Mom first—a fail on that count—and then she'd back me when I took them to Dad.

"Ry?" he prompts.

"I've got some ideas, Dad." I remember the breakfast he tried to cook, which was a first. Maybe today is the beginning of something new. "They may help us keep the team in Buckley."

CHAPTER

Twenty-Seven

IT'S ELEVEN P.M. AND I'M STILL AT THE STADIUM, CRANKING OUT reports. Dad is in his office, talking to someone on the phone as he paces behind his desk. Besides the clicking of my fingers on the keyboard and the hum of the ancient air conditioner, it's silent. And a little creepy with most of the lights off. When my phone rings, I almost jump out of my skin.

Sawyer Campbell.

He didn't text first. Which from anyone else would be super weird, but from Sawyer I have a pretty good idea what this means.

I debate not answering, but figure it's better to get this conversation over.

"Hey," I say, eyes flitting to Dad's partially open office door.

"I can't decide if I'm mad at you or not," Campbell says, voice hushed.

Well, that's one way to start a conversation. I'm pretty sure I'm supposed to say something in response, but I bite my bottom lip and hold it between my teeth.

He sighs. It's deep and tired-sounding. "Why didn't you tell me your mom sold the Beavers?"

Not mad, wounded, I realize. It hurt his feelings that I didn't tell him. My throat gets all tight and itchy, like it does when I eat pecans. "Does it matter?"

"Of course it matters. If something bad happens to you, I want to know."

I give a strangled laugh, tears pricking my eyes. "Really? That surprises me."

He's quiet for too long, and I can imagine him sitting on the edge of his bed in the Country Inn in San Antonio, elbows on knees, one foot bouncing. "What do you mean?"

"I mean..." I get up from my desk and walk out into the hall-way, where it will be hard for my dad to overhear. "I read the game report. You went two for four tonight. You're out of your slump."

Something creaks in the background. Probably the stupid full-size bed that his feet will hang off. "I hope so."

"Fantastic. I'm happy for you."

"You don't sound happy."

"It's just—" I have to swallow hard, mustering the strength to run through the script I've written in my head. "You didn't bother to find out how things went with my mom until everything in *your* life was back on track."

I pinch my eyes shut as soon as the words are out of my mouth. Nothing I'm saying is fair. I knew exactly what was at stake for him. I understood his frustration, but having him shut me out was a huge revelation: we don't have enough room in our lives for each other. We don't have space for hurt feelings or messy arguments. Neither of us can afford distractions.

"Ryan, I—"

"I've got a lot of work to do and it's late and—"

"Don't do this." His words hold a hint of a plea. "Don't sabotage us."

"There was never any *us*." I press my palm to my stomach, against the real, physical pain that truth leaves behind. I kept the rules. I knew the consequences. But I didn't expect doing the right thing would feel so wrong.

"What?" The question rides on a surprised exhale.

"You want to keep playing baseball. I want to keep working for the Beavers." I lean against the wall, letting it hold me up. If he saw me now, he wouldn't believe any of the words I'm saying. But he's not here, so only my voice has to be strong. "Nothing is more important than baseball, right?"

There's a long silence, so long that I start to wonder if we got disconnected.

"I guess that's true for you." He says the words softly, but they catch me like a fist to the throat.

"Yeah." I drop my head back against the cinder-block wall. I'm not going to counter or try to explain myself. Every second I'm on the phone makes it harder to hang up. "Well, I've got to get back to work."

"Can we talk about this when I get back? Face-to-face? Please?"

No. Yes. "I don't know. I'll be really busy trying to save the stadium."

Dad leans out the office door, his face confused. "Who are you talking to?"

"I've gotta go," I say into the phone, and end the call, not waiting for Campbell to say goodbye. I hid the truth from Dad about the sponsor meetings. I went behind his back. I'm not going to lie to him again. "It was Campbell." I walk back to my desk and wake up my computer. "He called to offer condolences about the team being sold."

Dad doesn't say anything, but he also doesn't return to his office.

"Did you need something?" I shoot him a quick glance before typing random letters on my keyboard, trying to look busy.

"He's a good kid, Ryan." Dad makes one of those weird frown–smiles, like he's saying something he doesn't want to. "You could do a lot worse."

His words stun me, and I stumble for a good response. "He plays for the team. So, you know, it's not something you need to worry about. We're just friends."

"I'm not worried about it. You're smart." He pats the top of my desk once, then returns to his office.

He's right. I am smart. Smart enough to stay far away from Sawyer Campbell from now on.

CHAPTER

Twenty-Eight

I'M FAIRLY CERTAIN IF SOMEONE TESTED MY BLOOD RIGHT NOW, IT would be eighty percent coffee. I'm jittery, my hands shake. My heart hasn't started palpitating yet, but one more cup might do that. I slept three hours on Wednesday night and caught two hours on the lumpy office couch last night. Meredith went home for a couple hours yesterday to see her kids but came back once she got them to bed. I don't actually know how Dad is functioning; he's slept even less than I have.

I managed to rope Mia into helping me pull some of the portfolios together after the sales staff crunched all the data. We haven't had time to talk about what happened with Campbell, and I'm grateful. Not only will she be pissed, but if I have to lay it all out again I'm afraid I'll change my mind.

I haven't seen him yet—their bus got in super late last night—but knowing that I won't be able to avoid him at the game tonight is a stronger kick than the coffee that Dad brews. And that's saying something, because I think Dad's been reusing the filters.

But first the meeting with Chestnut Oil Company. Dad has reviewed everything I'd written, passed it by the rest of our sales staff, and made a few adjustments. If we can get Mr. Chestnut to commit to signing a long-term naming-rights contract that will cover the cost of the needed renovations and the events center addition, then Black Keys can't legally move the team until the contract expires.

I dash home long enough to shower and change my clothes—a red A-line skirt and a sheer white blouse with a silk camisole underneath. My hair is still wet, so I pull it up into the highest ponytail possible and tie it into a knot. It actually looks pretty good.

A shower and clean clothes don't soothe my nerves. If anything, it makes the inevitability of this meeting that much more terrifying.

Mia's sitting at my desk when I return to the office, fielding calls like she does ground balls. "You look great," she mouths. "But—Buckley Beavers, can you hold? Thank you." She digs into her tiny quilted purse that doesn't look big enough to carry her phone and hands me a tube of lipstick.

Really, really red lipstick.

"Trust me."

"Okaaaay." I use the reflection in the side of her big water cup to apply it and look at her for approval.

She gives me a closed-lip grin but nods her head. "Oh, yeah. That makes you look at least…nineteen."

"You're an idiot."

"You love me."

I give her a hug around the chair. "I do."

Meredith has set up the owner's booth with tables for a fancy lunch spread. A rendering of the stadium with the events center addition sits on a tall wooden easel near the window that looks out over the field.

My palms are so sweaty that I don't dare wipe them on my skirt for fear that they'll leave smears on the material. I steal a napkin from the lunch table and dry them off.

Meredith radios from the parking lot that Mr. Chestnut has arrived, and Dad and I exchange a look.

"This is it," he says, giving me a grin that's bold and brave. The exact opposite of how I feel inside.

I nod, trying to send Dad all my positive thoughts.

Mr. Chestnut is an exact replica of Lucas, fast-forwarded twenty-five years. He's wearing a suit, a shirt with French cuffs, and cuff links that sparkle with diamonds.

He shakes our hands and gets right down to business. "I have to say, I was very surprised when Ryan called to ask me about my interest in sponsoring a facility that could host camps for children with special needs."

The look he gives me is more stern than friendly, and I battle the urge to crawl under the table. Instead, I say, "One of our players, Sawyer Campbell, brought up the possibility of using the stadium to replicate a program he's been involved with back home in Georgia. He's signed on to be the public face of Buckley's branch, but we——"

"Need the cash to make it happen." Mr. Chestnut glances toward the rendering, then back to my dad. "How much money are we talking about?"

My heart races like I've just finished my final kick of a five-thousand-meter run.

Dad passes him the portfolio, pointing out the different options, contract lengths, and pricing structures. Mr. Chestnut's eyebrows jump into his hairline.

"You're asking for a significant investment," he says once Dad has finished his spiel. "It's not something I can give you an answer on today."

I knew hoping for an immediate response was too much, but it doesn't stop me from deflating.

"Give me a week to run some things by my people," Mr. Chestnut says. "We can reconvene then."

Dad invites him to stay for the game, offers him some food for the road, and sees him to the elevator. All the good things.

I slump into the vinyl seat facing the field. Warm-ups are going to start any minute, and I need to get down to the field, but I can't move. My knees don't feel solid enough to hold me up.

Dad drops into the chair next to mine but doesn't say anything. We sit in silence, staring out the window at the rich green and red, the perfectly straight white lines and bases, the deep blue of the outfield walls.

"Do you remember the time you tried to ride on the back of the four-wheeler that drags the warning track? You were what, seven?"

"Eight." I hold up my elbow to show him the scar from being dragged along on the grate the field crew uses to smooth out bumps in the track. "Remember when we used the infield tarp as a slip-and-slide during that rain delay?"

Dad's lip twitches. "Which time?"

The batboys and I skidded across the slippery, puddled surface during plenty of rain delays. But one year when the Beavers were playing for the championship, Dad had wanted to keep as many fans in their seats as possible—I never realized it was probably because he was hoping for concession revenue—and turned tarp-sliding into a game. He put on quite a performance, sliding penguin-style. The crowd went crazy.

He drops his hand over mine. "I know you were hoping for an immediate solution, but these things take time. What Mr. Chestnut said was still very positive."

Tears well in my eyes, and one drips as I turn to look at him.

"This is my home, Daddy."

"I know, sweetie. And we're going to fight for it."

I rest my head against his shoulder, like I did when I was little and would fall asleep at the stadium.

"Do you think it'll be enough?" I whisper.

Dad's quiet for a minute. "I don't know."

CAMPBELL PLAYS BEAUTIFULLY. HE LAYS OUT FOR A LINE DRIVE, catching it with the lip of his mitt. He turns an amazing double play. He hits two home runs. He plays like he was never injured. Maybe better.

It's no surprise that the reporters want to interview him after the game. I'm so, so lucky that a journalist has driven up from Beaumont and wants to interview Ollie for their "Hometown Highlights" feature.

"Why don't you get the guys tonight?" I tell Mia as I move the inflatable sumo-wrestling suits from the back of the closet to closer to the door. Tomorrow is a double-header to make up for a rained-out game earlier in the season, and we have to prep for all the between-game entertainment. "I know you're dying to see Ollie."

"Aren't you dying to see Campbell, too?" She looks up from the parts box where she's trying to find the nozzle we use to blow up the suits.

"I'll see him later." I pretend to be super concerned with a patch on the seam, and she doesn't question me.

Once she leaves to go get the players for their interviews, guilt sets in. It wasn't a lie, exactly—I'll see Campbell on the field tomorrow—but Mia's going to be pissed when she finds out I'm hiding something from her.

She finds out much sooner than I expect.

The closet door swings open and hits the wall. "What did you do to Campbell?"

Mia's standing in the doorway with her hands on her hips, wearing her avenging goddess face.

"I..." My mouth works like a goldfish's, opening and closing as I search for an easy explanation. "Can you shut the door?"

She steps all the way into the narrow space and slams the door behind her. It's a small room anyway, but her anger makes it seem even more confining.

I lick my lips and try to explain. "I should never have let myself get close to Campbell. It was unprofessional. And so I told him that there was never any chance for us."

She waves her hands like a queen commanding me to continue, but I just shrug.

"That's it? That's your entire explanation?" She presses steepled fingertips to her lips and blows out a long, frustrated breath. "I'm going to say something that you're not going to like." She waits until I nod and then pushes on. "Your dad owns this baseball team. People are going to assume you got your job here because it's a family business. Not because you work harder than anyone in the world. Not because you're great at your job."

"Well—"

"There's no 'well,' Ryan. People are going to assume whatever they want because that's what people do." She drops on the floor beside me, her crossed knees almost touching mine. "What are you going to do when you take over the team someday and everyone believes it's only because you're Daddy's little girl?"

"But everyone who knows me knows—"

"Exactly. Everyone *who knows you* knows that you work for the Beavers because you love it." She takes the sumo suit out of my hands. "And are you going to let the opinions of people who don't know you run your life?"

My heart climbs into my throat. "No," I say, softly. This isn't the first time in our relationship that I've wanted to be a little bit more like Mia. She's smart and athletic and has an amazing family. But she also doesn't care about anyone's opinions. She's always been unapologetically Mia. "It's just...in this business, I can't afford to have sponsors or employees or other ownership groups doubt me."

"I know." She frowns and her shoulders slump a little. "You took a huge risk going behind your dad's back to find new sponsors, but sometimes the big risks are worth it."

We're not talking about baseball business anymore, and we both know it.

I pick the sumo suit back up, fingering the rough edge of the seam. "What did Campbell say?"

"He didn't have to say anything. When he didn't see you outside the locker room, the light in his eyes sort of flickered out."

"Dramatic much?"

She pushes my shoulder. "You know what I mean. He's usually so smiley, but then he looked so sad."

I drop my head into my hands. Imagining Campbell's dejected face is pretty much the worst. I deluded myself into believing that he'd be completely unfazed by what I said to him on the phone—that I'd be the only one hurting, that it was better for him not to have to think about me.

Sometimes the biggest lies are the ones we tell ourselves.

"You can fix this, you know."

"I still have to get through the meeting with Black Keys tomorrow." I peek at her through my fingers. "Help me?"

She grins, plotting already. "Always."

CHAPTER

Twenty-Nine

I T DOESN'T SURPRISE ME THAT BLACK KEYS ENTERTAINMENT
forces us to have a meeting on the same day as a double-header.
It's like they're trying to claim dominance. Or my mom really
wants to get rid of her shares that badly.

Dad needs to take a stand right away, proving that we're not
going to back down easily. The Beavers aren't going anywhere.

I borrow Mia's black dress again, and Ms. Vivi lends me a
double strand of pearls. It's ridiculous wear for a game day, but I
want to look my best even though I'm only going to be running
errands and getting the reports the lawyers need. When Mom
breezes through the door and sees me all fancy, her mouth drops
open in a surprised *O*.

"Mom." I accept her hug, although I haven't forgiven her.

Everything could go wrong. Mr. Jamison could say that this meeting is a mere formality, that plans are already in place to relocate the team. "Mr. Jamison, it's a pleasure to see you again."

He accepts my handshake, though he seems a little amused I offered it. They introduce me to the various legal teams, but I don't really care who they are. I only want to make sure I know which ones are on my side.

"If y'all will please follow me, we're meeting in the conference room today."

There was no time to repaint the hallway between the office and the room where we'd set up, no time to patch the scratches or replace the carpet, but some of the staff helped shift the boxes that lined the hall into stadium storage, so it looks a little less awful. Mia dusted the conference room table so that its former glory shines through the scratches and dents. The worktable against the back wall is covered in a stiff white tablecloth and a nice selection of cheese and meats from one of the local caterers.

Dad has been pacing the room for the last half hour, knowing that there's a chance it might be his last day as acting general manager. Black Keys can't take away his title, but they can undermine his authority. He puts on his salesman's smile when the group enters, and shakes Mr. Jamison's hand. I head for the door to let myself out.

"Ryan?" Dad is holding his hand out, signaling to the chair across from Mr. Jamison. "You're staying, aren't you?"

I stop, hand on the doorknob, and check Mom's expression. She gives me a half nod.

"Since you're a part owner, you really should be here." Her voice is soft, apologetic, but her words are like pouring lemon juice on a paper cut.

"I'm not an owner. I'm a part owner's daughter."

Mr. Jamison clears his throat. "Well, technically you're not an owner. *Yet.*" He pushes a slim folder toward me. "Your mother drives a hard bargain, and none of us was sure if the Faulkners were going to agree to her stipulations."

Nothing he says makes any sense. Not an owner yet? Does that mean Dad put it in his will and made it official? I'm not exactly looking forward to him dying so I can own part of the team.

Mom's bottom lip is trembling, but Dad is barely restraining a grin. "Open the folder, Ry."

I walk back to the table, eyeing the lawyers—who seem bored—and my parents for a clue. I flip back the heavy cover and see one sheet of paper with a thick, ornate border around curlicue text, which reads:

"This certifies that Ryan Marie Russell is the registered holder of two shares of the Buckley Beavers Baseball Organization." My voice quivers on the last word. I think I know what this means, but my brain can't process the facts. "Does this...is this—"

"Your mom only sold forty-nine of her shares to Black Keys,"

Dad explains, a smile finally taking over his face. "The other share is a gift from me."

A tear rolls down Mom's cheek, but she pats it away quickly. "Your dad will control the shares in your name until you turn eighteen." Her eyes dart to Mr. Jamison and then back to me. "At that point you can decide if you'd like to sell or keep them. You just have to sign."

My heart is hammering like the crowd's feet against the bleachers during a ninth-inning rally, pounding so hard that I can feel it in my fingertips. My name is there in big bold letters, and below it in smaller print is the word *Owner*. One of the lawyers offers me a pen, one of those fancy ones that looks old-fashioned, and I sign the document slowly and legibly.

I breathe out, releasing the burning in my lungs. I own a baseball team. I. Own. A. Baseball. Team. Iownabaseballteam!

When I look up, Mom makes this weird sound that's a cross between a sigh and a laugh. "I want you to be happy," she says, sending an almost tender look in my dad's direction. "I don't understand your passion for this team, but I'm not going to keep you from your dreams."

"As of today, those shares are worth about fifty thousand dollars. Make sure you thank your mom later." Dad clicks on my PowerPoint presentation, edited to leave out all the information that slams Black Keys. "Ryan had some interesting ideas of how we might fund the stadium renovation, which will also increase revenue in the off-season and beyond."

Mr. Jamison's head is tilted like he's surprised, but not opposed to listening to our ideas. He pulls out a black Moleskine notebook and writes something. Dad lays out the naming-rights contract—still not signed by Mr. Chestnut—the verbal agreement for a smaller sponsorship from Advanced Machining, and Sawyer's plan to help get the project rolling.

With every word Dad says, I see Mr. Jamison's body language change. He sits straighter. He takes more frantic notes and then asks for a copy of the slides.

"This is definitely not what I expected," Mr. Jamison says when Dad finishes up the presentation. "It looks like this organization is further ahead than I imagined. These are very promising concepts."

"Of course." Dad nods, shooting a wink in my direction. "Now if you'll excuse us, Ryan and I have a game to run."

THE GAME IS GOING SMOOTHLY. WE'VE GOT A DECENT CROWD FOR A double-header. I know that despite our meeting with Black Keys, giving Mr. Jamison a good impression of how we run the games is still important.

Mia bounces up to me after the third inning, a little earlier than usual. She takes the compressed air canister out of my hand and expertly loads it into the T-shirt cannon. "Come with me. I have a surprise for you."

"A good surprise?"

"Is there another kind?"

"Ugh. Yeah."

She pats my hand, something she's been doing way too often lately. "This is the good kind." She guides me to the tunnel that attaches her ticket office box to the stadium. Two people are sitting on the bench next to the employee lockers, where fans are *never* allowed.

"They were trying to buy general admission tickets, but I knew you'd want to seat them somewhere special."

The woman stands first. She's tall, even taller than Mia, with a narrow waist and wide hips. Her mass of dark brown hair is pulled back into a bushy ponytail. And then she smiles. Giant dimples, sparkly blue eyes, full lips.

"Brenda Campbell?" My voice squeaks.

"Ryan!" She throws her arms around me, enveloping me in the warmest, friendliest, most welcome hug I've ever received. "I'm so happy to finally meet you face-to-face! We're sorry to pop in on you like this, but we wanted to surprise Sawyer, so we didn't ask him to put us on the friends and family list. And we were happy to buy tickets, but your friend said your dad would be upset if we did."

"She's right." I extract myself from Brenda's arms, laughing as she says more in one breath than some people do in an entire conversation. She's exactly the same in person as she is on the phone. "I'm so glad Mia came to get me."

The boy behind her stands. He's close to my height, maybe an inch or two taller. Other than that, the resemblance is unmistakeable. "Sterling? You saved my computer files!"

He laughs and gives me a hug too, like we're family. "Sawyer told me about that. I'm glad he learned something useful."

"Where do you want to sit? If you want to surprise Sawyer, you can sit in the owner's booth. You can't see into it from the field, and it's empty right now. Or we can get you seats anywhere else in the stands."

They look at each other, and Sterling shrugs like he doesn't care.

"Or..." I pause, an idea unfurling in my mind. "Either of you want to ride an adult-size trike?"

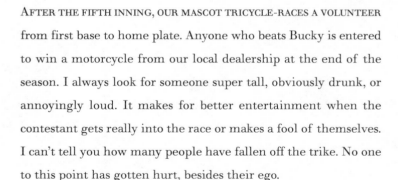

AFTER THE FIFTH INNING, OUR MASCOT TRICYCLE-RACES A VOLUNTEER from first base to home plate. Anyone who beats Bucky is entered to win a motorcycle from our local dealership at the end of the season. I always look for someone super tall, obviously drunk, or annoyingly loud. It makes for better entertainment when the contestant gets really into the race or makes a fool of themselves. I can't tell you how many people have fallen off the trike. No one to this point has gotten hurt, besides their ego.

I'm a little afraid Dad will be mad that I've switched things up, but when I radio Sterling's name to Meredith in the announcer's booth, I know I've done the right thing.

Usually the players don't even pay attention to the promotions, too focused taking their pre-inning infield practice while the pitcher warms up.

"This isn't going to screw him up, right?" I ask Sterling as Mia, Mason in the Bucky costume, and I wheel the trikes to the gate beside the home team's dugout.

Sterling snorts. "Have you met my brother? Nothing screws him up." He holds the gate open for me so that I can wheel the trike through.

Campbell gets stranded on third when our batter strikes out looking, and he has to jog halfway across the field to where our third baseman delivers his mitt to him. He's slipping it on when he hears the announcement. He catches the first infield toss, but his head comes up and looks toward the dugout.

I read his lips from across the field. "That's my brother."

His mouth is open, face all twisted up in baffled happiness. My heart clutches at the sight.

Sterling does an impressive bow before climbing onto the trike, and the crowd applauds and laughs. As the soundtrack of revving engines blares over the speakers, Bucky and Sterling take off, peddling toward home plate as fast as they can.

The beaver's giant butt hangs over the back of the trike, and his belly is wedged between his knees and the handlebars. Sterling wins, but only barely, and the audience cheers.

But so does Campbell. He pumps his fist overhead like his

brother scored the winning run in the World Series. Sterling points at Campbell as he jogs off the field. I'm not sure what that means in brother language, but the fans love it.

I wish there's a way we could give them a quick reunion, but it is really disruptive to the game, and I've broken enough rules.

For now.

The Campbells move to the owner's booth between games. They greet Dad, and some of the suite-holders, who think Brenda and Sterling are famous simply because they share DNA with Sawyer.

I have the entertainment to handle, so I don't get more than a hello and a mouthful of sandwich before I jog down to the tunnels to start prepping for the second game. Mia's gone back to the ticket office, so I'm deflating the sumo costumes alone when I hear footsteps and the swing of the promotion closet's door.

"Hey." Campbell peeks his head into the room.

The sound of his voice makes my heart lurch into a frantic rhythm. "Hey." I step off the sumo costume's belly and wave Campbell further into the closet. He's dressed for the second game in the gray-on-gray uniform with navy numbers and matching hat. "Don't you have to be on the field in ten minutes?" I've always heard that women love a man in uniform, but until he's standing so close that my toes are between his feet, I don't realize how true that statement is.

"Yeah." Half of his mouth is ticked up, and he takes both of my hands. "But I have to know something."

I look down at his cleats, trying to complete one of the half-formed apologies in my head. Maybe it's better if I let him talk first. "Okay?"

"How many strings did you have to pull to get my brother on the field?"

"It wasn't a big deal." The bottom of the half-inflated sumo suit is pressing against my back, so I can't scoot away without tripping on something. Not that I want to move.

"But it was." His arms wrap around my waist, and he pulls me into a tight hug. "Thank you," he says into my hair.

It was such a simple thing to do, but I knew it would mean a lot to him. I close my eyes, soaking in this feeling, letting myself memorize the press of his chest against mine. Measuring where my head fits beneath his chin. My hands slip under his arms and make their way up his back, snagging on the number stitched onto his jersey before finding a perfect resting place just below his shoulder blades.

"I was wrong about what I said the other night." I say the words against his chest, holding him so close that a whisper couldn't fit between our bodies. "I don't know what *this* is, but... I want it to be something."

The air between us changes, and this turns from a gratitude hug into something else entirely.

He pulls back to look at me, his mouth open like he's not

quite sure what to do. "What about your rules? What about the fraternization policy?"

"Some things are more important than the rules."

Sawyer hesitates, and then he decides. His fingers press me even closer, palm against my spine. His mouth is over mine, hovering, giving me the chance to back away.

I don't.

My lips brush against his, the briefest contact. Something that could be taken back. Something forgiven and forgotten, shaken off with an embarrassed laugh.

But I've made my choice. I want this. If people can't see me as a professional, as an *owner* of a minor league baseball team, then that's their problem.

I kiss him again, certain this time. His mouth captures mine, my bottom lip trapped between his. All the self-control we've managed in the past few weeks is lost in the rasp of my breath, the taste of summer on his tongue, the sensation of his hands against my ribs.

We're kissing like it's a necessity, like we couldn't wait one more instant, like we've been fighting a losing battle and have finally given up. But nothing about this feels like defeat. It feels like facing the inevitable and realizing it's a gift instead of a curse.

And then my radio chirps. It's not a call for me, but it's enough to shock us back to reality. His heart thunders under my fingertips; my breathing sounds ragged.

"I'm sorry," he says, straightening his hat that's somehow gotten pushed back on his head. "Actually, I'm not."

"Me neither." The words are true. "But you still should go so that you don't get benched."

Campbell steals one more peck before he slinks out of the closet. He looks far too suspicious, and I realize that if anyone guesses, it's going to be okay.

CHAPTER

Thirty

TWO MONTHS LATER

I LEAN BACK IN MY CHAIR AND PRESS MY FEET AGAINST THE BRICK half wall that separates me from the field. It's so nice to *sit* during a baseball game. To let the sun shine on my hair, which is down today and wavy thanks to Mia's magical curling skills. I take a deep breath and smell the hot dogs, the damp concrete from the late-afternoon rainstorm, and the sweet fragrance of the bagged cotton candy that hawkers are tossing to the people in the row behind me. It doesn't matter which park I'm in—this will always be the scent of home.

Mia elbows me and I open my eyes as the home team filters out of the dugout, cleats crunching on the concrete as they jog up the stairs.

"Oh, yum." She sighs and then takes a big bite of her licorice. I know she's not talking about candy—at least not the kind you eat.

The sight is drool-worthy, though. Sawyer takes a grounder, tosses it back to the first baseman, and cracks his neck. It's fun to watch him in his element. Everything about him is relaxed, completely engrossed in the game, but my pulse pounds like I've sprinted around the bases. It still happens every time he calls, every time I hear that syrup-thick accent, which gets even heavier when he's sleepy.

"Keep your eyes to yourself." I elbow her back. "*You* have a boyfriend."

"No, I don't." She takes another bite, even though I'm positive she hasn't finished the mouthful she already has. "I have a friend who is male, who sometimes hangs out at my house and eats all my mom's food."

"And that you make out with in the pool house whenever you think you can get away with it."

Mia smirks at me, but her teeth are pink and it's hilarious. "I'm fairly certain *someone* else broke it in first."

"Probably Marc," we say at the same time, and burst into laughter.

Three weeks ago, on the night Campbell got the call that he'd be moving up to Triple-A, we got caught kissing in the pool house. Mia had the soundtrack from *Star Wars* on her phone and started playing it as she peeked around the corner. "The Imperial March" was hilarious.

I feel light today, like when we left for Round Rock this

morning I shook off all my problems, leaving them in a gutter somewhere in Buckley. I'm not positive the Beavers will still be at John M. Perry Park in ten years, but they'll be there for the next five. Mr. Chestnut signed the naming-rights agreement, and there's a good chance with the addition and renovations, the team will stay in Buckley permanently.

Mr. Jamison is renting a condo in town and has turned the conference room into a temporary office. For as much change as he's bringing to the team, he's actually a really cool guy. He played baseball in southern California, and he's more laid back than I imagined anyone from Black Keys could be. He and Dad get along really well, which is both shocking and great. He's helping Dad see how we can mix the new and the old, how we can keep the Beavers' traditions and shake a few things up to improve revenue and ticket sales.

He's also arranged for me to attend the Baseball Winter Meetings this December in Nashville. It's a huge conference with classes that teach all the ins and outs of the business of baseball. I'll learn how other organizations run, get to do some networking, and spend a weekend away from home.

It happens to fall over my winter break and is only six hours from Cordele, Georgia. Mom has promised to drive down with me, and we're going to spend the week before Christmas with the Campbells.

And Sawyer.

That's the third big effort she's made at fixing our mother–daughter relationship. The first was giving me the shares. Black Keys wouldn't agree to the deal if they couldn't be a majority partner or at least have an equal portion, so she coerced my dad to give up one of his shares. Dad owns forty-nine percent, Black Keys owns forty-nine percent, and I own the last two. She wasn't even sure until the morning we met with Mr. Jamison if the lawyers and other stockholders at Black Keys would ratify the contract, but she was willing to sacrifice the sale if it meant I wouldn't get a portion of the team.

I'm still sort of in shock that she'd back out of something that big for my sake.

Letting me come to the game today—to see Campbell for the first time since he got promoted to Triple-A—was Mom's attempt at keeping a promise. I know she's really against me dating a baseball player and letting someone else's dream supersede my own. I've tried to convince her that will never happen, but she's got too much baggage on the subject. It helps that the Campbells are the best sort of people and Sawyer's impossible to dislike, but she still *had* to chaperone.

"Okay, okay, okay," Mom says as she edges past other fans. She's got a cardboard box heavy with drinks for the three of us, a loaded baked potato for Mia, a footlong for me, and a salad for herself. A salad. At a baseball game. A lot has changed over the last few months, but I guess I shouldn't expect too much too fast.

Mom claims she's here to spend time with Brenda, but I know this is another peace offering. She didn't have to bring me. She rescheduled a ton of training appointments with her clients so I can have more than one evening with Sawyer.

Brenda's sliding in behind Mom, carrying a box of her own. She tosses me frozen Junior Mints. My favorite.

I love this woman.

I don't tell her that they taste like her son.

The music for the first batter starts playing, and my mom says something to Brenda, and the two of them dissolve into laughter that's so loud it's almost embarrassing.

The first batter strikes out. The second hits a single. The third hits the ball into the gap between first and second. The second baseman fields it, tosses it to the first baseman, who pitches it to Sawyer. He leaps out of the way of the sliding runner and gets the tag all at the same time. Beautiful double play.

All four of us stand to cheer for him, and I see his smile grow as he jogs toward the dugout. He flips the ball to me underhand, and I catch it short of the fence. It's silly, but I clutch the ball to my chest like it's some great treasure.

Scarlett O'Hara was right about one thing: tomorrow is another day, but today is perfect.

THE END

Acknowledgments

FORGIVE THE BASEBALL PUNS, BUT THIS BOOK REQUIRED AN all-star team to get to production.

To my ace pitchers: My agents, Lindsay Mealing, Mandy Hubbard, and Garrett Alwert. Thanks for getting this story into the right hands at the right time. You folks are remarkable!

To the squad at Page Street: Ashley Hearn is the Cal Ripken/ Derek Jeter of editors. She fills the gaps, has great field vision, and has turned my story into something replay (or reread) worthy. My copyeditor, Alison Kerr Miller, snags all my mistakes like they're easy pop flies. I also can't forget Tamara Grasty, Max Baker, Sabrina Kleckner, Hayley Gundlach, Marissa Giambelluca, Lauren Knowles, and, of course, Will Kiester. Thanks for championing this manuscript and all the work that made it better.

To the design team at Page Street: Rosie, you are a power hitter! Y'all knocked this cover out of the park.

To the marketing and sales staff at Page Street and Macmillan: These are the folks that make the game run. You don't see their faces and you don't know their names, but without them there wouldn't be a book to enjoy.

To the book bloggers/YouTubers, Instagrammers, reviewers, librarians, teachers, and readers: Thanks for being that rambunctious crowd of supporters, for shouting from the top of your lungs about this book and my earlier stories. Thanks for making this job so fulfilling.

All joking aside, I've been incredibly blessed to work with so many talented, wonderful people.

This book is dedicated to my family, but they deserve double thanks. The first year I worked in minor league baseball, the Vallett family made everything happen. Dad served as the team photographer, Mom (and baby sister MeMe) handled promotions, my younger sister, Liz, was my intern/assistant/personal food-delivery service, and my little brother, Joel, was the best mascot you can imagine. Every story about Bucky the Beaver is based on his experience, but some of the best ones got edited out. I'm sure Joel would die if the world knew he blacked out from heat exhaustion and my mom kicked him when she thought he was faking. Oh, wait. I guess everyone knows now.

I'm incredibly grateful for the special relationship we all

share. For the way baseball made us an even more tightly knit family. Love you so much!

My four kids—Gavin, Laynie, Audrey, and Ady—inherited a whole bunch of awesome. They're funny, smart, and pretty darn patient. Thanks for letting me smother-mother you, read books aloud in ridiculous voices, and occasionally space out while you're talking. My life would be incomplete without you.

This story would have sat on my desktop for five more years without the help and encouragement of my friends and critique partners. I owe a debt of gratitude to Diana Wariner, Lynne Matson, Cheyanne Young, Kristin Rae, Katie Stout, Jessica Lawson, Lindsay Currie, and Nicole Castroman for reading and rereading this story. Thank you for your emails, plot chats, sanity checks, text messages, and phone calls. I could not do this without my crew.

While most of my writer friends are people I only see once a year, there's a whole slew of daily friends who keep me on my feet. Stacy Sorenson, Kara McCoy, Jennifer Wegner, Leah Christie, Caroline Lund, and my awesome sisters-in-law Brianne Stewart and Elizabeth Wallace are the ladies who remind me of how good life can be even when I'm away from my laptop. Hugs and cupcakes for you all.

And last but not least, I've got to thank my husband, Jamie. Thanks for not letting me give up on this dream. Let's take a vacation? I think we've earned it. Love you forever.

About the Author

BECKY WALLACE IS THE award-winning author of *The Storyspinner* and *The Skylighter*. She's a sucker for slow-burn romances, near-miss kisses, and ordinary people doing extraordinary things. Becky worked for a minor league baseball team, edited a sports marketing magazine, and toured internationally as a ballroom dancer before settling down in Houston, Texas, with her husband, four children, and one very fluffy puppy. If she's not writing, you'll find her baking sweet treats or reading on the elliptical.